JOURNEY INTO HELL

MIKE STRONG: FOR HIRE

JOURNEY INTO HELL

JOE DAVISON

4 Horsemen
Publications, Inc.

Journey Into Hell
Copyright © 2023 Joe Davison. All rights reserved.

4 Horsemen
Publications, Inc.

4 Horsemen Publications, Inc.
1497 Main St. Suite 169
Dunedin, FL 34698
4horsemenpublications.com
info@4horsemenpublications.com

Cover by J. Kotick
Typesetting by Autumn Skye
Edited by SL Vargas

All rights to the work within are reserved to the author and publisher. No part of this publication may be reproduced, stored in a retrieval system, or transmitted in any form or by any means, electronic, mechanical, photocopying, recording, scanning, or otherwise, except as permitted under Section 107 or 108 of the 1976 International Copyright Act, without prior written permission except in brief quotations embodied in critical articles and reviews. Please contact either the Publisher or Author to gain permission.

This is a work of fiction. All characters, organizations, and events portrayed in this novel are either products of the author's imagination or are used fictitiously.

Library of Congress Control Number: 2022933471

Paperback ISBN-13: 978-1-64450-524-3
Hardcover ISBN-13: 978-1-64450-875-6
Audiobook ISBN-13: 978-1-64450-525-0
Ebook ISBN-13: 978-1-64450-513-7

CONTENTS

Chapter 1 1
Chapter 2 11
Chapter 3 22
Chapter 4 28
Chapter 5 36
Chapter 6 42
Chapter 7 51
Chapter 8 61
Chapter 9 71
Chapter 10 82
Chapter 11 92
Chapter 12 102
Chapter 13 110
Chapter 14 116
Chapter 15 124
Chapter 16 132
Chapter 17 141
Chapter 18 147
Chapter 19 155
Chapter 20 158
Chapter 21 164
Chapter 22 167

Chapter 23 173
Chapter 24 177
Chapter 25 184
Book Club Questions 189
Author Bio 191

CHAPTER 1

VALKYRIE CITY—1950 FIVE YEARS AFTER THE
SECOND WORLD WAR

Valkyrie City sits soaking wet from eight straight days of rain. The rushing floodwaters usher the dirt, grime, muck, and trash into the sewers below the street. It's a bath the city desperately needed. The neon lighting up downtown gives the city a radiating rainbow glow. Mike Strong, the hero of Valkyrie City (as some like to put it, others would put it another way) sits in his desk chair, staring out the window. His piercing, albeit bloodshot, blue eyes seem to glow in the dark. He slouches as if he's had a few too many and clenches his perfect jaw, which many people liked to hit. He watches as the ice in his rocks glass swirls with the rocking movement of his wrist. The larger than average raindrops pound against his window with the speed of a Thompson machine gun, a sound Mike was all too familiar with.

The city hasn't seen rain like this in a few years and it'll wash off the streets if nothing else—maybe we lose the stench, Mike thinks. *It's as if the sky opened up and released the cleansing rain, knowing the city was full of evil and needed to be bathed. From Hastings Tower in the north to South Wharf, the city is full of bad people doing bad deeds. If you're born in the city, you'll be just fine. You learn the ins and outs fast in a town like this. But, if you're a transplant, it's gonna be pretty hard. The learning curve is one you just might pay for with your life. It's the rich eating the poor here and, in some cases, that's literally what is happening. The things that go on behind closed doors in this city would shake the socks off some folks. If the common street gangs don't get you, maybe the vampires will. Or, if you're lucky, a werewolf. But as fate would have it, it's the damn demons. They don't play by the rules. Angels ain't no better. I think I hate angels the most. At least with a demon you know they're going to lie to you—or try to eat you. Angels stand over you watching you die unwilling to step in, can't interfere with fate. So, children die, mothers and fathers die, and they just stand there self-righteous and indignant. What the hell do I care? I can't be killed anyway. So, fuck you demon bastards. Let the rain drown you sorry motherfuckers. Just bring the big fella up once. Let me knock 'em around a few. It's the least I could do for all he's done for me. With this gift and all. Maybe I think too much.*

The rain rattles the window, sending Mike back to his time in Germany, fighting Nazis. He slowly goes catatonic to the rhythmic pattern of the rain. Soon he is somewhere else altogether.

The explosions echo.

GERMANY—THE 6TH OF JUNE 1944

The whistling of the incoming missile was a warning for every soldier to take cover. A much younger, muddier, and blood-covered Mike Strong runs through the muck, jumping over dead soldier after dead soldier. His only thought is to make it to the bunker before another bomb lands on someone he knows, or worse, himself. The mud is thick, and every step is like lifting fifty-pound weights with his feet.

BOOM!

Soldiers go down one after another. The soldier closest to him is shredded by debris. He knows right away it was Mac Christinsen— the bandaged right arm gave that away. A real nice guy from the Bronx. Mike doesn't have time to mourn now. He watches as good American men drop from gunshot wounds all around him. He knows at any moment one of those very bullets could have his

CHAPTER 1

name on it. Shots ring out. A bullet goes through his shoulder, but it doesn't slow him down. He has to take it. He is a few feet away from the bunker now. He endures the burning and stinging in his shoulder and uses it as fuel.

More and more soldiers die.

With every passing second, a fifty-caliber machine gun booms as the Nazis fire onto the Higgins boats. Hundreds of helpless soldiers leap off the floating coffins.

The large caliber rounds pierce the metal and kill the soldiers who don't abandon ship ten at a time.

BOOM!

A grenade goes off, blasting our runner onto his back. The mud softens his landing, but the concussion makes his brain shake like a child holding a rattle. The wind is knocked out of him and he tries to take giant gulps of air. His vision blurs and time slows down as he watches more of his friends go down. A Nazi soldier emerges from the bunker with an MP40, firing heated lead and copper. His grin says it all.

He enjoys killing Americans.

Our runner rises up from the mud; the surrounding scene is horror exemplified. Pulling himself out of the mud felt like the devil was trying to pull him down to hell. A Nazi is blown in half in front of him. His body contorts as his limbs fly in different directions. It's only a few yards to the open door but first, he'll have to take out several Nazis. With speed and agility, he pulls out his sidearm.

It's a Colt 1911 .45 caliber. The gun fits perfectly in the palm of his hand. The counterbalance makes it easy to look down the sight even as the ground rattles with explosions, Mike fires and nails a Nazi in the face, blowing out the back of his head.

Mike is at full speed again and all he hears is his own breathing and the metal-on-metal clink as he fires. One, two, three Nazis fall into the mud, dead. As he turns, a Nazi fires at him, the bullets slamming into the mud with a damp *thwip*. Still, his feet pull out of the mud by sheer will alone. He will not be stopped.

Another American goes down in front of him and Mike simply leaps over the dying hero.

A Nazi standing in the doorway is his last obstacle. He ducks and strafes to the right, evading a blow from the stock of a StG 44.

JOURNEY INTO HELL

He jabs his pistol under the chin of the Nazi and pulls the trigger. The soldier's helmet explodes, splattering him with brains and blood. Both Mike and the Nazi tumble and slide into the concrete bunker, slamming against the wall. Mike groans; the concrete is much less forgiving than the mud.

Inside, the bunker drops down a few steps. He aims at three Nazis firing giant guns out of the portholes. Suddenly, a Nazi steps close, aiming his Luger at Mike's head.

"Beweg dich nicht, American!" the Nazi says with a grin.

Mike puts his hands up, his finger looped around the trigger guard on his 1911. "I almost made it," he laments.

"Den mund halten," the Nazi orders over the explosive firing of the machine guns.

Mike notices a huge knife strapped to the Nazi's boot and, in an instant, kicks him in the knee and snatches up the knife. The Nazi drops to one knee as Mike flips the knife around in mid-air, catches it, and jabs it through the Nazi's neck. As the Nazi falls, Mike spins his gun around his finger like a cowboy. He fires, hitting the other Nazi in the back of the head.

Mike spins to his feet as the last Nazi tosses a grenade at him. He doesn't flinch. His mission is done—he secured the bunker. Mike watches as the grenade bounces off the wall and back toward the Nazi. He fires, hitting the Nazi in the head. The Nazi slumps to the ground, landing on top of the grenade. The corpse takes the brunt of the explosion, sparing Mike's life but covering him in blood, dust, and concrete.

The dust settles. Mike exits the bunker. To his surprise, there are ten American soldiers waiting for him. He looks at his unit and smiles. He wipes the blood off his uniform's nametape, which reads STRONG. He breathes heavily, wiping the viscera off his face. His shoulder aches, and he rolls it around and cracks his neck.

He looks up to see a missile careening toward him. It is the last thing he sees before darkness engulfs him.

Mike is sucked down into a dark liquid whirlpool. He starts to stretch and contort, his muscles and bone bending against physics. His mind is flooded with images of raging fires and people burning.

CHAPTER 1

The face of a horned demon appears before a bright white light blinds him. He slams to the ground and the viscous surface engulfs him. Mike reaches up through the gooey texture, pulling himself to the surface. He is covered in a black oily substance that sticks to his skin like bubble gum. He struggles to his knees and looks down at his right hand. It has a strange scar on it now. A line down the center with two shorter lines crossing it at the top and one at the bottom. It looks like a crucifix that is both upright and upside down at the same time. His skin is smoking.

Mike grabs it with his other hand and the pain sears up his arm, to his chest, and into his neck. His screams do not help with the pain. The skin on his face burns and his eyes turn black as they bleed the same oily dark goo he is kneeling in. He clambers to his feet in the sticky black water. Mike looks down at his reflection. It moves oddly, as if it's going to rise out of the pool. Then it does. It reaches out with its right arm, pulling itself out of the murky depths. Mike looks at a weird backward version of himself. Then its skin sloughs off and it's the Devil. The demon grabs Mikes face and pulls his flesh off.

VALKYRIE CITY

The small apartment is noisy. A large oscillating desk fan whirls back and forth on a small kitchen table where an empty bottle of whiskey languishes next to a well-used ashtray. The sound of the city bellows in through an open window. An open pack of Ox Head cigarettes sits next to a battered trench lighter, the gold paint chipped. The living room is big enough for a loveseat, an end table, a lamp, and a dresser. The latter is topped with folders, pieces of paper, and a shotgun. The bedroom is just to the left of the living room, and it, too, is rather small. A wooden vanity, complete with a wash basin, sits across from the twin-sized bed, where Mike wrestles with his nightmares.

He finally wakes. His throat is dry. He is soaking wet from sweat. He stares up at the ceiling fan as it slowly rotates above him. The neon lights from outside flood the room with rainbows. Propping himself up on his elbows, he breathes heavily.

The sheet does little to hide the perfect outline of his toned body. Mike swings his legs over the side, sitting up. There's another bottle of whiskey on the nightstand, most of the amber liquid gone. He guzzles what remains, tossing the bottle toward the trashcan in the corner of the room. He misses and the bottle shatters against the wall like a snowball. Mike shakes his head, looking at the mess. Mike stands, stretches, and yawns. He exits the room only to come back with a small broom and dustpan. With a sigh, he sweeps the floor in the nude. He checks to make sure he swept up all the glass, and feels confident he has done so. Walking to the small kitchen, he dumps the contents of the dustpan into the wastebin. He puts the broom back in the corner. He greets his coffee maker as if it's an old friend, giving it a smile and a wave. He brews a pot of coffee.

Mike inhales the coffee like it's his life source. When he is done, he grabs a towel hanging on the bathroom door, wiping the sweat off his skin. He is careful to give his undercarriage special attention. He tosses the towel on to the bed and pours a second cup of coffee. He's still hot, and the coffee isn't helping. He throws open the bedroom window and the cool October breeze cools his skin. Mike pensively sips his coffee, looking out at the city.

Valkyrie City was built with everlasting paradise in mind. It was supposed to be the shining, glorious angel who guides you to Valhalla. Maybe once it was, but now it is mostly wet, cold, and dangerous. The city is full of gangsters, criminals both large and small, corrupt police, corrupt politicians, and something far worse: things that go bump in the night. There are creatures that consume human blood and flesh while hiding behind human faces. Things far worse than the Nazis I fought for the world's freedom, Mike thought, swishing the coffee in his mouth for a moment.

The buildings are old and brick. Except the ones that are boarded up and gutted, their steel pilfered during the Great War. The lower West Side is the most dangerous, populated by lowlifes, thieves, and drug addicts. That's where Mike spends most of his time.

Mike listens to sirens in the distance while a couple argues in the alley below. He turns, looking at the clock. 3:30 *in the morning*

CHAPTER 1

and people are fighting. Some poor kid probably has to hear all that. This city is going to pot.

He walks over to the coffee pot, pouring another cup of the steaming gold into his mug. Mike is starting to get a chill now. He flings on his bathrobe one-handed, careful not to spill his coffee. He steps out onto the fire escape and lights a cigarette, taking a long drag. *Oh, that's the stuff.* He blows the smoke out with a sigh of relief. Shutting his eyes and leaning back against the cool steel of the stairs, Mike balances the warm coffee cup on his right knee. The sound of the city relaxes him. The more he is surrounded by chaos, the better he thinks. He flexes his right hand. It's stiff and sore.

He rubs his hand, looking over the many scars, including the branding on his right palm. It's a war wound he'll never forget. His hand blurs out of focus as the memory rolls over him.

GERMANY—JANUARY 1945

Mike and his team make their way down a dirty underground corridor. The concrete walls are soiled with muck and water drips from stalactites hanging overhead. A blast rings out in the darkness and the walls crumble around them. Breathless and dazed, Mike lays in a pile of rubble and dust. Everything is muffled. He can hear screaming but has no idea who it is.

He watches through hazy eyes as one of his soldiers is raised in the air by what looks like an enormous octopus's tenacle and slammed to the ground. Mike rolls onto his back and props himself up on his elbows just as the same soldier is tossed at him. Mike takes the hit. The cracking of concrete and men screaming is all he can hear. Pushing his now dead comrade off him, Mike rises to his feet. Suddenly, a tentacle grabs his leg and drags him through the rubble.

VALKYRIE CITY—1950

With a gasp, he snaps his eyes open. "This fucking curse!" he laments. Inside the apartment, his phone rings. He grabs his coffee cup and steps back inside. He grabs the phone. "Mike Strong," he says into the receiver.

"I can always count on you, Strong," a female voice says.

"That you can. Are you burning that candle at both ends, Detter?" Mike asks playfully.

"You know this pencil pusher. I can never sleep until I've uncovered all of the evidence."

"And what are you investigating this time?" Mike steps back outside with the rotary phone, the cord snaking behind him.

"What do you know about Johnny Martoni?" she asks.

"I know he's a lower-level criminal looking for a leg up." Mike lights another cigarette.

"Is that a cigarette?" Detter asks.

"I know. I'll stop tomorrow. What about Martoni?"

"Well, I have it from a good source that Martoni might be trying to make some serious moves and climb up the ladder faster than expected," she says.

Mike thinks for a moment. "How's he gonna do that? He'd have to shoot his way up the ladder! Not to mention he's so short he'll need a *step stool* just to get to the lower rung!"

"You are hysterical, Strong. Well, he's suspicious of a rat in his gang. He's also let it be known on the street that he's expanding."

"A rat, huh? The fattest of the rats in his gang is probably Leo Guzzo. He strikes me as an opportunist!" Mike chuckles.

"How are the nightmares?" Detter asks with sincerity.

Mike doesn't speak for a moment, puffing on his cigarette. "Horrible," he admits. "Cloudy. A forgotten life from years ago. Thoughts I don't need and memories I don't want. Each one renting a room in my brain for the long haul."

"It's time to evict some of those memories," she says.

"Yeah, well, I'm out of whiskey and have..." He looks inside his pack of smokes. "One cigarette left, so I guess I will be stopping today."

"Meet me at 9:00 at Joey's!" she suggests.

"Alright, Detter, it's a date. I'll buy the pancakes!" Mike says with a smile.

"See ya at nine, Strong,"

"Tell your fiancé I said hello!" Mike adds.

"I will. He's working on some Port Authority story."

"You are like two peas in a pod," Mike chuckles.

CHAPTER 1

"Oh yeah, you know us. A real power couple in the journalism world."

"Becky Detter, in my mind, you're a shoo-in for the Pulitzer!"

"From your lips to God's ears! See you in a few, Mikey."

"See ya in a few, Detter!" He replaces the phone in the cradle, setting it aside. He sips his coffee and puffs on his cigarette. *Now that's a dame. Becky Detter you are pure magic in a world of darkness.*

Shots ring out from a nearby alleyway. It's a sound Mike is all too familiar with. He takes a long pull from his cigarette, looking out over the hazy city that screams for help. The lights bounce off the haze, giving it a sickly yellow hue. *This city needs one big match!*

Mike turns to close his window. A very pretty woman in a bathrobe stands on his balcony. She waves at him.

"Natasha, you okay, sweetheart?" Mike asks the blonde-haired woman.

"I heard you talking on the phone, and I can't sleep." she says, pushing her way into his apartment.

"No, come in," Mike says sardonically.

"Thank you. It's warm in here. What's your heat set at? Three hundred degrees?" She pulls out a pack of smokes, lighting one.

She asks while climbing in through my window in a bathrobe!

Mike quickly pulls out an ashtray, placing it on the table. Natasha sits, puffing on her cigarette. "What is your deal with her?" she asks, gesturing at the phone.

"Detter? We're work friends." Mike says, putting on an undershirt.

"Her fiancé also is a reporter, no?" Her English is broken with a thick Russian accent.

"Eighty-five percent of relationships start in the office!" Mike jokes, slinging a button-down shirt on.

"You're always alone, Strong." Natasha remarks, clearly judging him.

"Thank you. I'm in a relationship with myself. And coffee."

"You two have sex?" Natasha snickers, blowing out a cloud of smoke.

"No, I only drink the coffee." Mike says.

"I meant with the reporter," Natasha clarifies.

"No. It's strictly professional, no funny business." Mike loops his tie around his neck, knotting it beneath his Adam's apple.

"Where are you going at 4:00 in the morning?" Natasha stares at him.

"I need smokes and liquor. And more coffee." Mike says. He sits to put on his socks.

"You need a girlfriend."

"You making an offer?" Mike asks, grabbing an old pair of combat boots.

"Why you wear those ugly things with your nice suits?"

"I trust these boots. They're comfortable and they can take—and give—a beating." Mike laces them tightly.

"All men wear dress shoes but you!"

"You gonna talk about my shoes all day?" Mike smirks.

Please don't offer sex because I need to leave and get a jump on the day. I won't be able to resist!

"When you need a woman's touch, let me know. I get bored taking care of my mother."

"Well, that certainly is a fantastic offer, Natasha." Mike says.

"I don't want a boyfriend, but we can fuck whenever you want. In my country, sex isn't always attached to love. I too, love no one." Natasha says, revealing her naked breasts beneath her bathrobe. Mike stares at them in all their glory. He takes a deep breath, loosening his tie. *Well, that answers that.*

He tosses the tie. Before it lands on the dingy carpet, he and Natasha are locked in an embrace that would make the Gods blush. Her tight body glows under the neon lights, her breasts heaving. He strokes her thighs, then picks her up, dropping her unceremoniously onto his pull-out bed. Natasha smacks his face hard, and he grins.

"Come to me, American. Let me show you what a Russian woman can do with her tongue," she purrs, her kisses trailing down his stomach.

"Let me show you what I do with my tongue," Mike counters, grabbing her by the throat. He pushes her back on the bed, burying his face between her thighs.

"Yes, please." Natasha moans.

CHAPTER 2

The door chime rings as wide-eyed Becky Detter gleefully bursts into Joey's. She looks around, expecting to see Strong in one of the booths. Her cute yellow coat dress is as bright as her personality.

"Damn it, Strong!" she mutters under her breath, sliding into the first booth with her leather briefcase in tow. She tucks her brunette hair behind her ears. She pulls out a folder, a large notepad, and a number two pencil.

She waves at a very pretty, dark-haired woman. Her hair is slicked back and parted on the left. Her lips are a shiny, candy apple red. Her yellow paper hat, pinned in her hair, matches her white-and-yellow uniform.

"Whatcha need, Becky? Coffee?" Joanna asks.

"You know it, darling!" Becky winks, waving with her pencil.

"I'll have that up for you faster than a jackrabbit jumping off a tin roof in the middle of August!" Joanna grabs a coffee cup and spins it around her finger. She slides a saucer onto the counter with the other hand. With a twirl, she pours the coffee into the cup and slings the pot back onto the burner. She snags the saucer and a napkin and, in a wink, brings the coffee to Becky's table.

"You should have a traveling show, Joey!" Becky says with a gleeful smile. Becky notices Joey's nails are red, matching her lips "Your nails are impeccable!" she coos, grabbing Joey's hand.

"I'm gone for two minutes and you're getting proposed to!"

Becky and Joey look up to see Rachel, a tall, willowy redhead with thick curls. She is stunning, even while wearing the same yellow uniform as the other waitresses. "No, ma'am. I was just admiring her nails!" Becky laughs.

Rachel lovingly drapes her arm around Joey.

"I know. I'm kidding. Besides, Joey and I are just friends!" Rachel says, giving Becky a wink. Joey puts her hand on top of Rachel's, the gesture making the beautiful silver ring on her finger glisten. While Becky loved her boyfriend, Joey and Rachel were the couple that made her believe love conquers all. In truth, she is a little jealous of their love for each other.

"You ladies are amazing, and the coffee is the best in town!" Becky says, pointing her pencil at the two women.

"Are you ordering something to eat or just doing homework?" Rachel asks sweetly.

"Waiting on Strong again?" Joey asks.

"Always—the story of my life. Waiting on him is like ninety percent of my day" Becky snorts.

"I'm sure he'll want to eat!" Joey says, walking back behind the counter with Rachel.

"What's the word on the street?" Becky asks, looking around to make sure the diner is empty. The girls are her eyes and ears. Most of Valkyrie City's criminals eat in the diner and are too stupid to notice that Joey and Rachel are anything other than waitresses.

Joey unfolds a newspaper left behind by a patron, revealing the headline:

MIKE STRONG DOES IT AGAIN! FINDS MISSING ARTIFACT!

"You tell us. You're the reporter." Joey chuckles.

"I only write the small stuff. I need the *big* stuff. Any word on Johnny Martoni or his boss, Gustavo Geonetti? You get a lot of their goons in here, right?"

CHAPTER 2

Rachel hustles out of the back of the restaurant, carrying a stack of napkins "Actually, I did hear something. Lucy St. George over at The Dice Club was in here the other day and said she saw Johnny and his boys get into a huge argument over a snitch in the gang!"

"It's the mob, there's always a snitch!" Becky laughs.

The door jingles as Mike Strong steps in, the rising sun giving him a halo of sorts. Joey and Rachel start clapping and hooting in jest. Mike takes off his fedora and waves with it like a pageant winner on a parade float. "Thank you, ladies! I'm appalled and dishonored to be here!" Mike jokes. He tosses his hat, bounces it off his bicep, and back into his hand. Then he flips it, putting it back on his head.

Joey raises her eyebrows at Becky. "Talk about a traveling show!"

"Coffee, ladies! Two eggs, some bacon, maybe some home fries?" Mike slides into the booth across from Becky.

"Nice trick!" Becky quips.

"Thanks! I learned it while the Nazis were shooting at me."

Becky gives him a look.

"Seriously!" Mike shrugs his shoulders. "What?"

Joey sets Mike's saucer and coffee cup on the table. "Always a charmer, Strong!"

"I thought my powers didn't work on you two?" Mike smirks.

"You're pretty smooth, buddy!" Joey says before sashaying away.

"Why do you hate me?" Becky asks in a gruff voice.

"What are you talking about?" Mike pours a mountain of sugar into his coffee cup.

"I've been here for like twenty minutes. When we talked on the phone, you were already dressed. You didn't even bother to put on a tie!"

Mike cocks his eyebrow, touching his neck. "Yeah, I was. Then I wasn't," he mumbles, before sipping his coffee. He pulls his tie out of his trench coat pocket with a grin "But I brought it!"

Becky pulls a gold cigarette case out of her briefcase, flipping it open. She selects a black cigarette but before she can find her matches, Mike offers her a flame from his gold trench lighter. Then, he lights his own cigarette.

"Joey, fill 'er up, please," he calls, holding up his coffee cup.

"I literally just gave you that!" Joey exclaims from across the restaurant.

"Whatcha got for me?" Mike asks Becky as he sets his coffee cup back on the saucer. He eyes the newspaper in her hands.

"Not much," Becky admits, flipping the paper around so that he can read the headline. Mike snickers. The he notices the column below the fold. "What's this?"

"Here you go," Joey croons, pouring Mike a new cup of coffee from her pot. Becky grits her teeth, frustrated by the intrusion.

"Looks like Phillip got that Governor's Ball gig you wanted," Mike murmurs, reading the byline.

"I know. I'm pissed at my Uncle Ralph! Why would he give him the scoop I've been trying to get for two months?" Becky folds her arms.

Mike grins. *She's cute when she's angry.*

"Word on the street is that he likes balls. The bigger the better!" Joey jokes before heading back behind the counter. She slots the coffee pot back into the percolator.

"Speaking of 'on the street.' What've you heard about a few teen-aged girls gone missing?" Mike asks.

Becky reaches into her briefcase, pulling out a stack of folders. Thumbing through them, she puts one on top of the pile. "Here it is. This one. Amanda Hutchingsonton, twenty-two years old, disappeared three days ago. She is the daughter of a super wealthy judge from the Upper East Side. Cute girl."

"Amanda Hutchingsonton, that's a mouthful. Hutchingsonton? That's got to be fake, or someone didn't get their papers filed correctly when they made port." Mike skims the report. Amanda disappeared near the harbor. *What is a cute girl like that doing by the docks?*

"I know what you're thinking." Becky says. "Why is a cute girl like that down at the docks? No one knows, apparently." She sips her coffee.

"How much homework have you done on this?" Mike asks just as Joey places a plate of food in front of him. "Smells great, doll!"

"Very little. I haven't even talked to the parents yet. Not sure I can. I've got to get an article in about Abbott Vertchello's sentencing for those murders upstate by three o'clock today."

CHAPTER 2

"He's that guy who killed all those college kids right?" Mike asks around a mouthful of bacon.

"Yeah, nine kids he killed. They're throwing the book at him—seven life sentences."

"That's a waste. Take him out back and put a bullet in his head, that's what I say."

Joey is hovering. "Coffee?" she asks with a smile.

"I can't say I don't disagree with her," Becky says.

"I also don't not disagree?" Mike says, confused. "The reason I ask is because some broad came into my office—"

"You mean Natasha?" Becky interrupts with a laugh.

Suddenly, the hairs on Mike's arms stand up. For a moment, the room goes quiet and time seems to stop. Mike looks over his shoulder as a new customer walks in. He sits down at the counter, adjusting his dark suit. With a devilish grin, Mike nods at him. His ears pop and he finds that he is midway through answering Becky's question:

"Huh, she lives above my apartment. And no, it wasn't Natasha. Anyway. This lady said her son had been missing for a week and the police don't want to touch it for some reason."

Becky flips through the folders, pulling out another one. She hands it to Mike. He opens it to reveal a photograph of a young man. The name "Jason Savini" is jotted alongside; the same last name as the woman who was in his office. She'd introduced herself as Christine Savini. Mike reaches into his trench coat pocket, pulling out his small notepad. "This woman, Christine Savini." Mike says, tapping the name on the folder. "She came in and said her son was working that area. He hasn't been seen in weeks."

Becky stares at him. "As in prostitution?"

Mike nods.

He notices Becky looking over to the man at the counter. When she looks back at Mike, her mouth is downturned. "What is he?" she asks.

"He's from the underground. Probably looking for some sorry sap who needs a wish granted," Mike says.

"He's a Genie?" Becky asks, wide-eyed.

"Hardly." Mike sighs.

JOURNEY INTO HELL

The door to the cafe bursts open as five sailors barge in, singing some discordant tune. They are sloppy and clearly drunk. Joey and Rachel immediately go into customer service mode. Rachel pulls out her lipstick, using her reflection in the toaster to map her lips. Joey pulls her neckline down to reveal more of her cleavage before walking toward the men. "Sailors! My favorite!" Joey guides the men to a booth in the back. "You boys in town long?" she asks. The men stare at her and Rachel, smiling like goofballs.

Mike doesn't even notice the men. He's too busy reading the missing persons folder. As his eyes scan each word, he gets a little more upset.

Suddenly, something shatters, breaking Mike's concentration. The sailors are getting a little rambunctious. One of the men tries to give Joey a kiss. Joey dodges his onslaught of drunken pecking like a prize fighter. "Alright, fella. Let's just sit down," Joey says with a smile.

"You don't like me?" The sailor staggers.

"What would your mother say if she saw you like this?" Joey asks.

"Ma? My maather is a wholesome lady! I love ya, maaa!" the sailor shouts.

"Gentlemen, can you take your friend back to the ship?" Joey asks. "He's looking a little green around the gills and I'm not about to clean up any vomit."

"It's his birthday! He's looking for some love!" one of the men complains.

"Happy birthday! How old are you? 19?" Joey asks. "Did you drink all of the alcohol in town?"

"I'll have you know, I'm 21 today!" The drunken sailor belches. "I'm the oldest of all of us, you see."

The men laugh and smack the table. One of the sailors catches Mike staring. "What are you looking at, old man?"

Mike looks around as if to say, "Me?"

"Yeah, you!" The man shouts, jabbing his finger in Mike's direction.

"Sir, please. Let's just keep this friendly," Joey cajoles.

Rachel walks up to the table. "If you guys don't calm down and eat something, you're going to have to leave."

CHAPTER 2

"Leave? We're American soldiers! You can't kick us out!" one of the sailors exclaims, indignant.

Mike glances at Becky. She sips her coffee, tapping her pencil's eraser on the table. "These guys would be a cakewalk for you. Don't bother." she says.

"Look at us again, old man, and I'll show you what for!"

Mike smiles and waves at the sailors before turning back to Becky. "You're right. It would be a waste of time." Mike sips his coffee, discovering the cup is full again. Mike smiles. Becky looks past him. He can see in her eyes that something is wrong. Becky puts on her glasses, and, in the lenses' reflection, Mike can see two of the sailors approaching him. They glare at Becky and Mike.

"You got a problem?" one of the men asks.

Mike casually sips his coffee, while Becky pretends to read through some notes in her book. Neither look at the threatening men.

"Hey, you deaf or dumb?"

"Get up so that we can show you a beating in front of your girlfriend!" his friend adds.

"He's not my boyfriend!" Becky says coolly, writing something down.

"When you say it like that, it just makes me feel bad," Mike quips.

"Well, maybe you need a boyfriend??" The sailor leers.

Mike laughs at the audacity of this guy. "Man, you've got to give it to him!" That was good.

Becky looks up over her glasses at him. "Seriously? I wouldn't let this Milk Tooth take me to the firehouse if I was on fire."

"What was that, lady?"

"You heard her. Beat it, guys, before someone gets hurt," Mike says sternly.

"That's it, old man. Get up!" Milk Tooth says.

"No." Mike takes a long drag of his cigarette.

Rachel approaches the table slowly, trying to implore the men to vacate the premises. "Gentlemen, please. We understand you guys only get like one weekend a month on shore, but let's start the day off with a smile."

"What kind of shit is that?" the sailor asks.

Mike stands, getting in the sailor's face. "Watch your mouth around women, you young, inexperienced, wet behind the ears, mama's boy! Get out of here before I feed you a knuckle sandwich!" Mike hisses.

The two men back up but puff up their chests. "What's the big idea, fella?" Milk Tooth asks.

"The nice lady asked you to calm down or leave. Now, you have a third choice." Mike smiles.

The other trio of sailors approach. They smell like they took a dip in a pool of vodka and haven't dried off yet.

Mike takes a deep breath, squaring off. "I don't want to fight you boys. I wouldn't want you to go back to base with black eyes and broken noses. And I'm positive that Admiral Alexander wouldn't want that either."

Don't make me kick the living shit out of you five dumbbells and make you go back to base looking like Dalmatians.

As Mike waits for the men to make a move, his eyes drift toward the gentleman in the suit and fedora sitting at the counter. The man nods at him before taking a bite of his pie. Mike connects the dots. *Ah, a demon. He's bad news. One of those demons that doesn't follow guidelines; a free thinker out for blood—literally.*

Mike would wager the demon had been whispering into one of the soldiers' ears, goading him to pick a fight. *That's how they feed on humans: bad decisions. If I had a dollar for every bad decision I've made, I'd be a millionaire.* Distracted by the demonic presence, he doesn't see the punch being thrown until it is too late. It connects with Mike's jaw like a wrecking ball slamming into a brick building. Mike's back teeth and jawbone crunch. Mike takes the hit but doesn't falter. He stands, as sturdy as an oak tree.

Something special about Mike Strong is that he can take a hundred punches from a human. It's one of the unique gifts he received during the war. He has to play the part, though. The demon giggles and gives him a thumbs up. When the next punch comes, Mike dodges it with ease. "That's two," he warns the sailor. "I don't give three. Let the demon go, boy. He'll only bring you down. He'll take your life and make everything you eat taste like shit."

Only one of the sailors truly understands what Mike is saying. He locks eyes with Mike. "You've got a demon, pal," Mike continues, addressing him and him alone. "And he ain't nice. Has he been making you do stupid shit? Got you wrapped up in whatever

CHAPTER 2

offer he's made you? Did he promise you money? Women? Men? Whatever it is, let it go."

The other men back up in confusion.

Becky reaches into her briefcase, pulling out a mirror. She peers into the reflection, scanning the crowd behind her. Then, there! "Shit!" Becky says.

"What are you talking about, fool? Monsters?" the sailor says.

"I didn't say 'monsters'. I said 'demon.' He goes by Gurthrual, right? He makes you do shit. Steal maybe?"

Joey and Rachel watch in silence. This is not the first time they've seen Strong fight a demon. But they know it could get ugly. They both take one giant step backward, getting behind the counter. Rachel presses a red button on the underside of the cash register. A compartment under the counter flips open to reveal a sawed-off shotgun. Joey and Rachel lock eyes.

Mike reaches into his trench coat's inner pocket. He pulls out a necklace and slips the chain over his head. Then he pulls out a ring, sliding it onto his finger. He claps his hands together. "Grut slaog frem'qui," he intones, his eyes glowing blue.

"Gurthrual! Let him go. Show yourself and we can talk about it," Mike says. The man at the counter has vanished, but Mike knows he's still close by. "I know you're here; I already saw you." *The bastard had better show himself.* Mike looks over his shoulder at Becky. "Gurthrual. He's a low-level demon, known for possessions. Turns good people bad fast."

Suddenly, the room goes cold. Mike's breath is a puff of steam.

"What is happening?" one of the sailors asks fearfully.

"Well, your boy here got himself a good old-fashioned empathy demon." Mike turns his attention to the possessed sailor. "Did you lose someone recently?"

"My mom died while I was in boot camp. I was doing it for her. She needed money," the sailor says.

"What did you give away?" Mike asks.

"What?" the sailor asks, shaking.

Meanwhile, Becky flips through the pages of an old book she had stashed in her briefcase. She scans the stained pages, looking at various creatures, words, and symbols. The amount of information contained within the tome is overwhelming. Finally, she finds the name "Gurthrual" alongside some symbols.

"Got it!" Becky shouts. "Incantation or ex-possession?"

"Possession." Mike answers, keeping his eyes on the young sailor.

Becky slides the book across the table and Mike glances at it. The pentagram on his right hand begins to glow. "Grunta crisnota esesanta!" Mike slams his hand against the sailor's chest and his skin goes translucent. The sailor's veins bulge and his eyes suck into their sockets. It sounds not unlike a bursting watermelon. His mouth opens so wide that his jaw dislocates.

The sailors watch slack-jawed as their friend twists and bends. His spine snaps backward until both his hands and feet touch the linoleum. His stomach expands as the demon's face presses through his skin. "Strong!" the demon bellows.

"Shit," Becky breathes. She pushes everything into her briefcase, getting ready for anything. The four other sailors book it out of the cafe and down the city street.

Gurthrual tears through the skin of the sailor's stomach, slithering out. The body of the sailor falls limply to the floor.

Gurthrual stands up. He shakes the viscera off of his fedora, putting it on. He stares at Mike as he straightens his suit. Mike stares back at him. "Mike Strong, it's been a while," Gurthrual says, his sharp teeth glinting.

Mike takes his cigarette from the ashtray. "Taking lives and making strife, huh? You piece of shit!" Mike takes a drag.

"You say that like I'm evil," Gurthrual says.

"You are."

"Why? Because I use humans for my own purposes? That's not on me. That's on *them*. It's not my fault they can't differentiate their own inner monologue from demons. You understand that, I'm sure."

Don't I! "Clever demon. But you're *just* a demon to me. I'd put a bullet in my mouth just to watch you burn in hell," Mike says.

"What bugs the shit out of me, and so many others like me, is that you aren't afraid of us. How can you possibly look pure terror in the face and not be shaken to your core?" Gurthrual asks.

"Are you kidding me?! I watched a hundred men die in front of me. Thousands more perished. And for what? Because one of you dumb fucks took control of a depressed painter and we all tried

CHAPTER 2

to destroy the world together. I'm not afraid of any of you. You all have to die— angels, demons, monsters, werewolves, whatever the fuck else is out there."

"The righteous has spoken. You talk like a demon, yet you act like an angel," the demon remarks with a toothy smile.

"I'm kind of the middle of the road," Mike admits.

"You act like humans are blameless. They summon us and we do as they command. Of course, that comes at a price. And yet, they make the deal every time! *Every time*! Suckers! Oh and your friend—you know, that Austrian one with the 'stache and comb over—he was our best pupil. He did a lot for us. He almost broke the seal. Imagine that! What then, hotshot? You survived the war, so what? You got shot a few times, so what? You shut a door to another dimension and got some powers, so what? Like everything, you too will die. I'll still be here making humans kill each other, rob banks, stab hobos, talk quietly to children, shake babies to death. Yeah, keep shaking that baby, it'll stop crying eventually. *So what? What then, tough—*"

Click. BOOM!

Mike lowers his Army-issued Colt 1911, the same weapon that got him through the war. The same weapon he was holding when he touched a certain artifact.

The gun smokes. The shell casing bouncing off the floor is music to Mike's ears. *Plink!* The demon falls down dead, its brains and skull fragments spattered all over the floor and walls.

Mike looks down at the demon, its dark black blood pooling. It steams and seems to simply absorb into the linoleum. Mike holsters his gun, the red glow on the handle slowly dissipating. He flexes his hand, watching the pentagram fade, too.

Becky grimaces at the mess. Joey and Rachel immediately know what to do. They rush into the back, grabbing a plastic sheet used to ship non-perishable foodstuffs. They lay it on the ground beside the body. Becky drops to her knees, pushing the demon onto the plastic sheet. Together, they roll him up then take their gruesome package through the kitchen and out the back door.

Mike looks down at the dead sailor, his midsection a wet mess. "I hope it was worth it, kid. You've got about another million years in hell, so good luck!"

CHAPTER 3

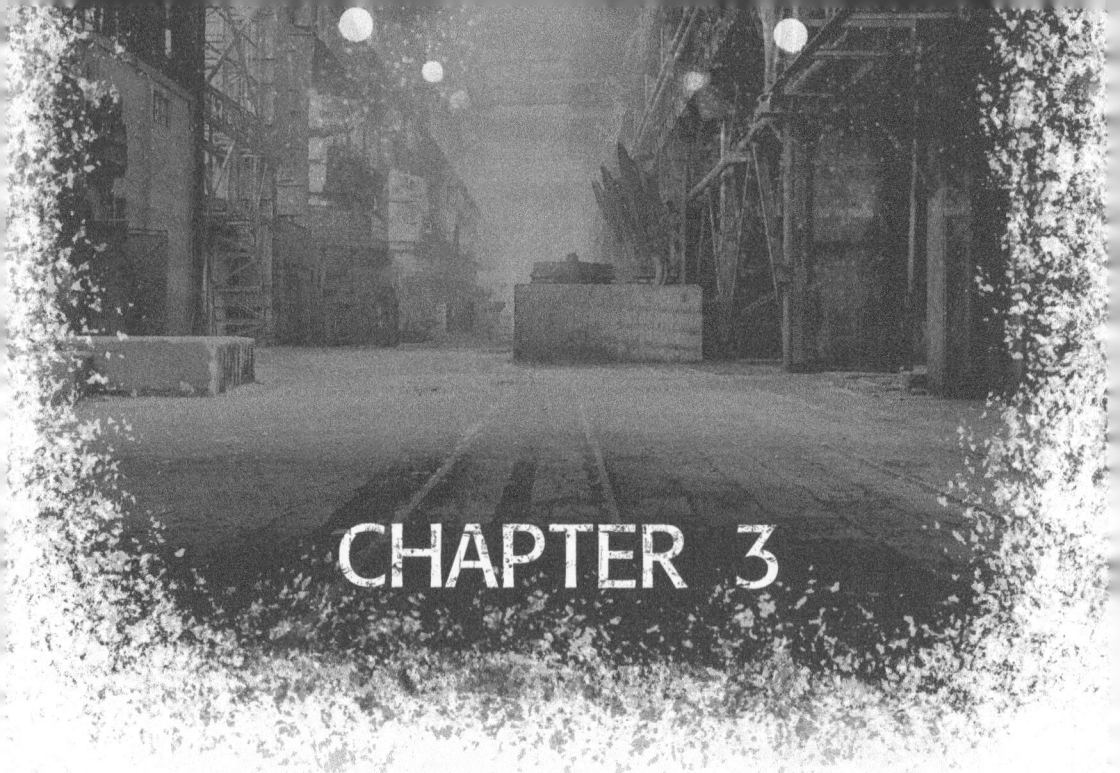

The southwest side of Valkyrie City is the most dangerous area. Hoodlums, gangsters, thieves, and all the other petty lowlifes end up here eventually. Low-income walk-up apartments and tents make up every street and corner. If you want the hard drugs—opium, heroin, meth—it's all here. Shoot it, drink it, eat it, snort it. The southwest side is a virtual shopping plaza of bad decisions.

It's pouring. Huge ships unload large shipping containers. Dock workers yell at each other as they work for a meager wage to try and keep their families fed. In the midst of these hard-working people is the cancer—the man who owns it all: Gustavo Geonetti. He's a ruthless, worthless, blight on the face of the city.

The mob boss to end all mob bosses, his retaliations are some of the worst. If you cross him, you will lose not only a finger but probably a whole hand. Cross him and you're dead and tossed in the drink. If you're lucky.

Gustavo Geonetti sits in the back of his Rolls-Royce as the rain beats against the roof. Two men approach the car, the small man wears an expensive suit, the other holds an umbrella out over his head. This is Johnny Martoni, an underboss. His henchman, who goes by Leo Guzzo, opens the back door so that Johnny can step

CHAPTER 3

into the vehicle. He is careful to keep the umbrella poised over Johnny's head.

"Close the door. You're getting the inside of my car wet," Gustavo orders in his deep voice. Johnny raises his eyebrows at his boss. *No shit*, he thinks, but shuts the door.

"It's raining cats and dogs out there. What am I supposed to do?" Johnny asks, shaking Gustavo's hand. He pumps it too enthusiastically.

"Jesus! Seriously? Johnny, you're like a child. You want to be an adult but your actions say otherwise. That's one of the most annoying things about you," Gustavo grumbles at the overexcited man.

"A child? I'm a damn man! A man!" Johnny replies, insulted.

"A man would keep his mouth shut and listen to what I'm about to tell him. A man would do what he is supposed to do. He wouldn't buy his broads fur coats and pearls, flashing his money around like a kid in a candy store. You've also gotta keep your men in line, Johnny..."

"My men are in line! My men are the best. Each one of them would take a bullet for me," Johnny interrupts.

"See, that's what I'm saying. You just talk and jabber on like a leaky faucet. The never-ending babble that pours out of your mouth is tiring." Gustavo takes a huge puff off his thick cigar.

"Gus—" Johnny starts but Gustavo smacks him across the face.

"Gus? *Gus?* I'm your fucking boss, not your friend! Don't ever address me like you're my pal, you shit stain. Your actions are giving some of the other bosses cause for concern. You walk around like you own the city, son! *You* don't own this city—I do! You understand? You follow me? You dumb-dumb! You will address me as Mr. Geonetti! You got that?" Gustavo screams at the small-framed man as he backhands him over and over again.

"Yeah, yeah! I got it! Mr. Geonetti! I got it!" Johnny cowers into the seat.

"You've got to rule your men with respect." Gustavo says calmly, relighting his cigar.

"Mr. Geonetti, I rule my guys with fear. They fear me!" Johnny says, blood pouring out of his nose.

JOURNEY INTO HELL

"Fear? No one fears you. And if you think your men do then you are mistaken. You need loyalty *and* fear. Your men have to understand that if they cross you, you will fucking kill them and their family. All of 'em—wife, kids, dog, cat, even their fucking goldfish. You got me? The consensus is that you ain't got no control of anyone in your gang. How do I know that, you ask? Well, I'll fucking tell you. One of your men is a snitch. We got word from one of our friends at precinct ninety-nine that one of your men is an undercover cop. A cop! You have a cop in your gang, Johnny. Fear? You ain't got fear. Loyalty? You're a joke to them. Change it up now, Johnny, or I'll drop you like a fucking bowling ball covered in cement." Gustavo blows a cloud of smoke.

"I understand." Johnny says, looking out the window at the pouring rain.

"I hope you do. Clean your house, Johnny. You've got a week." Gustavo spits tobacco out of his mouth.

"Don't you fucking hate that? When the tobacco gets in your mouth." Johnny says, trying to find a friendly leg to stand on.

"Shut up. End of the week, Johnny. Get out." Gustavo pushes Johnny out of the car into the rain. Leo tries to cover him with the umbrella, but Johnny trips and falls into the mud, ruining his white suit.

"Shit! God damn it! Help me up!" Johnny screams.

The window to the car rolls down. "Give me the umbrella," Gustavo says coolly, holding his hand out to Leo. Gustavo pulls the umbrella into the car and drives off, leaving Johnny cold and wet. The message is clear.

"Fuck me!" Johnny says, standing up.

"That didn't go as planned, huh, boss?"

"Shut up, Leo!" Johnny grumbles, storming off.

Leo hurries to catch up, opening the car door for Johnny. "Where to?" he asks.

"The penthouse." Johnny says, getting into the car.

Leo drives through the city with its towering skyline, Johnny sulking in the backseat. The rain makes it hard to see. The narrow streets are crammed with vehicles of average folks making their way to work. Johnny is fuming, his face red.

CHAPTER 3

"I'll show him. I got control, Leo! I got control!" Johnny says as he snorts a line of white powder.

The Hastings Towers are upscale apartments for the elite. The high-rise is a shining beacon of hope for some and a zit on the chin for others. The poor hate those inside and those
inside snub the poor. Johnny is no different.

The uniformed valet greets Johnny Martoni's car with a huge umbrella. "Got a little wet today, Mr. Martoni?" The valet smiles.

"No, you nitwit, I went swimming in a suit!" Johnny says sarcastically, shoving his way past the taller man.

"Fair enough, sir," the valet says, doffing his dark blue brimless cap.

"I'll park the car and be right up, Mr. Martoni." Leo says, his forearm resting on the steering wheel.

"Good." Johnny says, already striding into the huge building. The lobby is reminiscent of a museum. The floors are made of marble and the towering pillars look like something from Greece. There is a giant statue in the center of a centaur pouring a jug of running water into a fountain, a mermaid lounging alongside.

Beyond the fountain is a large sitting area with red leather couches and chairs with gold trim. There are several paintings on the wall. One, in particular, is a recreation of Jacques Louis David's *The Lictors Bring to Brutus the Bodies of His Sons*—a mournful depiction of Brutus sentencing his sons to death by burning in stark red hues.

As Johnny passes by the 15 foot tall recreation, his shoes squeak. An older man lounging in a high-backed chair with a newspaper laughs as he walks by. "Cram it, old man!" Johnny growls.

"Nice suit!" the old man snickers.

An elevator operator cranks open the golden gate, allowing Johnny to step inside. The elevator has a cherry-wood floor and a matching handrail. The mirrored walls are etched with roses and filigree that resembles thorny vines.

"Fifteenth floor, sir?" the operator asks.

"That's my floor, isn't it?" Johnny snaps. The operator ignores his outburst, pressing the button for the fifteenth floor. Then, he cranks the golden gate shut and the elevator rises with a loud clanking of chains and counterweights.

JOURNEY INTO HELL

Johnny Martoni's apartment is perhaps the swankiest crib in town. The foyer is polished marble with a purplish hue when the sunlight hits it just right. The sunken living room has four stylish, black leather couches in a cross formation with a large coffee table between them. On the coffee table is a three foot tall ceramic statue of *St. Michael Vanquishing Satan*. On the far side of the apartment is the kitchen, the cabinets a muted gray and the appliances black. The whole apartment is dark in color and mood. Just like Johnny Martoni.

The large wooden door bursts open as Johnny storms in. He yanks his tie off and throws it on the floor. He kicks off his shoes and they go flying across the living room, almost knocking over his beloved statue. His suit jacket and white shirt puddle on the floor. Johnny doesn't notice the beautiful woman sitting at his kitchen table in a red and white polka-dotted sundress. Her beautiful auburn hair is styled in bouncy curls that rest elegantly upon her shoulders. Her big brown eyes widen as she watches her dripping wet lover cross the living room. With a huff, he disappears into his bedroom.

Those gorgeous red lips gape in shock, cigarette smoke billowing out of her mouth. She sits still. The magazine she had been reading lays forgotten on the tabletop. The kitchen's giant, easterly-facing window bathes her in soft light, bringing out the reddish highlights in her hair. The embers of her cigarette burn in the ashtray.

"Everything alright dear?" Lucy St. George calls.

Johnny sticks his head out the door of his bedroom. "No! How long have you been here?" Johnny asks, fighting with his wet socks. He finally manages to peel them off.

"Since about 10 o'clock this morning. I thought you were going to be here," Lucy shouts across the apartment, her heavy Bostonian accent echoing off the walls.

Johnny walks out of the bedroom, buttoning a fresh, dry shirt. "We got problems, doll!" He tucks his shirt into his pants.

"By the looks of it, I'd say so. What happened?" Lucy asks, getting up and walking over to the drink cart.

"Geonetti thinks I don't have control of my boys! And that ain't good! 'I'm a liability,' he says. I'm a liability? What the hell is he

CHAPTER 3

talking about. I get shit done. I move heroin, booze, numbers, and that new shit. What's it called? Those fucking Nazis were hooked on that shit. Meth! I move that too!" he crows, cinching his tie tight.

Lucy looks up at her man, handing him a scotch on the rocks. His right eye is black and blue, and his lip is swollen.

"Did he hit ya, babe? That lunatic. He's gonna get what-for, that's for sure. No doubt about it." Lucy fills a washcloth with ice from the bar cart's ice bucket. She leans in, putting the ice against his mouth.

"Problem is, I know I've got a rat. I have to have one. No way someone didn't tip off the coppers last week. We could have had those paintings and been gone. I know it." Johnny takes a gulp of scotch.

"Take it easy, freight train. You've still got to get to the station." Lucy says, examining his swollen eye.

"I'll show him. Maybe I will clean house—all the way to his house!" Johnny paces.

Leo walks into the apartment, tracking water on the floor. He loiters in the foyer, waiting for Johnny to acknowledge him.

"Leo! Call a meeting tonight at The Dice Club. I want Jacky, Pete, and Louie there. You too, darling. Let's paint the town the red!" Johnny grabs Lucy by her shoulders, laughing manically.

CHAPTER 4

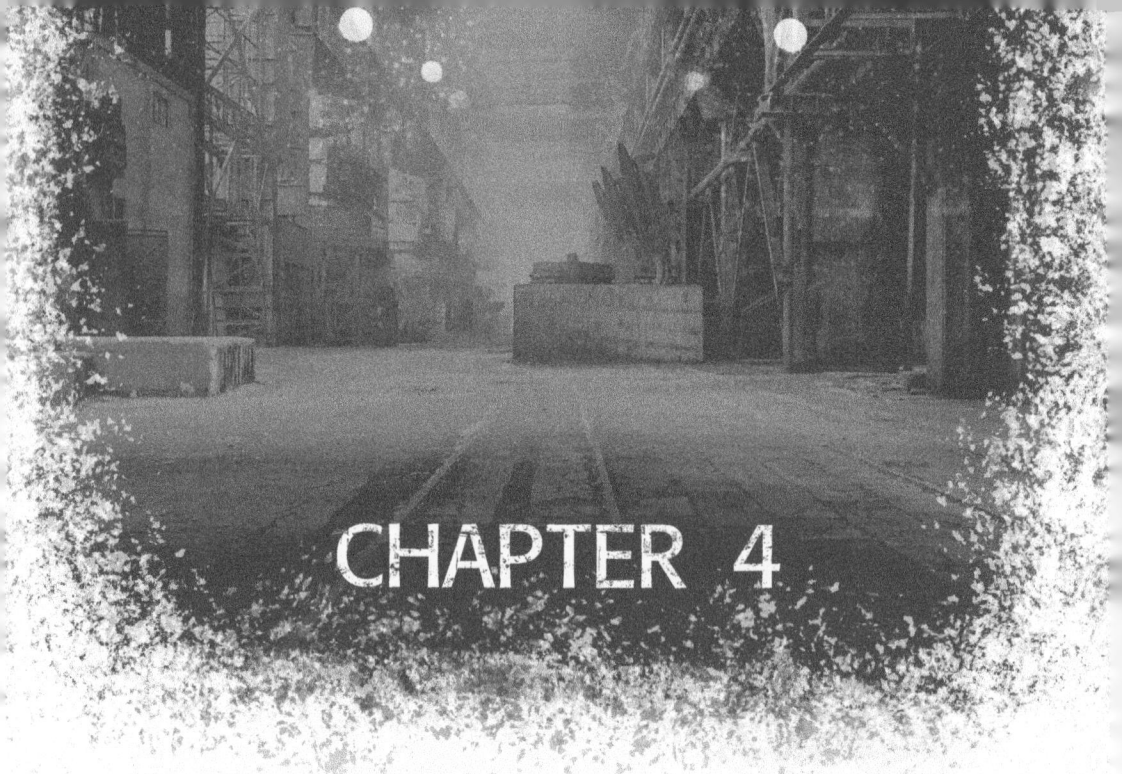

The sound of the tank rolling by makes Mike jerk awake. The concrete that he'd been using as a pillow hurt his head anyway. The smell of the burning town made it hard to sleep peacefully; he was plagued by nightmares. Several American soldiers march behind the rumbling tank. Mike rubs his eyes, watching as the world burned before him.

"Strong! I've got orders for you."

Mike is greeted by a tall man in dirty military fatigues. He holds out a folder. "You're Second Lieutenant Strong, correct?"

Mike stares at the man, not comprehending.

"It's my understanding you are the only one left in your battalion. I am sorry to hear about your loss," the messenger says mournfully.

"It's alright, kid. We all knew what we were signing up for. Easily could've been another guy standing here. But now, it's me." Mike takes the folder.

"You're on a plane at 0600," the messenger continues.

"A plane? To where? I just got here!" Mike asks.

"I'm not at liberty to say, sir," the messenger says, standing at attention.

"Sir? You've got silver bars there, First Lieutenant." Mike salutes. "You outrank me!"

CHAPTER 4

"Not any more I don't, sir." The messenger inclines his chin toward the folder.

Mike opens the folder and two pins with attached silver bars fall out. He stares at the pins in his hand for a moment, then looks at the messenger. "Captain?"

---

6 a.m. came early for Mike. Even the sun was still sleeping. The sound of the twin engine UC-78 Bobcat was loud and made it very difficult to hear. Two officers greet him outside the idling plane.

"Nice to meet you, Captain Strong." An officer says. The nameplate on his chest reads Fairchild and, judging by the bars on his shoulders, he's a First Lieutenant.

"Please, won't you join us?" The Lieutenant motions to the aircraft.

"I've got a choice?" Mike smirks.

Both the men shake their heads. With that, the three men climb into the cramped Cessna. Mike sits in the fourth seat in the back. He is as snug as a bug in a rug. His shoulders squeeze together, and his knees are now one with his chest.

"Snug." Mike remarks, but his companions hardly hear him over the engine.

"I'm sorry." Lieutenant Fairchild says, craning his neck to look back at Mike.

Mike just waves a hand as if to say never mind. Outside, a soldier shuts the main door to the plane and pounds on the window. The pilot gives him a thumbs up. Mike watches out the window as another soldier yanks two yellow wooden blocks out from underneath the front wheel. The plane creeps forward. Mike doesn't have much faith in the Cessna's ability to do much of anything except crash into bullets.

Mike looks out the window as the plane lifts off the tarmac. The devastation in the surrounding area is far too immense to fathom. There are literal holes in the earth and entire neighborhoods reduced to rubble. As the plane treks across the landscape, Mike stares at the world on fire.

What is to become of us? To think, a month ago I was teaching a bunch of college kids. Mike's eyes water. Looking at the carnage forced him to think about more than he wanted to.

He refocuses on the interior of the plane. Both seats in front of him were occupied by an officer. Fairchild sat in the seat directly in front of him and an officer he hadn't met yet is beside him. The seat next to Mike is empty except for a manila folder with his name stamped on it in large, red letters. Mike's curiosity gets the better of him and he picks it up. It's heavy and there seem to be some papers and what feels like a few photographs inside. Lieutenant Fairchild turns.

"That's yours. Read it." he instructs before turning back around.

Mike unwinds the red string keeping it sealed when Lieutenant Fairchild abruptly turns back around. "Also, don't be surprised by what you see. Some things in this world are just too outstanding for one to believe without outside influences."

Mike slowly opens the folder, not sure what to expect. He slid out a cover letter addressed to him and some 8x10 photos of strange symbols, artwork, and a group of men and women in dark robes standing in a circle around a huge funeral pyre.

Mike thumbs through the photos. *Why are they showing me pictures of witchcraft and Nordic runes?*

Mike studies a picture of a stone tablet engraved with ritualistic symbols. He chuckles when he reads the caption written in black marker across the top of the picture. *These are not Egyptian hieroglyphs,* he thinks, shaking his head. He turns the picture upside down to reveal an ancient form of spellcasting. He turns his attention to the letter addressed to him:

June 10, 1944

Captain Michael Strong,

> *The world is suffering, and we are calling on you: the Soldiers, the Sailors, the Airmen of the Allied Expeditionary Force! If you are holding this letter, it is because you offer a unique skill or profession that will benefit the safety of Life, Liberty, and the Pursuit of Happiness in the greatest country in the world: the*

CHAPTER 4

United States of America! We must defend our liberties from this ruthless, heartless, fascist radical known as Adolf Hitler and his army of Nazis. Now, go forth and fight for not only the United States of America, but the entire world! Good luck and Godspeed!

Dwight D. Eisenhower,
President of the United States of America
In God We Trust!

"The world is on fire and all because one insane lunatic wants to be a king!" Mike looks out the window as gunfire illuminates the copse of trees below. Mike knows each flash of light precipitates a man's last breath.

The plane lands on the tarmac with a bounce. Mike is rattled awake as it skids down the runway. *How long have I been out?* He wipes his mouth. Looking out the window, he can't see much of anything.

Through the cockpit's window, Mike can make out some large lights ahead but that's about all. The plane turns to the right as it rolls slowly toward its destination. As the engine stills, Mike rubs his ears and shakes his head. He can't believe how loud those engines were.

"We're here!" Lieutenant Fairchild announces. "Did you enjoy your flight?"

"Oh yeah, it was swell. We didn't get blown up!" Mike smirks.

"Not today." Lieutenant Fairchild follows the other officer out of the plane.

Mike pulls himself between the seats, his dirty fatigues smearing dirt across the cloth. He hit his head on the ceiling as he exits the plane. The two officers watch as he rubs his head.

"Watch that first step, it's a doozy!" Lieutenant Fairchild laughs.

Mike grimaces.

"Captain Strong, I don't think I introduced Major Leland Charland," Lieutenant Fairchild motions to the man who had been sitting beside him for the entire flight.

Mike salutes the tall, dark-haired man. Major Charland salutes back. "No need for formalities at this point. From here on out, we are undercover, so to speak," Major Charland says in a deep voice.

"I don't follow."

"It'll all be explained inside," Major Charland replies.

Mike looks around but doesn't see any kind of building, hut, or even a tent. "Inside? Inside where?"

Major Charland laughs as the ground opens up with a *whoosh*. A piece of earth about twenty feet wide rises like a horizontal garage door. The hydraulics hidden in the earth rumble and bright spotlights shine into the dark forest. The door reveals a hidden bunker. Mike notices the steps leading into the bunker are made of ancient stone. He follows Major Charland down into the structure and immediately recognizes the art on the wall.

"This is ancient Gaul," Mike remarks.

Major Charland stops, examining the artwork depicted on the wall. "What's that, now?"

"This artwork is made by the Gaul people. Fifth Century. We're still in France then, I take it?"

Major Charland and Lieutenant Fairchild laugh. "You just know this stuff off the top of your head?" Lieutenant Fairchild asks.

"Yeah," Mike says, sucking on the inside of his cheek.

"Well, now I know why you're here," Major Charland says, patting him on the shoulder. "C'mon. This way."

The stone hall opens up into a huge, stone room with all kinds of artifacts. There are Grecian statues, paintings, ceramics, stone sculptures, and a ton of soldiers boxing items up to be shipped. "Why do you have all these priceless artifacts?" Mike asks. Then he spots something amazing. "That's the Galia Gladius!" Mike picks it up.

The entire room stops what they're doing, watching him swing the sword around. "This is amazing. Where did you find this?"

"We didn't. All these artifacts were on a train headed to Romania. We intercepted, or rather our men—" Major Charland motions to a group of six men sitting around a table, drinking tea. "—stopped the train and retrieved the stolen artifacts. We'll ship them back to America for the time being."

CHAPTER 4

Mike admires the golden hilt. A smile lights up his face. "This is the Galia Gladius, the sword of a would-be prince. It's based on a Celtiberian sword design. However, this has a 30-inch blade, the rest were only 27 inches in length. It's supposed to have beheaded a Leviathan. It's said that those who use it become obsessed with killing." Mike rattles off the facts like its common knowledge.

A soldier walks over, sticking his hand out to Mike. Mike hesitates but gives the man the weapon in his hand.

Major Charland stares at him. "You're odd for a..." He checks his notes. "...a teacher of theological studies at Harvard."

"Sorry to disappoint you." Mike says, clicking his heels together like a soldier at attention. "You're kind of what I expected."

"Follow me." Major Charland makes his way to another corridor that leads into another large stone room.

"Have a seat," Major Charland points to a vacant chair next to several seated soldiers.

Mike wedges in between two large men. He is uncomfortable; clearly, as are the other ten soldiers seated at a table made for two. Mike looks around. He doesn't recognize anyone. Some of the men look like they haven't slept in days. Not like you can sleep with bombs going off every ten minutes.

"Gentleman, we have brought you here because each of you has a certain skillset relevant to this particular mission. Now, I know what I can tell you and I know what I need to tell you.

"Our first mission is in Romania. We will storm a bunker in the mountains. Inside, there are men working to destroy the planet itself. We have gathered intel on the fact that Hitler is collecting artifacts from all over the world to help aid in his victory. These artifacts may be religious in nature, or in some cases, supernatural. I personally don't believe in that kind of stuff, but when an axis of evil like Adolf Hitler is consuming countries like a child eating chocolate, we must act no matter how bizarre the belief.

"That is why you are here. To help explain this further, I'll introduce you to our newest trusted colleague and Nobel Prize-winning physicist Albert Einstein." Major Charland says, turning to a very recognizable face stepping out of the darkness. Mike sits up in his seat.

"Holy fuck!" he exclaims before clapping his hand over his mouth. "S'mourry," Mike says, his voice muffled beneath his palm.

Albert Einstein's hair is disheveled, as if he just escaped from a sanitorium. He is wearing a dress shirt, sweater vest, and dress pants. Where one would expect loafers, he's wearing combat boots, the laces untied. As he starts to speak, his thick German accent is hard for the soldiers to understand. Several of the soldiers look at each other in confusion while Einstein explains the mission they are about to embark on.

"Unified Field Theory. There are fields—or, rather, one unified field—that affects all four of the fundamental forces in the universe, including gravity and electromagnetism. This field is beyond our comprehension. We can't measure it.

"The laws of nature are not quantifiable. What we once thought to be true is now false. I have studied physics for decades and I am humbled by my own misconceptions. What is it if not magic? I'm now a believer of the unseen. I present to you a series of images the likes of which you have never seen." He clicks the projector, and the first image appears on the bunker's rough-hewn wall.

The men sit in shocked silence as he clicks through the images. Each one is more absurd than the next. Mike perches on the edge of his seat, trying to understand what he is seeing. *What in God's name is this man talking about? Is he talking about magic? Sorcery? Witchcraft? These are not real things.* Some of the symbols on the projector are ones he recognizes, and some are obscure. Perhaps they are from ancient civilizations he is not privy to. It's the images of men and women that are the most disturbing. One shows a woman being sacrificed while watched by a group of cloaked figures. Another is a man in a hooded cloak slicing a goat's neck. A third shows a woman laying on a pedestal as a man pours blood onto her naked body.

Mike raises his hand.

The last image is dark and overexposed. A young girl stands with a man and a woman, her midriff exposed. A face with angular features presses through her rounded stomach.

"Excuse me!" Mike shouts, waving his raised hand like a child tired of waiting his turn. The entire room is startled and wakes up.

CHAPTER 4

Some of the other soldiers jerk upright in their chairs, wiping their drool-slick mouths.

Einstein looks up, raising his bushy eyebrows. "Go ahead."

"Are you suggesting that Hitler is using *witchcraft* to win the war?" Mike asks.

Einstein pulls his glasses down to the tip of his nose, looking over the rims. "I have come to the conclusion that the theory of relativity must include an expansion of the imagination," he says.

So, is that a 'yes'?" Mike asks.

"Gentlemen, what we are about to do is go up against pure evil itself. And we're going to need more than bullets to stop it," Major Charland interrupts. "I mean, they're gonna help. A lot." The soldiers snicker. "We leave at 0600 hours for Romania. Sleep tight and eat up. Chow is in the room down the hall and the shitter is up top by whatever tree suits you. Remember, eat when you can eat, shit when you can shit, and sleep when you can sleep!" His voice rings through the cavernous room long after he stops shouting.

Mike remains rooted to the spot, occupied by what he has just seen—and heard. The exiting men brush past him, but he doesn't even notice. He is somewhere else. His mind races at the fact that magic and witchcraft might be real. He thinks of all the past religions he's studied and passages he's read. "Am I in a different reality?" he says aloud, but no one is around to answer.

CHAPTER 5

The rain chills Becky to the bone. She darts from one awning to another, leapfrogging down the sidewalk to *The Valkyrie Herald*. The Herald is the most prestigious newspaper in all of Valkyrie City, and not just because Becky Detter is the nosiest, in-your-face reporter that any Private Investigator would want on their side.

Becky's white high heels clack on the sidewalk as she darts to yet another awning. The shopkeeper gives her a nod. "Wet enough for ya?" he asks with a chuckle.

"No! I wish it would get colder. Then I could ice skate. I'd finally get to work on time!" She winks. She holds her very own newspaper over her head and scurries back out into the drizzle that was once a downpour. Becky looks good in her sky-blue skirt suit and thin white belt. Her red leather trench coat protects most of her outfit from the water. The loud color clashes with her outfit, but it is fashion forward and, somehow, works perfectly.

Cutting across the busy street, Becky finally makes it to her building. The massive 110-story building is the largest in the entire city and is named *The Spear of Light*, mostly due to the huge spotlight that shines skyward. The moniker also refers to the city's name and the weapon used by the Nordic Angels of Death.

CHAPTER 5

Becky shuffles into the lobby with a few other sodden personnel; they all shake off from the rain. Becky tosses the wet newspaper into the trash bin by the door, making her way to the wide, tiled staircase. Her office is on the third floor.

"Good morning, Gary!" She nods to an old janitor trying his best to keep the floor dry.

"Good morning, Ms. Detter. Where in heaven is your umbrella?" the nice old man asks.

"It wasn't raining when I left my house!" Becky shoots back.

"You're gonna melt in all this rain, honey. You're made of sugar and just as sweet!" he says with a crooked smile and wink.

"Gary, you sure know how to talk to a woman!" Becky rounds the staircase to the third floor. The office of The Valkyrie Herald is loud, consisting of three rows of five desks, all occupied by crafty, fast-talking reporters. Some are on the phone, while others type on their Brandowitz 940 typewriters, making the room sound like it's under machine-gun fire.

She squeezes between several desks to reach her own, smack dab in the center of the room. Each is laden with scribbled notes, papers, folders, and trash. Journalists are pack rats by nature; there's no telling what will inspire a story. Becky finally reaches her desk amongst the commoners in the bullpen, flopping her heavy briefcase onto the blotter. She sighs in relief as she sinks into her chair. The familiar clacking of dress shoes amidst the rapid fire of typewriter keys announces her fiancé's presence. He leans over the back of her chair, giving her a kiss on the forehead.

"Good morning, my lovely wife-to-be!" the tall, handsome man says. Becky spins around in her chair to look up at Phillip Aldameyer, the second-best reporter *The Valkyrie Herald* has to offer. His suit is a lovely gray with checkerboard cross-stitching. His white shirt underneath his matching vest is neatly pressed. His red bow tie oddly matches the trench coat she is wearing.

"Hello, my love!" She grins.

"I trust your morning was fine?" Phillip asks. Becky thinks for a moment, knowing she must lie to him about the goings on with Mike Strong. He won't believe her if she dared to mention demons.

"It was fine. Wet." Becky says, rising to give him a tight hug. Phillip locks eyes with another male colleague. Their stare is deeper than it should be. No one notices, least of all Becky. Phillip awkwardly wraps his arms around his fiancée, returning her embrace.

"I have a busy day, my love. I'm off to interview the Chief of Housing on what is to be done about Hannigan's Port. What a dreadful place."

Becky steps back a little with justified dignity. "Those poor people have had enough issues with the city. Where are they supposed to go? Disappear into the woods and live like Robin Hood?"

Phillip adjusts his bow tie, taking a gulp of air. "Well, no. But they must go somewhere, darling. They can't live in tents and under all the bridges of Valkyrie City!" He smooths the wrinkles in his jacket and carries on.

"I love you!" Becky says, her arm sliding down his sleeve as he presses past her. Phillip turns, bringing her in for one more hug. "I love you, too!" The moment is broken by a bellowing voice.

"Becky, my love! Can I see you in my office?" The deep voice belongs to the editor-in-chief and owner of *The Valkyrie Herald*, Ralph Detter, Becky's uncle. Phillip uses this opportunity to escape as fast as he can.

Ralph Detter's shirt is unbuttoned, and his tie is loose, even though it's only 8:30 in the morning. He is holding a cup of steaming coffee and, just like her, there is a pencil tucked behind his ear. As he heads back into his private office, Becky leans over her desk, pushing some papers aside to look for her notepad.

She finally finds the leatherbound pad and rushes into her uncle's office. Ralph sits behind his huge oak desk. There's a large, bronze bucking bull paperweight in the corner. The inscription on the base reads "The Bull!" He examines a stack of papers with a magnifying glass. To his left rests a messy stack of dingy folders, clearly not belonging to him. They are wrapped in twine and dog-eared from frequent use and improper storage. Becky looks at him with her notepad ready and pencil poised. "What you got, boss?" she says with gumption.

"What do you know about the missing persons scene?" he asks in a gruff voice, sitting back in his oversized chair.

"Can't imagine it's much of a scene if everyone is missing?" Becky says, cracking herself up.

CHAPTER 5

"I have a stack of papers here that the police chief gave me. He would like you, specifically, to look into this matter." He takes a sip of coffee.

"Why me?" Becky asks, sitting down.

"I'm not sure. Do you have a connection to someone missing?" Ralph asks.

"No, I do not. At least, I don't think I know anyone who might be missing. Then again, how would I know? They're missing!" She guffaws, slapping her knee.

"Well, this is your top priority now. The chief is very adamant that we tackle this as soon as possible. He doesn't want the civilians to get word of a possible murderer on the loose." Ralph coughs.

Becky slides to the edge of her seat, pulling the stack of folders closer to her. She looks over the top folder, reading the name on the tab: *Jessica—Baltimore*. There are some numbers and a case file: **MP-1664-Z1**. Untwisting the twine, she opens the folder, examining a photo of a young girl with a wide smile.

"Cute girl, too bad she's just a case file now," Becky says, disgusted.

"Exactly. There're thirty-five missing persons case files there. Find out what is happening and do it quickly," Ralph says.

"Oddly enough, I met with Mike Strong this morning for breakfast—sort of, anyway, He had a woman come into his office looking for her son. What was his name?" She thinks for a minute. "Jason Savini!" She thumbs through the files looking for Jason Savini's name. She doesn't find it. "Well, if it's related to Strong's case then things could get hairy. This sounds like a detective's case workload. I'm just a reporter, Ralph! What do you want me to do? Arrest someone?"

"No. I want you to uncover who is taking all these people," Ralph says, folding his meaty arms.

"I'm not a cop." Becky insists, standing up with the case files in-hand.

"Nope. But you are one hell of an investigative journalist, and you seem to have a knack for hearing things on the street. Someone has to know something." He smiles.

Becky chews on her cheek for a moment. "You know, boss, some days, things just line up." She gives him a wink and walks out of his office.

JOURNEY INTO HELL

The small room is dark until Becky pulls on the small, beaded chain. The light doesn't help much; it's still a little too dim in the small storage closet that Becky is about to turn into her command center. Becky pushes several file boxes against the back wall. The dust plumes in the air, obscuring the yellow hue of the flickering light. Taking some boxes off a shelf, she finds a window that is covered up. Becky quickly removes the rest of the boxes and moves the shelf to the other wall. With a grunt, she rips the wooden plank off the window and is hit with a blast of sunlight.

"Well, that's better!" she says, still holding the wood plank. Now, to deal with the clutter! She opens the door to the room and starts pushing old boxes into the hallway. After a while, the hall is full of boxes, rickety old chairs, and the sun-bleached plank of wood.

Becky rests for a moment, wiping her brow. Looking back into the room, she is satisfied with her new office area. There's a small table with a chair, a lamp, and several filing cabinets. She unfolds a huge map of the city, thumbtacking it to the wall. Then she starts going through her folders.

With each new missing person's case, she puts a pin in the map at the location where said person was last seen. Once finished, she steps back to look at the map. There doesn't seem to be a pattern—at least not one she could discern. "I certainly hope Strong has a few answers," she says to herself.

She adds each person's picture to the corkboard next to their respective thumbtack. There are over thirty pictures on the wall now. Becky is in awe at the amount of people who have gone missing in the past several months. The last thing Becky does is write the names of each of the victims under each photo.

Becky looks at her watch. It's 1:45 in the afternoon. Exiting the closet, she trips over the boxes she forgot she'd stashed in the hall. She squeezes past the mess and makes her way toward the bullpen, where it's as loud as a bandstand.

She scoops her purse and jacket off her desk, intending to go to lunch. Uncle Ralph stops her. "How far did you get?" he asks.

"Not far. Mainly just set up my work area so I can start to make sense of all of it. There's a lot of missing people, Ralph!" Becky leans on her desk.

CHAPTER 5

"I know. I'm worried it's more than just missing people," Ralph murmurs, straightening his tie. He looks particularly dapper today; he doesn't typically wear a tie, much less an unwrinkled shirt.

"You got a hot date?" Becky asks.

"If lunch with the mayor and police chief is a date, then yes," he replies.

"Sounds like I should come. I *am* hungry." Becky smirks.

"You're more than welcome. I could use the backup." Ralph says, grabbing her by both of her shoulders.

"Lead the way, daddy-o!" Becky says.

CHAPTER 6

Mike strolls along the wharf, studying the people. He passes a slew of merchants selling the catch of the day to the locals. *Now, that's a smell only a mother could love.* Mike wrinkles his nose. He stops at a vendor selling Atlantic salmon. "Hey buddy, you ever see this kid around?" Mike asks the stout fisherman, showing him a photograph of Jason Savini. The man shakes his head and Mike continues on his way.

He turns to a couple buying some melons. "Excuse me, do you come here a lot?"

"About once a week, fella," the man replies.

Mike tips his hat in greeting. "Have you seen this young man?" He shows them the photo, but they also shake their heads.

Mike steps out from under the awning of the vendor aisle into an open concrete area. He sees a few men that look like they may be searching for a John or two. *There's a couple of working stiffs!* He chuckles. *Working stiffs. I kill me.*

"What can I do for you?" one of the men purrs.

Mike smiles. "I'm not here for that, mister. Have you seen this kid around?" Mike shows him the picture of Jason Savini.

"Who wants to know? You a copper?"

CHAPTER 6

"I don't have a badge, if that's what you're asking," Mike replies smoothly.

The man seems satisfied with that answer. "I'm Gary."

Gary, huh? Not the name I was expecting. "Mike Strong," Mike says.

"A pleasure." Gary replies, looking Mike up and down.

"So anyway, have you seen the kid?"

Gary studies the photograph again and calls over another gentleman loitering across the street. The man walks up, giving Mike a once over. "Handsome," the man observes.

"Mike Strong, Starlight. Starlight, Mike Strong," Gary says, gesturing between them.

"He sure is. I bet he's as strong as they come," Starlight laughs. Gary playfully swats Starlight's arm.

Yeah, this is more like it, Mike thinks.

Starlight takes the photo, looking at it. "Yeah, that's Ginger. Well, his street name is Ginger, I think his real name is like William, or Bill, or Billy, or Mac, or Buddy."

"Jason?" Mike suggests hopefully.

"That's it! Jason! Nice kid. Smart. If I remember correctly, he went with an older John about a week ago. Some gangly old dude. You'd be surprised how many old men need *a lot* of young men," Starlight says.

Mike thinks for a moment. "Did you recognize the old man?"

"Yeah, he's been around before. He comes late at night," Starlight replies.

"How late?" Mike asks.

"Well after midnight."

"Oh, you mean the German gentleman? He gave me the heebie-jeebies," Gary asks.

"That's right! He is German," Starlight agrees.

"Thanks a lot for the help," Mike says, tipping his hat.

"Anytime, Mike Strong," Starlight croons. Both men wave goodbye to him.

Guess I'll have to come back tonight and do a little stakeout. Great. Nothing better than sitting in the shadows for eight hours waiting on a German. Mike gets back into his car, tossing the photograph into the passenger seat.

Looking out his window, he spots two mafia goons staring at him. One he recognizes as Pete Zumba, one of Johnny Martoni's men. Pete unabashedly meets his gaze. *Oh nice, Pete Zumba is here on the docks.* Mike starts his Plymouth Fury and the car roars to life. As he drives off, Pete Zumba points menacingly at him. *Yeah, do something you goon. I dare you!* Mike flashes Pete a smile.

The drive is the one thing Mike loves about his city. The wind whipping his hair with a cigarette between his lips brings him peace. He stares out the window at the small city with a big name. *It'll never get old. I hate how much I love this city. What with all its murder, drugs, and monsters. So very odd how all this came together. That war changed more than I'd like to admit.*

The light turns red. He looks at the pentagram on his hand, a reminder of what happened in Romania; an ever-present connection to the past that keeps his future on its set path. *Without this birthmark, who knows what would have happened.*

"How fucking long is this light?" he grumbles. He takes one last drag of his cigarette, tossing the butt out the window. When *"If you got the money, I got the time"* by Lefty Frizzell comes on the radio, he cranks the dial.

Mike rocks his head from side to side, singing along. The light finally turns green, and he steps onto the accelerator. The skyscrapers tower over him, Mike looks over to see a huge billboard for one of his favorite comics called *Future Girl*! The image is that of a very pretty, curvy lady in a pastel-colored spacesuit, a bubble helmet tucked under her arm. Her pink, purple, and blue suit hugs her figure. The caption reads "*Future Girl!* Now a Saturday Morning Hit TV Series!" *I'm not going to miss that!*

As he drives along the freeway, he is in his element. Suddenly, a rusty Ford F150, complete with a large tow boom and dangling chains, roars past Mike, merging in front of him.

Mike recognizes the truck as well as the logo on the back windshield. He looks into the rearview mirror, spotting a second, larger truck tailgating just behind him. It's a GMC 350 COE, dark green with a yellow driver's side door. It's mean and ugly, with a huge, smashed metal grill. It looks as though it was punched in the mouth

CHAPTER 6

and is now missing some teeth The hitch and boom on the back are massive, used for towing other tow trucks. It is a beast and barrels at him like an angry freight train.

Shit, Mike thinks. *Why do these guys gotta mess up my afternoon? Just a peaceful drive through my beloved city and some "overbite" has gotta come out swinging.*

He sighs.

If there is one thing Mike hates more than the gangsters in this city, it's The Wreckers, a radical gang of werewolves posing as a towing service. These junkyard dogs are ruthless, mean, and ready to attack at a moment's notice. Their gang uses tow trucks as an extension of their aggressive demeanor and muscle. Mike put several of their pack members down for good about a year ago. They've been hunting him ever since.

Looking back in the rearview mirror, he sees the cab-over truck riding his bumper. *Why today? These knuckleheads need some flea medicine.* Mike accelerates, almost hitting the F150 in front of him. He merges into the right lane, spotting an exit ahead. *I can make that,* Mike reassures himself.

Mike's Plymouth Fury takes over the lanes like a cannonball and barrels right for the exit. The cab-over merges as well, side-swiping another vehicle. The driver doesn't seem to care; he simply keeps pushing after Mike. The lead Wrecker slams on their brakes, going into reverse on the open freeway. Cars slide and swerve out of the rusty truck's way.

Mike clears the exit, hauling ass. He blows the red light at the intersection, sliding left. The gas pedal touches the floor and the car roars like a rabid tiger. Mike can see that the cab-over is keeping up with him. *Gotta shake these mutts!*

Traffic is light so Mike sets his cruise control at 75 miles per hour. He zooms past a speed limit sign that reads 35.

"Whoops." he mutters. Mike pushes down on his bench seat until it clicks. The middle of the seat opens, revealing a hidden compartment with all kinds of unique weapons stashed inside. On the side of the compartment there are six clips for his 1911. Mike grabs the one that is labeled "Dogs". He pulls out his pistol from his shoulder holster, popping the clip out and replacing it with the "Dogs" clip. He puts the regular clip in the free slot inside the compartment.

Shutting the compartment with his free hand, he steers with the other. Just then, a car pulls out to take a right, and Mike has to cut the wheel to the left in order to miss it.

He veers into oncoming traffic for a moment then back into his lane. He racks the slide on the pistol, chambering a round. He slides the gun back into his shoulder holster. Mike is cool as a cucumber, singing along to *If You've Got the Money, I Got the Time*. He pulls out a cigarette from its case.

The wind is blowing extremely hard through his car, so he must lean into his steering wheel to use his lighter. With some fumbling, it finally sparks, and he gets a good puff of nicotine into his lungs. He sits back up in his seat just in time to be rammed by the cab-over. His cigarette falls out of his mouth and into his lap. "Shit!" Mike shouts

He frantically tries to pick up his cigarette before it sets his car—or his slacks—on fire. The cab-over rams into him again. Mike looks in the rearview mirror, shouting at the goons in the truck. "Stop hitting my car, ya riffraff!"

Mike finally finds his cigarette, putting it back in his mouth. He takes control of his car again and makes a hard right without looking out for pedestrians, cars, or baby buggies. Thankfully, no one is hurt. The cab-over does the same, its wheels screeching on the asphalt. *Man, this driver is good.* Mike gives the driver a thumbs up in the rearview mirror. The driver flips him off. *No one can take a compliment anymore.*, Mike snickers.

Mike turns right again, sliding into a narrow alleyway. He speeds a few blocks, then makes a hard left, smashing into some wooden crates and debris. Bits of wood go flying into the air like shrapnel. The cab-over is still right behind him. Mike puffs on his cigarette as the alley comes to a dead end. "Shit," Mike groans, sliding his car sideways to a shuddering stop.

Mike is out of his car before the cab-over reaches him. As the truck bears down on him, Mike takes a stand in the middle of the alleyway. "Do it, you son of a bitch!" Mike shouts, his feet planted on the asphalt.

The truck rumbles at him at full speed. Mike is unwavering. "Hit me!" Mike screams as he aims his pistol at the windshield. The truck seems like it's going to plow right through him, but suddenly, the

CHAPTER 6

brakes engage, and the truck stops only inches from Mike, spraying him with dirt and orange dust from its hood. Mike shuts his eyes to avoid the onslaught. He spits out some dirt, brushing off his clothes.

The men in the truck get out "We're going to beat you to death, Strong!" the driver says. Mike knows him as Edgar Harding, a small-time crook until his bite. After that, he became a big-time problem. The passenger is Jack Craig, also a small-time crook turned real bad boy.

"Better get in line, buddy," Mike says grimly, stepping back.

"You can't kill us, Strong. You know that?" Jack Craig sneers, making his way around the front of the massive truck.

"Our boss wants to talk," Edgar says, punching his fist into his hand.

"Well, I'm not in the mood for talking." Mike squares his feet for a fight. Jack roars. His fist connects with Mike's jaw, sending him up and over the hood of his Plymouth Fury.

Damn it! Mike thinks as he sails through the air.

He hits the ground hard, landing on his back. He lays there for a moment, trying to regain his breath. *I should just kill these barking guard dogs and be done with it.*

Mike stands just as Edgar grabs his by the lapel, slamming him upside down on the hood of his own car. Mike looks up to him. "If you don't stop, I'm going to put a bullet in your brain, Fido!" Mike says coolly.

"Tough words for a guy who is losing," Edgar says, punching Mike in the gut. Mike moans in pain, curling up like a pill bug and falling off his hood. He stands up, moaning. "Stop hitting me," Mike grumbles.

"You're coming back with us," Jack Craig insists, smacking Mike's pistol out of his hand. The pistol slides under the Plymouth. Mike glares at his hand as if angry at it for letting the gun go. Edgar pulls back his left hand to punch Mike in his mouth, but Mike sees it coming from a mile away. Mike grabs Edgar's fist and twists his wrist up and back. With his free hand, he swiftly palms Edgar's throat, crushing his windpipe.

"I told you to stop punching me," Mike says as Edgar chokes. The big man only stares at him, confusion contorting his features. Mike knows he's only got a few moments to take out Jack because, unlike regular goons, werewolves heal real quick-like. Mike spins around, ducking instinctively as Jack throws a haymaker at him. Mike slams his fist into Jack's stomach, landing a double right for good measure. With a solid uppercut to the jaw. Jack is knocked onto his ass.

Mike turns his attention back to Edgar who seems ready for another beating. Mike's knuckles connect with Edgar's ribcage, two ribs snapping like kindling. Edgar moans in pain. Mike turns around just in time to kick Jack in the face as he struggles to regains his feet.

These dumb bastards are going to do this all day if I don't either end them or make like a tree and leave, Mike thinks as he punches Edgar in the stomach.

Mike grabs Edgar by the back of his neck. He drops down hard onto his knees, pulling Edgar's head into the front fender of his car. Edgar's skull makes a loud cracking noise, denting the fender. While on the ground, Mike looks for Jack. He's standing again, distracted by his heavily bleeding nose. Using this opportunity, Mike kicks Jack in the kneecap and he falls face first onto the pavement. Mike grabs Jack's hair and starts punching him repeatedly in the face.

"I told you boys to stop. Now I'm going to have to mess ya up real good," Mike says through gritted teeth. Jack's face crumples with each punch. Despite his bruised, bleeding knuckles, Mike doesn't stop his onslaught. Jack's blood splatters his face and neck.

Suddenly, Edgar grabs Mike by his head and twists, trying to break his neck. "I'm going to break your neck, Strong!" Edgar screams.

He thinks he's going to break my neck, Mike thinks woozily as the pain radiates through his body.

Mike pushes back into Edgar, propelling him into a stack of pallets. He spins around, headbutting Edgar in the jaw hard. Edgar's teeth shatter in his mouth, giving Mike enough time to step back and assess the situation. Edgar rolls to his feet but is facing away from Mike. As Edgar turns around, Mike bull rushes him. They slam into the brick wall of the nearby building with a thunderous crack.

The hit is so hard that some of the bricks crumble. Edgar is rattled and he's had enough. With a roar, he stiff arms Mike, knocking him back a few feet. Mike watches warily as Edgar transforms into his true form. His skin tears, revealing the muscle and bone underneath. As Edgar roars, his face extends into a snout. Huge teeth

CHAPTER 6

break through his human gums. His hands grow, his fingernails becoming thick and black. The human flesh falls to the ground like discarded clothing. Now, Edgar stands about nine feet tall, his legs meaty with muscle. Thick hair grows all over his body.

Mike sighs.

Edgar backhands him and Mike hurtles into a third story fire escape, crashing through the wrought iron railing. Mike lays on the metal for a moment, disoriented. He is about to stand up when Edgar leaps up to join him. He slams his huge, clawed foot onto Mike's chest.

Mike has no choice but to end its life. Before Edgar can strike, Mike opens his right hand and the pentagram starts to glow. Something slides out from under the Plymouth Fury and through the air, catching Edgar's attention. Edgar's gaze follows the object into Mike's right hand. It's his trusted Colt 1911, fully loaded with nine-millimeter rounds made of silver. "Bye, Edgar," Mike says, pulling the trigger.

The bullet punches through Edgar's skull and his huge, monstrous body falls backward off the fire escape. Mike lays still, watching as Edgar changes back to human form and dies. Breathless, Mike stands, cracking his neck and adjusting his trench coat. He looks down to see Jack Craig getting up and, without hesitation, Mike leaps off the third-floor balcony to the ground below.

Jack is ready to fight, but Mike fires into his chest twice. Jack falls backward into a pile of trash. "Right where you belong," Mike says. His face bloody and bruised, but his hair perfectly coiffed, Mike looks around. The coast is clear—there are no witnesses. Mike gets back in his car, taking a breath.

He opens the hidden compartment and replaces the clip into its slot. He puts the other clip back into the gun and puts the gun back into his shoulder holster. Looking out the driver's side window, he realizes he's going to have dickens of a time getting out of the alleyway. Mike starts his car and tries to pull around the cab-over but has to back up.

He pulls forward again. Then backs up again. Then he pulls forward again. Then backs up again. Then pulls forward. Then backs up, readjusting his tires. Then pulls forward again. Then backs up again. Each time he cranks his steering wheel, he grunts in pain.

He pulls forward again, adjusting his wheels. With a scrape of the rear fender, he pulls away free. Mike looks at his watch, shaking his head. "That literally took twenty minutes. Next time, I'll just kill them to start with."

If The Wreckers are after me, this problem ain't over. I might as well head to the source and see if I can't settle this in a nonviolent kind of way, Mike thinks.

He pulls out of the alleyway, lighting a cigarette. Though, *I'm probably going to have to kill the whole lot.* He takes a long drag, smoke pouring out of his nostrils. *From bad to worse. Story of my life.*

He turns onto Main Street, keenly aware of the ache in his body.

CHAPTER 7

Becky steps out of the brown and tan Rolls-Royce Silver Wraith, looking up at the prestigious Salvaggio's restaurant in all of its glory. Her eyes widen. Salvaggio's is an upscale Italian restaurant set high on the hill in the middle of downtown. Its lavish entrance has a marble staircase flanked by four, 20-foot-tall columns leading up to heavy French-style doors made of dark wood. A three-foot-tall brass bust of Leonardo De Vinci sits proudly on the top of a pillar at the plateau of the staircase. Only the rich can eat here.

Walking through the doors into the main foyer, a diner would see a series of hostesses all dressed in black suits and tuxedos, with their hair pulled back tight or parted and combed neatly. The maitre d', chef, and sous chefs are all trained in Italy, and it shows: they are the pinnacle of fine dining. The food is perhaps the most impeccable in all of Valkyrie City. Reservations are made six months in advance, and Lord help you if you are a minute late.

Becky and Ralph are escorted up the large marble staircase and greeted by Gerome Alexander Harper, the mayor of Valkyrie City. His short, dark hair and beard is immaculately groomed. Becky admired his bright green eyes and his radiating smile, both striking against his dark skin. His deep voice can command a room and, for someone with his job, that's a good thing. Becky smiles as he bends at the waist, kissing the top of her hand.

"M'lady Detter, so good to see you!" the mayor says.

Becky curtsies coyly. "Oh, Mr. Mayor, you are such a charmer!"

"Don't let my wife know!" he says with a laugh.

The maitre d' opens the door, waving the mayor, Ralph, and Becky into the massive restaurant that looks more like a museum than an eatery. The first thing Becky notices is the huge painting on the marble floor. She recognizes it straight away as a recreation of Da Vinci's Saint John the Baptist. It takes up the entire foyer.

She is in awe of the dark molding, made of Italian stone pine, on every corner, banister, and table. The setting is dim and intimate. The maitre d' escorts them to a table in the center of the room. Becky immediately recognizes Gustavo Geonetti sitting at a circular table in the back with several other gangsters and a dark-haired woman with her back to them.

She can't see her face, but Becky assumes it's Wendy Washington, a vocalist at The Dice and a well-known beauty. She's one of Geonetti's groupies. As they sit down at the table, Becky looks up to see the police chief enter in full dress and regalia, his medals hanging off of his uniform. He is an attractive man, the epitome of tall, dark, and handsome. His eyes hide his past and Becky knows it.

Becky is familiar with him because he and Strong have had some serious interactions before. She's always liked him, though she's itching to uncover his well-kept secrets. Before he sits down, the police chief s makes sure that Gustavo Geonetti sees him. The two men make eye contact, the tension palpable.

The police chief takes off his hat, tucking it under his arm. He sits, picks invisible dust bunnies off of the brim, and then hands his hat to the maître d' for safekeeping.

"Are all the men in this city handsome, or what?" Becky says.

Ralph laughs, patting his thick midsection. "Why, thank you!"

They all laugh for a moment, but it's the police chief who cuts it short. He is all business. "We have to do something about this city, mayor."

The mayor surveys him intently. "I'm trying to push funding from the property commission to the police. It's hard. People want luxury housing even if it means sacrificing their security and well-being.

CHAPTER 7

I've got these millionaire realtors breathing down my neck, I've got city officials wanting to spend five million on an art sculpture to put in the middle of Balder Park rather than fighting crime."

"A five-million-dollar sculpture?" Becky asks incredulously, nearly spitting out her water.

"We have so much crime that it's perfectly okay for the number one gangster to sit in the same room as the mayor and police chief. That is a problem," The police chief says loud enough for several nearby tables to overhear him. The mayor waves his hand subtly to shush him. "Mr. Mayor, I understand you have to play it safe and keep the community happy on all fronts, but soon our good city is going to fall into that eyesore we call a wharf and sink into the ocean," the police chief says curtly.

"What if we start addressing the district attorneys? Those bastards are defending these criminals for a ton of money. Ricky Carter just got off on three murder charges. *Three*. He's walking free on our streets," Ralph suggests.

Becky sits quietly, eating the free bread. "This bread is good," she says. The men look at her, clearly unenthused by her interruption. "I'll just keep eating," she mutters, pulling her bread apart.

That's when she notices a large man walking up to Gustavo Geonetti's table. They whisper. Geonetti is clearly upset about something. He waves to two of his goons and they get up to follow the larger man, who she doesn't recognize.

Geonetti tosses his napkin onto his plate of food, slamming his fist on the table. His outburst gets most of the restaurant's attention, including Becky's tablemates. Geonetti sees them staring and waves.

He stands, as do his remaining goons; the woman does not. Geonetti snaps his fingers, and she reluctantly rises. Becky was right, it is Wendy Washington in all her beauty. Even Becky finds her attractive. "I'm not a lesbian but I wouldn't stop it from happening," Becky murmurs.

Ralph turns his head looking at her. "What?"

Becky looks around, confused. She hadn't realized she'd spoken aloud "What?" she parrots, embarrassed.

Geonetti strolls up to their table. She pulls her purse in tight against her chest, putting her hand inside the front pocket where her snub nose .38 revolver sits patiently. The best thing about Becky is that she is so unassuming, though she's far spunkier than people give her credit for.

"Gentlemen, forgive me," Geonetti says. "I just received some terrible news about some friends of mine. They were killed in broad daylight."

"That's terrible news. I'm sure they were just innocent men doing innocent things," the police chief says with a smirk.

"It truly is a tragedy. They were good men—honest and hardworking. You should converse with some of your officers, chief. Maybe that'll get to the bottom of it. It's so weird that they would just be shot to death in an alley for no reason. It seems this city is full of rodents. We need a good janitor—take some of the filth out to the curb. Valkyrie City has got all of these gumshoes mucking up real progress, if you know what I mean. Mayor, it would do the city good to expand. Bring in more business, as it were," Geonetti says.

"That's what I love about you, Gus! You're always thinking of the community. You know what? I will look into it. What were their names?" The police chief stands up. "Let me shake your hand," he adds, sticking his hand out.

Geonetti looks at his outstretched hand, knowing he's been put on the spot. He shakes the police chief's hand. "Edgar Harding and Jack Craig. Well, you fellas have a great lunch!" Geonetti says, turning to walk away.

"Jack Craig? You don't mean the six-time petty thief and gun runner, who's a known affiliate of The Wreckers. *That* Jack Craig? I'm so sorry such a *good* man was killed for no reason. I'll be sure to put my best men on it straight away," the police chief says curtly.

Geonetti turns back, meeting Becky's eyes. Her hand still inside her purse, she curls her fingers around the pommel of her weapon. "You'd better make sure you're in before dark, missy. You never know what kind of evil lurks out there in the shadows, and not just the monsters under your bed. *Real* monsters. It's better to be safe than sorry," Geonetti says.

Becky smiles at him "I'm surrounded by tough men and a lot of bullets. I'm sure I'll manage."

Wendy Washington laughs, which pisses Geonetti off. He grabs her arm, digging his fingers into her skin. "Remember your place, doll." With that, he drags her out of the restaurant.

CHAPTER 7

Becky watches him drag the pretty dame out onto the sidewalk. "I'd bet twenty to one, Strong had something to do with Edgar Harding's and Jack Criag's unfortunate deaths," Becky says, tossing her napkin on her plate. She rises, slinging her purse strap onto her shoulder.

Ralph mournfully stares at his empty plate. "We haven't even ordered yet."

"I've got to go, boys! It's been a real hoot!" Becky grabs another breadstick. "For the road, ya know. Girl's gotta eat!" With a final wave of her breadstick, she hustles out, desperate to see Mike Strong.

The police chief looks at the mayor and they both shake their heads.

"We have to end shit like this, Gerome," The police chief says.

"I know," the mayor replies, unable to shake the sunken feeling in the pit of his stomach.

Becky hails a cab. A bright white Cadillac cab swings in front of her. "Where to, doll?" the cabbie says with a smile.

"Crown Center, please. And fast!" Becky slides into the backseat.

"Not to worry, miss. I'll get ya there lickity split!" the cabbie says, stepping on the gas. The cab pulls on to the main stretch of road leading through the city, turns onto Main Street, and heads east toward the business district. Crown Center, where Mike Strong's office is located, is just past the business district in the dried-up neighborhood.

The business district is bustling; pedestrians on the march from one meeting to the next crowd the sidewalks and storefronts. The thirteen city blocks that make up the district act like a parking lot most of the time. Cars at a standstill line the streets, clanging trolleys straddling the median like they own the place.

Becky stares out her window, looking at the chaos. She thinks about her future and the future of her city. Did she want to marry Phillip? Did he love her? She was sure he did, but sometimes, his actions seem forced and fake. That she was almost sure of. Before too long, Becky dimly hears the cabbie say something. She looks up in surprise to see they had stopped.

"Got here in no time and safe and sound! All for the low fare of two dollars and fifteen cents!" The cabbie grins.

"Thanks, pal! Here's a little extra for rushing!" Becky hands the man a five-dollar bill.

"Wow! Thanks, lady. You have a beautiful day, beautiful!" the cabbie says before pulling away from the curb.

Becky stops to adjust her dress and coat, eyeing the dilapidated, twelve story office building. "Mike, I wish you would move," she murmurs under her breath. Inside, the building is just as decrepit, with stinky carpet and paint peeling off the walls. A floor chart listing the various offices hangs beside a massive bloodstain.

It looks like someone blew their brains out in the lobby and no one bothered to clean up the mess. Becky traces the blood stain from the wall to the floor, and across the carpet. The person in question was dragged out the front door. Becky returns her attention to the addresses on the wall. There's a list of incompetent lawyers, shady accountants, and Quack doctors. Mike Strong is there too, with "P.I." written beside his name.

She makes her way down the narrow, dimly lit hallway to the elevator. She can feel her high heels sinking into the moist carpet. She realizes there is a scrap of paper stuck to her foot. She lifts her shapely leg to rip it off. "Gross," she says, trying to resist the urge to wipe her sticky fingers on her dress.

A tattooed young man steps out of an office into Becky's path, his arms laden with paperwork. He is escorted by a man in a cheap suit. "Read over the disposition and remember what to say. The most you could get is five years, but you're a smart kid. You'll get a smack on the wrist!" the man says. As the clearly frightened kid walks by, Becky realizes he is in the military; his walk and posture give him away.

"If I was you, kid, I'd get a different lawyer. Good luck!" Becky calls as she steps into the elevator. She just catches the kid's resigned frown before the doors slide shut.

Becky stands in the center of the elevator, watching the floor counter scroll until it reaches the fifth floor. Ding! The very dented and stained doors shake open, revealing a stark hallway with a flickering old light. There are bullet holes pockmarking the walls and bloodstains on the carpet. As she walks down the hall toward

CHAPTER 7

Mike's office, she slows just in case anyone might be there instead of Strong. It's better if she has the element of surprise.

She reaches his door, finding it closed and locked. She fishes her keys out of her purse and opens the door. The place is empty. She walks in, firmly shutting the door behind her. She snoops at his desk in the back room, perusing his scribbled notes and tossing out some trash.

"This place needs an atomic bomb." Becky says.

She sits down in his high-backed leather chair. She kicks back, putting her feet up on his desk. Tilting her stylish hat down over her eyes, she allows herself to rest for a moment.

She jerks awake as the front door to Mike's office is smashed in. She hurriedly sits up, looking through the partition window that separates the rooms. She sees two very large shadows.

"Time to skedaddle!" she yelps. Becky moves quickly to the other side of the room, putting her back against the wall. "Trapped like a rat on a sinking ship!"

The only way out is the window and fire escape. As Becky moves for the window, the men see her. Darting past the door, she gets a great look at both men. The fat one is Leo Guzzo, his face wrapped in cheeks and chins. His nose looks like he'd recently been hit with a shovel. Leo is Johnny Martoni's right hand goon. He's known for being not too smart, but he's a brute, to say the least. The other man is Jacky Ribbasa, his wide chin and big nose make him look like a rhinoceros and hippopotamus had a child. He's another Martoni goon. Becky stops in her tracks.

"Hey, fellas. You looking for that scoundrel Strong too?!" she asks, though her act is unconvincing. It doesn't help that Leo Guzzo has had run-ins with Becky and knows who she is.

"Cut the chatter, you pipe organ! Where's Strong?" Leo says.

"Pipe organ? That hurts, Leo," Becky whips back, trying to figure out a way out of the office and away from these idiots.

Leo stomps toward her, angrily. "You're that snappy reporter! I remember you!" He grabs her arm.

Becky scoops a brass paperweight off of Strong's desk, hitting Leo in the knuckles. He instantly lets go.

"Bitch!" Leo groans, shaking his hand. Becky swings at him again, smashing the knuckles on his other hand. CRACK!

"Bitch! Stop that!" Leo says, shaking his other hand.

"You can't handle a small broad?" Jacky chuckles.

Leo catches the paperweight on Becky's third swing. Wrenching it from her hand, he tosses it out the window, smashing the glass.

"Well, Mike is not going to be happy about that," Becky snorts.

Leo grabs Becky by both of her arms, picking her up off the floor. He turns, putting her down between Jacky and himself. "Where's Strong?" he asks again, through gritted teeth.

"How should I know? I'm also looking for him," she snaps. "You dumb goof!"

"Maybe we should take her and use her as bait," Jacky suggests.

"If you don't take your damn hands off of her, I'm going to chop them both off and feed them to you!" Mike Strong stands in the doorway with his gun raised. He is beaten and bloody.

"You're going to get a knuckle sandwich!" Becky says to Leo.

Jacky pulls his own gun from its holster, putting it against Becky's head. "One more move and I'll blast this cute little noggin all over your walls, dick!" Jacky says.

Mike moves like lightning, striking Jacky in the face with the butt of his gun. Jacky's nose splits as wide as the Grand Canyon, blood pouring out like a loose faucet. "My nose!" Jacky screams, stepping backward.

"Your neck is next, Jacky!" Mike shouts.

Leo shoves Becky at Mike. Mike lunges to catch her, but she is agile and manages to spin out of his way so he can take Leo on. Both men raise their weapons, pointing them at each other's faces.

"Shoot!" Mike says with a cocksure smile.

Jacky grabs Mike in a bear hug from behind, squeezing him extremely hard. Mike isn't fazed by this, but he plays along. He needs to see what Martoni's next move is.

"Stop moving. Come with us and we'll let the reporter go!" Jacky says into his ear.

Leo slams a right hook into Mike's jaw.

Mike takes the hit and plays it off. "Yeah, do it again, tough guy!" he says, spitting blood. He turns his head, searching for Becky. "Get out of here, sweetheart. I'll handle this."

CHAPTER 7

"You are all out of your minds if you think I'm letting you take Mike Strong, ya baboons!" Becky says. She reaches for her purse but realizes her purse flung off her shoulder in all the commotion. She looks around frantically.

"Becky, get out of here. I've got this," Mike says in a mater-of-fact tone that only she can understand.

"Fine. But I'm not happy about it. I hope you dumbos find your coffins at the bottom of a cliff," Becky says in a huff.

Jacky kicks her purse toward her, gasping when he feels something heavy bump his foot. "Leo, the purse! A gun!"

Leo goes for the purse just as Becky does. They both grab the straps, but Leo is stronger and pulls it out of her hands. "Missed it by that much!" Becky moans.

Leo opens the purse to find some lipstick, napkins, and a breadstick, which he holds up for all to see. "Girl's gotta eat?" he asks, before putting the breadstick back. Finally, he finds her snub nose .38 revolver. "Nice toy. I hope you're good with it," He laughs.

"Good enough. Maybe I'll show you one day—put a bullet right between your eyes," Becky says.

Leo thrusts her purse at her with a grunt. "I look forward to the day, missy. Now run along so we can show your boyfriend a good time."

Becky stares at him for a moment, confused. She grins. "I don't think he thinks of you that way."

"Yeah, guys. I didn't know it was *that* kind of a party. I know some gentleman down on the docks though, if you're interested," Mike says.

Jacky pushes Mike away but keeps a hold of his arm. "What are you talking about?" Jacky asks, alarmed.

Leo points to the door. "Go, lady! Before I toss you off the balcony."

"Fine. Mike, *dear*, I'll see you for coffee in the morning," she says, walking out the door.

Leo turns his attention to Mike. "How's your face feel? Because it's killin' me! Is that blood? Is your nose broken?" Leo asks mockingly.

Mike Strong winces as Leo hits him squarely in the face. He spits blood onto the carpet. Leo hits him again and again, rocking

Mike's head from side to side as though his neck is a spring. Mike grins as blood pours out his mouth. Soon, everything goes black.

CHAPTER 8

The haziness wears off in fits and starts. Mike brushes debris off of him, coughing up a plume of dust. Looking around, he discovers half the building has collapsed. The smoke has cleared, and the fires are no larger than campfires, so he's been out a while. "Baker?" he calls, looking for his compatriots. "Charland?" No one answers.

He gets up, pushing a concrete slab off of his leg. His hearing is still muffled from the explosion that probably killed half of his unit. Suddenly, a large hand grabs his shoulder. Mike turns to see his Major.

"Leland! You're alive," Mike says in a raspy voice.

"Yeah, thankfully. C'mon. We have to be at the rendezvous point in two hours," Leland says.

"Where is everybody?" Mike asks, wiping away the rivulet of blood threatening to drip into his eye. He palpates his forehead, finding a cut that is bleeding badly.

Leland looks his face over. "You're fine. Foreheads bleed a lot."

The two men stagger out of the ruined bunker. The rest of the unit is outside, largely unscathed; only he and Leland were trapped inside. Several of the men are also covered in dust and debris. Mike looks over Unit 66 as they dust themselves off. One of the men is his Unit Commander: Captain Johnathan Maxwell. He's a tough son of bitch, even though he's an objectively small man. He is a hell of a fighter and one hell of a leader.

Mike admires him because, so far, they haven't died. Next to Captain Maxwell is Lieutenant Eddie Baker, a short, stocky, wise-cracking Boston Baked Bean who was once an Olympic boxer, Mike watched him get hit eight times in the face by a Nazi and it didn't even phase him. Mike likes Baker the best. They are kindred spirits who get punched in the face a lot. Not by choice.

"Alright men, we've got to get moving," a gravelly voice says. "Thankfully that mortar didn't kill us." It's Major Gus Simmons, a bald, older man with a thick mustache, wide neck, broad shoulders, and a scar down the right side of his face that isn't quite done healing. He sloshes his way down a muddy hillside "We ain't got time for lollygagging and chatter. Get those boots up and start marching." He steps over fallen Nazis. "We have to secure this establishment by dawn."

Mike starts walking with his commander and fellow soldiers. The path ahead is dark and thickly wooded. The remote countryside is crisscrossed by mountains. Unfortunately, it seems as though every inch is crawling with Nazis.

Another soldier, a Midwestern corn fed kind of guy by the name of Michael Campbell, pauses to look at a map with his flashlight.

"We're in Chernivtsi, Ukraine right now. We need to reach this point of the Siret River in Romania in about two hours," he says, watching the weary men march by.

The men keep going in the darkness for about three miles with no incidents. As they walk, they come across the Romanian border. There, they come face-to-face with a small unit of Nazi soldiers and two Panzerwagen ADGZs—armored, six-wheeled vehicles with mounted .45 caliber machine guns.

Mike Strong takes a knee with the rest of the men. They wait quietly as Major Simmons converses with Major Charland.

"Alright, boys. We've gotta take out these Nazis. Baker, Strong, and Campbell take the left flank, while myself, Charland, and Geyer will take the right," Simmons says. Mike glances over to see Steve Geyer, a tall, funny-looking guy from Kalamazoo, dart across the small dirt road.

CHAPTER 8

Two other soldiers hang back from everyone else. Simon Archer is a German American with dark hair and eyes. He's deadly in combat, and unsettlingly mysterious. The other is Philip Walkins, a fit Californian who speaks like a poet; he never shuts up about the art of surfing and soul-searching.

The Nazis at the border have no idea the men are about to pounce on them. Major Gus Simmons makes his way back to Strong and Baker who are crouched down amidst some brush. "Okay, you two go around far left, and try to get behind them." Major Gus Simmons traces a curved route with his arm.

He turns to the other men, making a circle motion with his hand. Mike and Baker nod and sneak off into the darkness. The cold and snow blows at their backs like the breath of death. Clambering over some fallen trees, Mike sneaks quietly with his partner moving like his shadow alongside. They dart from brush to brush. Mike intently watches the men at the makeshift guard shack.

Mike counts at least a dozen men. He stands tall against a huge Norway spruce that still has most of its needles despite the chill in the air. It resembles a large Christmas tree. *It'd be nice to be home for Christmas instead of staring down Nazis*!

Baker moves for cover again. The men circle back around behind the Nazis and stare at their backsides. Mike sees an opportunity and takes it. Sneaking up on a Nazi who is changing the back passenger wheel of a Panzerwagen, he grasps him in a headlock. Before the Nazi can call out, Mike snaps his neck. The man falls dead without a sound. Baker slides up behind the Panzerwagen. "Nice work." Baker says.

"Thanks, now only like ten more to go!" Mike whispers.

Mike looks up over the Panzerwagen toward Major Simmons' hiding spot, giving a thumbs up. Then he ducks back behind the vehicle. "Think he saw you?" Baker asks.

"Probably not, but let's wait a minute," Mike replies.

As if on cue, the wind howls, throwing a wall of snow across the border crossing. It's the perfect cover for the soldiers to attack. It's now or never. Mike kneels beside the Panzerwagen's tire, tightening the bolts the Nazi didn't have the chance to tighten.

"What are you doing?" Baker hisses.

"Making sure we've got a vehicle. We still have like ten miles to go and trekking through this blizzard is going to get just as unbearable as watching grass grow," Mike grunts twisting the tire iron one final time.

Baker jumps into the back of the Panzerwagen, positioning himself behind the mounted machine gun. He racks the chamber and the clacking of the metal gets the Nazis' attention. Mike leans against the side of the vehicle, casually lighting a cigarette.

"Hello boys," Mike says.

"Scheisse!" one of the Germans shrieks, bringing up his MAS-38 machine pistol.

"Offenes feuer!" another Nazi screams. Before the Nazis can respond to his command, they hear the racking of several weapons behind them. Unit 66 steps out of the bushes. The Nazis open fire, diving for cover. Baker fires the mounted machine gun. Bullets slam into the snow with an echoing THIP, THIP, THIP!

Three of the Nazis take cover behind the other Panzerwagen, shooting indiscriminately at the American soldiers. Major Simmons slides up to one of the Nazis, kicking him in the shins. Then, he kicks him in the groin for good measure. As the Nazi doubles over in pain, Major Simmons grabs the man's head, pulling him down into the snow. He makes quick work of him, snapping his neck in one swift motion.

Mike pulls out his sidearm, leveling it at another Nazi. The bullet splits the skull of the soldier, and he falls into the snow. Bullets pummel the vehicle, just barely missing him. Mike dives headfirst into the snow. Above him, Baker fires incessantly, the light of the exploding gunpowder illuminating the surrounding area. The scene is both majestic and horrifying.

Major Charland is on a Nazi in an instant. The Nazi aims his Luger pistol at him, but he smacks it away. He grabs the soldier's arm, twisting it so hard it snaps at the elbow. Then, he flips the soldier over his shoulder into the snow, stomping on the man's face until it has the consistency of pudding.

Meanwhile, Captain Maxwell grapples with two Nazis at once. As one throws a punch, Maxwell ducks. He comes up underneath the Nazi's swinging arm, hitting him with an uppercut. He knocks the man backward. The other Nazi levels his pistol at Maxwell's

CHAPTER 8

head. Without a moment's hesitation, Maxwell tackles him into the snow, pounding on him with both of his fists. The Nazi's Luger skitters across the icy ground. The Nazi pulls a knife from his belt, trying to stab Maxwell in the neck. Both men grasp the weapon, playing a deadly game of tug-of-war. The point presses against Maxwell's stubbly neck, drawing a drop of blood.

Maxwell rolls, knocking the Nazi off balance. His advantage lost, Maxwell yanks the knife out of the man's hand, stabbing him in the carotid artery. Blood sprays out like a water hose. Maxwell throws the knife at the other Nazi who catches it and throws the knife at Major Charland. Simon Archer catches it in midflight, returning to sender.

The knife sticks in the Nazi's forehead. He drops like a rock.

"That was just... huh..." Major Charland mutters.

Archer looks at Captain Maxwell, who is still sprawled on the ground, covered in snow and blood. Maxwell's raised eyebrows say it all.

Campbell and Walkins are positioned behind the concrete structure of the guard post, firing their rifles at the remaining Nazis. Most are fleeing, shooting their guns over their shoulders. Campbell drops to a knee, getting a bead on one of the Nazis. He squeezes the trigger, blowing off part of the man's scalp. Walkins, however, does not shoot. He chews at his bottom lip. "Shoot them, Walkins!" Campbell screams over the sound of gunfire.

"I'm not shooting anyone in the back. That's the coward's way, Campbell," Walkins yells back.

One of the Germans turns, firing his machine gun at the guard post. Bits of concrete blow off the building, flying like shrapnel. Walkins puts a bullet in the middle of the man's face.

"Happy?" Walkins asks.

A Nazi gets the drop on Mike, punching him in the jaw, but Mike can take a hit. The Nazi was not expecting that. Mike returns the favor with a right hook to the man's face, followed by a left to his ribs. Then, he puts his pistol against the Nazi's chest, pulling the trigger at point blank range. His back blows out like confetti.

The gunfire slows and stops. The wind howls, blowing snow into their eyes and reddening their cheeks. Mike scans the area, as do all the soldiers.

Major Simmons stands up. "Clear?"

"Clear," the men of Unit 66 reply. The only enemies in the vicinity are cold and dead.

The chaos is over. The men regroup in the middle of the road. They breathe heavily, clouds of vapor spewing from their mouths. "Good job, men. That was like clockwork," Major Simmons says.

Baker pops his head out of the Panzerwagen. "Found the keys," he announces cheerfully.

"That's great. Now we've got a ride. Someone find the keys to the other one," Major Simmons orders.

"Got 'em," Archer says after looking into the other vehicle.

The men waste no time piling into the vehicles. Mike, Baker, Campbell, and Leland get in one. Simmons, Walkins, and Archer get in the other one. Baker steps on the accelerator and takes off down the narrow road through the Romanian countryside. The view would be breathtaking but it's dark and the men are too tired to look out the windows.

Mike sits wedged in the back with Leland. The cold chills them to the bone. Leland pulls out an envelope from his satchel, looking over the photos inside.

"What do we got?" Mike asks.

Leland hands Mike the stack of photos. The one on top is of an older man with a long black beard, thick eyebrows, and shoulder-length hair. He looks a lot like the paintings of Vlad the Impaler. Mike notices he's wearing a strange headdress adorned with gems and a heavy cloak with a sigil on the left lapel.

Mike flips through the photos. He stops at a picture of a woman who has been cut from ear to ear; it looks as though a creature is peering out of her cracked skull. A man stands over her, a knife in-hand.

On the floor, there are various sigils, including a pentagram. Mike notices a large ring on the man's right pinky finger. Mike recognizes the sigil on the ring as the Baphomet Star, the sigil of a Templar deity.

"Occultists? What do they have to do with the war?" Mike asks.

"We're not sure, but intelligence says Nazis are using anything and everything to try and win this war," Leland says.

CHAPTER 8

"That shit is not real, Major. I should know. I've been studying the occult for years. I'm a professor, remember?" Mike says, thumbing through the remaining pictures.

"I know. That's why you were handpicked for this job. Everyone in this Unit has a special skill specifically related to these missions," Leland says.

"Missions?" Mike asks.

"This isn't our only one. Our job is to end Hitler and everything he stands for. That includes snuffing out sub-factions of his military—those put in place to tip the balance in their favor. Hitler is certainly using everything at his disposal," Leland says.

"Including the Devil."

"Well, God certainly isn't helping him out, now, is he?" Leland counters.

Mike looks away, thinking about the possibility of angels and demons.

Finally, the vehicle shudders to a stop, the brakes grinding. Leland puts everything away in his satchel. The men get out of the Panzerwagen, stretching their cramped muscles and cracking their necks. The sun is coming up, revealing more of the scenic landscape. Mike looks out over the mountains and snow-covered ground. The steep Carpathian Mountains were to the right of them towering into the sky with its snow-covered mountain tops. It looks like a living tapestry. Mike turns his attention upward looking at the vast sky and its millions upon millions of stars.

"'O thou art fairer than the evening air clad in the beauty of a thousand stars.' Christopher Marlowe, English playwright," Walkins says stepping close to Mike.

"'For my part I know nothing with any certainty, but the sight of stars makes me dream.' That's Van Gogh," Mike smiles.

"Okay, guys. We need to get to Rogojesti. It's between here and here," Campbell says, jabbing at two points on his map. The soldiers crowd around Campbell and the map. "This place," he draws a circle around a small town with his finger. "It's due east of this big-ass lake. Lake Rogojesti, I guess. There's a hidden bunker and we need to destroy it."

"We're hiking from here. I didn't expect to run into border guards, so I don't know what to expect from here on out. Be ready for anything, and I mean *anything*," Simmons says, a thick cigar bobbing between his teeth. "Let's go, ladies! We ain't got all day."

The men follow behind him, making their way across the countryside; the freshly fallen snow crunches beneath their boots. Mike wipes his face, finding blood on his glove. His forehead must still be bleeding. He feels lightheaded.

The landscape becomes blurry. He sees a steel beam sticking up out of the ground in front of him. He looks over at Leland, who is now dressed like a gangster, wearing a white and blue pinstriped suit, a fedora, and a long trench coat, Mike's head feels like it's on a swivel and he can barely keep his eyes open. He staggers. Suddenly, it feels as though he's punched in the face. He drops to his knees with a groan.

"Strong, you've gotta get up, buddy!" Baker says, clapping him on the back.

Mike looks at his hands. They are drenched in blood and dripping onto the rocky ground. Mike looks up to see a strange man standing over him in a cloak; he is inordinately tall, his shadow shrouding Mike in darkness, huge ram-like horns sticking out of his forehead. The man reaches his hand out, blue flames leaping from his palm. Mike looks back up at Baker who is screaming at him now. "Get up! Get up!"

Mike lays in the debris. Sound comes in and out, as if someone is turning the radio dial. His eyes burn and his body feels like it's on fire. He reaches out into the fog, hoping Baker can see him.

Baker grabs Mike's hand. They are in a concrete bunker now. Baker pushes Mike down the hallway as the constant hum becomes deafening. Mike turns around to see Simmons gutted and dead on the floor. A huge Nazi flag spread on the floor beside him is burning.

Mike looks down the corridor to see a hideous monster standing eight feet tall, its veiny muscles pulsing. Its head is elongated like a deformed wolf. A long snout and sharp teeth snap, saliva trickling onto the floor. Its body is charred, yet it still walks. Mike stares at the thing that's not an animal but not a human. As it walks toward him, it moans. With each step, pieces of the creature fall off. Underneath, the creature's skin is pink and healthy; the charred skin is giving birth to a new life like razing a forest to promote new growth.

CHAPTER 8

The corridor starts to vibrate. As Baker pulls Mike behind him, Mike is hit in the head by falling debris. He tries to shake it off but must squeeze his eyes shut until the pain passes. He opens his eyes to see Leo Guzzo's ugly face. Leo grabs Mike's head, punching him in the jaw.

Mike closes his eyes again. When he opens them, he finds his pistol in his hand. As he raises it, the metal becomes red hot. He can't seem to let go of it and the skin of his palm cooks. The pain is unbearable and Mike screams, thick, bloody saliva bubbling from his mouth. Mike fires in slow motion, each bullet casing ejecting from the chamber of his gun. The sound is muffled by the loud hum that seems to be coming from everywhere.

Mike and Baker drop to the ground. Finally, Mike drops his gun. His palm is burnt and bubbling, a pentagram burned into his flesh. Mike looks back up as Baker tosses their last grenade. The explosion decimates all the men, and they burn into a vapor. The raging fire consumes Mike.

His eyes go wide as he watches his skin peel away and his muscles melt into goo. He screams, the sound evolving into maniacal laughter. Leo Guzzo crouches beside him. "Oh, you're still here?" Mike asks dreamily.

Leo Guzzo stares at him in confusion. "Yeah, buddy. I wouldn't miss this for the world!" He punches Mike again and Mike's head rocks back and forth. Leo punches so hard the force knocks Mike, and the wooden chair he's strapped to, onto the ground.

Mike's head hits the concrete. He pushes himself up off the ground as Baker pulls on his webbed utility belt. Mike stumbles to one knee, a small pieces of concrete cutting through his pants and into his flesh. Looking over his shoulder, he watches as sections of the corridor explode behind them.

The force blows both Mike and Baker through a section of wall in front of them. As they roll to a stop, Mike loses his gun amidst the rubble and debris. As they try to get up, the floor beneath them collapses and they crash deeper into the bunker. Mike lands on a concrete sacrificial table and the wooden top splinters. The table is ornate, shaped like a cross.

Mike moans in pain, staring back up through the hole. A bright light shines down, becoming brighter and brighter until Mike is forced to close his eyes. Another explosion rattles the table, and Mike is keenly aware of pain that radiates through his entire body. When the shaking stops, Mike opens his eyes to see Leo Guzzo standing a few feet away. He is deep in conversation with a shadowy figure.

Mike sniffs, finding that his nostrils are clogged by congealed blood. His mouth is cut and swollen. He feels like the bottom of a trashcan—he expects he looks like it too. He tries to breathe slowly but passes out.

CHAPTER 9

Becky stands in the elevator, upset that Mike would let himself get taken so easily. "What a moron!" she says, stomping her foot. *He must be up to something.*

The elevator door dings, and she steps out in the old musty lobby of the old musty building. Walking outside, she realizes that she doesn't have her car. "Oh scuttlebugs!" she yells. She leans out over the city street, eyeing an oncoming cab. Hailing it with an agitated flick of her wrist, the cab pulls up. Becky urges the driver to roll down his window.

"Hey listen, this is gonna sound weird. But I need you to park for a moment."

The driver nods. "Yeah, okay. I'm runnin' the meter though." Becky shrugs. The cab pulls into a spot and Becky climbs into the back seat.

"Now, we wait," she says.

"It's your dime, doll," he replies, keeping an eye on the meter.

Becky watches as the goons escort Mike out of his building. They usher him to a dark, four-door sedan with tail fins. Before they shove him into the back of the car, Jacky puts a sack over his head. Jacky gets in the back seat with Mike as Leo gets in the driver's seat.

Becky taps the cabbie on the shoulder. "Follow that car." The cabbie smiles, putting the car into gear. "Not too close," she adds.

"I know how to follow someone. You think this is my first 'follow that car' experience, lady?"

"Okay, sheesh, calm down, big fella." Becky replies.

The cab pulls out onto the main road, following the black sedan. They take the on-ramp, heading southwest. Becky notices the sign on the interstate reads 318 South Wharf. *We're going to the docks.*

The cabbie trails behind the sedan down the interstate. They turn onto the exit ramp, leading to the industrial side of town and the wharf. The sedan takes a left, putting the docks and water on its right. They continue for another few miles. Suddenly, the cabbie slows down, pulling over to the side of the desolate road.

"What are you doing?" Becky asks, alarmed.

"There are no other cars on this road. It'll certainly look like I'm following them. We need to stop for a moment," the cabbie explains.

"Wow, you *have* done this before."

"It's Valkyrie City, darling. Everyone is following everyone else." He laughs.

This gets a chuckle out of Becky.

They wait until the sedan makes a right turn down a side street. Then, the cabbie takes off again, making his way down the isolated marina at a snail's pace. As he gets close to the street, they discover that the sedan has pulled off at a warehouse.

He drives past the side street. Becky catches a glimpse of Leo punching Mike in the gut. *Bastards!* The cabbie keeps driving for about a block and stops. "Shall I wait?" he asks.

"Not unless you wanna risk your neck and possibly get shot by Mafia goons," Becky says, opening the door.

The cabbie seems to consider the proposition for a moment. "Nah," he replies.

"Well, see ya someday," Becky says, getting out of the cab.

"If you're lucky," the cabbie says before pulling away.

Becky is left standing on the side of the road as the sun starts to set. She takes off toward the warehouse, slinging her purse strap over her shoulder. Clutching the bag tightly, she strolls alongside the chain-link fence, looking for a gap. It would be easier than jumping over. Finally, she finds a gate.

CHAPTER 9

There's no padlock. Becky looks up and down the street, not quite believing her luck. She pulls the old rusty latch up, scurrying toward the warehouse. She presses her back against the rough brick, trying to catch her breath. Becky sidesteps with her back pressed against the wall. She reaches the end of the wall and peeks around the corner. The sedan is parked outside but there is no sign of Leo, Jacky, or Mike. Becky can see, just under the dim light hanging on the wall, that there is a metal door. She thinks for a moment looking at the parked cars. Then she smiles.

Mike dimly hears the door shut. The toes of his boots slide across the poured concrete, his captors holding him up by his armpits. Mike tries to listen for whatever sound he can, but it is hard to think over his heartbeat pounding in his ears. Leo's last punch dazed him. Suddenly, he is shoved to the ground. *I can only assume I'm in a fishing warehouse*, Mike thinks. *I can smell the ocean and feel the concrete.* Mike's head is pulsating, and spots and flurries obfuscate his vision. Not that there's much to see with a bag on his head.

Mike shakes it off. "Pretty pathetic to kick a guy with a bag on his head." Mike says, his muffled voice dripping with sarcasm. Someone picks him up, placing him in a wooden chair. Someone else wraps rope around him, tying it tight. Seemingly for laughs, he gives Mike another thump to the head. Mike rocks back and forth in the chair. Abruptly, the bloody sack is ripped off of his head, and Mike gulps fresh air.

"You look like utter dog shit," Leo remarks.

"I'm going to beat you back to Brooklyn," Mike mutters.

Jacky carries a tin bucket over to Mike's chair, setting it beside his feet. He places Mike's feet inside of it. Leo heaves over a bucket of mixed concrete. He pours the thick, sloppy mixture on top of Mike's boots. "You're about to go for a swim with the fishes, Strong," Leo crows. "Let me know if you see anyone you know down there."

Becky is about to make her move when headlights shine in her direction. A bright red Chevrolet Corvette swings into the warehouse's parking lot. Becky ducks down, pressing against the side of the brick the best she can. "*Martoni,*" Becky whispers. She slowly peeks her head around the corner to watch Johnny Martoni get out of the driver's seat. "It seems we are way outnumbered here," Becky groans. As the short man makes his way inside, Becky realizes she has limited options now.

The heavy metal door shuts with a bang. Johnny Martoni walks in with a swagger that almost has him dancing. Johnny is delighted to find Mike Strong tied to a wooden chair, beaten and bloody. The yellow hue of the overhead light illuminates Mike but casts a shadow on his surroundings. "I smell an asshole," Mike says.

Martoni stops, waving Leo over. "I wanna watch as you toss his interfering ass into the drink," Martoni says, agitatedly chewing on his cigar.

"Untie me and I'll take on all of you in a fist fight." Mike spits blood across the concrete.

Jacky punches him in the side of the head. "I'll go first," Jacky chortles, making Martoni and Leo laugh.

"Hey Guzzo, you wanna get your ass kicked?" Mike chuckles.

Leo grabs Mike's face with both hands. "Mikey boy, you're like thirty minutes from breathing underwater. I can't wait." Leo says, hocking a globule of spit onto Mike's face. Mike whispers something, but Leo can't quite hear him. "What was that?" Leo asks.

"Come closer. It's hard for me to talk," Mike says, his voice raspy. Leo leans in close, nearly pressing his ear against Mike's chapped lips. "I said: 'you're going to squeal like a pig when you die.'"

Leo stares at Mike for a moment. Then, angrily, he grabs the back of the chair, dragging Mike and his concrete shoes across the warehouse. "What are you doing, Leo?" Martoni asks.

"He's going in now. He's a piece of shit! You're a piece of shit, Mike. A real worm," Leo huffs.

Martoni looks at Jacky. "Did you get anything off of him?"

Jacky pulls out Mike's military-issued handgun. "Just his iron."

Martoni takes the weapon from Jacky, looking it over. "This is nice." He tosses it across the warehouse, and it clatters across the concrete like a pebble skipping across water. "He doesn't need this anymore." With that, he follows Leo—and his prisoner—out of the back of the warehouse.

Becky sneaks over to Leo Guzzo's sedan, hiding behind it. From this vantage point, she can see the huge wooden doors for truck deliveries. She gets an idea. Opening the driver's side door of the sedan, she gets in, careful to keep her head down. After a brief

CHAPTER 9

search for the keys, she blindly reaches underneath the dashboard, tugging on the bundle of wires there.

Mike squints through the blurred vision he had so elegantly acquired. Leo places his chair at the edge of the long dock. Martoni sidles up beside Mike. "I can't believe this is it. This is the end of the hero Mike Strong," Martoni says. "I've been waiting years for this; you piece of shit. You have been a thorn in my side for far too long, Strong."

"Don't count your chickens before they've hatched, Johnny," Mike manages, his speech garbled. He's pretty sure he has a concussion. Jacky smacks Mike in the back of the head. "Hey, what gives?" Mike asks, indignant.

"Shut up," Jacky replies with another smack. Jacky bends down, prodding the concrete. It seems solid.

"How's it look?" Leo asks.

"Not bad," Jacky says.

"Can we dump him or not?" Johnny asks.

"Yeah, I think so." Jacky pushes harder on the quick-drying cement.

Martoni leans over into Mike's face. "Strong, it's been a pleasure. But I need one less thorn in my side. It's nothing personal—just business."

"Hey Johnny, no problem. Just a thought, though. Geonetti is gonna kill you one day. You're a mess and he knows it. You're a liability, that's for sure. You, with your hot red Corvette and flashy clothes? Geonetti thinks you're about to burn out, or up, or *both*." Mike can barely keep his head up. *If I can get this cuckoo bird to get fired up, maybe I can get out of this mess. I hope he buys this buckshot I'm firing at him.*

Johnny stares at him "You truly are an honest man, Strong. Too bad we didn't work together."

Beyond the dock, the clear night sky and the flickering stars mirror the lights of the skyscrapers reflecting in Valkyrie Bay; it's a cityscape yin-yang. *At least, if I die here, this will be the last thing I see*, Mike thinks, looking out at the still water.

As if he can read his mind, Johnny spins the chair and metal tin Mike's feet are encased in. The sound of the chair legs scraping on the dock makes Mike wince. "Look at that view, Mikey. You couldn't have died on a more picturesque night."

Mike stares at the city in front of him. *His* city—the one he'd sworn to protect with every ounce of his being. *She sure is beautiful. This ci—*

Martoni kicks him into the bay.

Mike hits the water hard, water pouring into his mouth and nostrils. He is yanked down by the tub of cement attached to his feet. The chair crumples on impact, smashing the back of his head like a Major League home run. Mike is disoriented. Everything seems to slow down underwater. Mike feels himself hit the ocean floor. *Got to be about twenty feet down.*

He shakes his head. Then, with his free hand, he rubs his face, trying to open his eyes. It's dark—the kind of dark that makes you think sharks are lurking, waiting to devour you. Or the Loch Ness monster. Or maybe something else altogether, some otherworldly monstrosity full of piss and teeth.

Mike tears his eyes away from the abyss, looking down at his feet. He tries to pull them out of their prison, but to no avail. He can feel that the cement has completely solidified around his ankles. He keeps pulling, but all he can do is hop around the ocean floor as though he's in a potato sack race. His trench coat floats behind him like a cape.

Suddenly, he hears an enormous splash from above. The concussion of the impact pushes water down on top of him, making him turn somersaults on the ocean floor. Mike looks up to see Leo Guzzo's Chrysler New Yorker diving straight toward his head, the headlights resembling the eyes of a demonic shark.

What the hell? Mike flails his arms. *Gotta move.* In a fit of sheer panic, he hops faster and faster, trying to get out of the sinking automobile's way. A flurry of bubbles escape his mouth as he screams.

Leo and Martoni crash into the water as well. The sedan, now nose down in the sand, slowly starts to tip in his direction. The huge car slams next to him, sending up the thick murky bottom in a soupy cloud. Mike is suddenly blind and deaf in the underwater world.

When the cloud clears, he looks back up to the shadowy figures pulling themselves out of the water. The murky water also reveals a familiar face clouded in darkness. Mike knows this figure

CHAPTER 9

all too well. "I have waited a long time for this, Strong," the specter hisses to him.

Mike stares at the horrifying figure. He can't help but to smile. *Ah Death, my old friend.*

"It is but a moment's time before you die, and I shall relish in your last suffocating breath," Death says. Mike stares at the gnarly face of a million-year-old dead man, the murky plume of sediment making a perfect cloak and hood. Mike brings his hand up, looking at it strangely. Death tilts his head. Mike shows Death his middle finger. *Go fuck yourself, Death. You're going to be waiting a long time.*

Death laughs at him. "What is it about you that makes me like you so much?" Death hisses.

My good looks? Bob, can I call you Bob? We've been here before—a few times. There's only one way for me to punch a ticket and drowning ain't it. Right, those are the rules. That's the curse, isn't it? Go fuck yourself. Mike thinks the words but he knows Death can hear him.

Mike stretches out his arm, raising his hand high over his head with his fingers spread wide. The pentagram on his palm starts to glow. Death watches in anticipation.

On the dock, Jacky pulls Martoni from the water as Leo helps himself up. Jacky struggles to lift Martoni, pissing Martoni off a little.

"What the hell was that?" Martoni screams. "That car came out of nowhere!"

Jacky takes off running for the front of the warehouse. "I'm not sure, boss." Jacky calls over his shoulder.

Martoni stands on the dock, looking into the water. He can't help but laugh. "Well, now he's got a car on him. What a blessing."

Leo laughs a little but then frowns. "That was my car."

Martoni claps his hand on Leo's soggy shoulder. "I'll buy you another one, Leo. Strong will forever have a memorial now: a Chrysler New Yorker on his chest."

Suddenly, Mike Strong's Colt 1911 skitters past them and drops into the water with a *plop*. Confused, Martoni looks back at Jacky, wondering why the goon kicked the gun in their direction. Except, Jacky is still inside the warehouse.

"Whatever. This is the second time I've been completely soaked today!" Leo moans, Martoni laughs, smacking Leo on the back. "Stop being a baby."

Mike's gun slams into his outstretched hand. Aiming it at the concrete around his feet, he opens fire. Chunks chip off as the loose, still wet cement inside seeps out. Mike tries to kick his feet again, and this time, his right foot breaks free. He fires again and can pull out his left foot.

Mike is completely free now. He starts swimming toward the surface, pausing long enough to turn and flash his middle finger to Death one more time. *Not this time, you old bastard,* Mike rushes to the surface, bursting out like a breaching whale. He inhales as much oxygen as he can.

He breathes deep, looking around to see if any of the mafia bozos are still around. He can hear voices, but they are deep in the warehouse. Mike floats under the massive dock, straining to hear what they are saying.

Martoni looks at the debris field left by the sedan. It had busted through the wooden garage door, leaving shards of wood and a generous helping of dust in its wake.

"What the hell happened?" Jacky asks.

"Maybe the brake slipped?" Leo offers, shaking his head.

"Doesn't matter. Get your asses to The Dice. We've got a meeting tonight," Martoni says, walking toward his car. He twirls his keys around his finger.

Becky is still outside, hiding behind Martoni's Corvette. "I hope Strong is alive. I'd better get the hell out of here before I get shot," Becky mutters, darting off into the darkness.

Leo stands in the lot, reminded, once again, that his car is at the bottom of the bay. "Hey boss, how are we getting back?" Leo asks. "Can we ride with you?"

"Take a cab, Guzzo," Johnny says, sliding into his sleek convertible.

Leo hurries toward his boss's car. Martoni can't leave—not before he's said what he needed to say. Johnny pulls out a pack of smokes from his glove box, lighting one. "What is it?" Johnny asks.

Leo glances toward the warehouse, making sure Jacky is still out of earshot. "I spoke with a buddy at the Ninety-Nine. He overheard

CHAPTER 9

the Police Chief talking to someone on the phone. Someone who knows an awful lot about our goings-on. Someone in our gang."

"Reeko?" Johnny asks.

"I'm not sure, boss. But it's someone close to us. We need to be careful," Leo urges.

Jacky walks out of the warehouse and Leo steps away from Johnny's Corvette. "No idea what happened. Why did the car do that?" Jacky asks.

Johnny starts his car, the engine roaring. He glances over to Leo and Jacky, revving the engine a few times. Then, he slams the car into gear, stomping on the accelerator. The back wheels kick up dirt and, in a matter of seconds, the car is out of sight down the deserted street.

Leo and Jacky stand at the entrance to the warehouse. "Someone tampered with my car," Leo says. They both stare out into the empty parking lot.

"We need a ride," Jacky mutters.

"No shit."

Mike hangs onto the huge wooden pylon beneath the dock, trying to listen for more familiar voices. He waits a few minutes and decides to make the long swim back to the sea wall.

The wall crumbles under his weight as he pulls himself and his now 300-pound trench coat out of the water. He lays on the cold ground for a moment, catching his breath. He can still see the warehouse on the horizon.

Mike holds his gun aloft, the glimmering stars above his only source of light. He shakes some water out of the chamber then slides it back into its holster. Looking at the sky, he sighs. This was not how he planned to get his exercise today. He rolls to his stomach, getting up to his knees with a huge moan. His face feels like someone used a sledgehammer on it for three days straight.

He pours the water out of his combat boots before putting them back on. When he stands, they sink into the muddy bank. Mike reaches into his inside trench coat pocket, pulling out his pack of smokes. They are completely soaked. He squeezes the pack and a ton of water weeps between his fingers.

Mike sighs, tossing the entire pack to the ground. He staggers across an empty lot that is now being used as a tent city. A homeless man grunts, turning over on his mat as Mike walks into a narrow alleyway. *So, Johnny's gonna be at The Dice tonight. Wonder what his plans are? I've got to find Becky. She's probably worried sick about me. I need a shower and some dry clothes—and a cup of coffee.* Mike makes his way down the alley, leaving a soggy trail of footprints behind him.

Mike makes his way to the corner, looking up and down the street for a taxi. No such luck. *Looks like I'm walkin.* He passes by mom-and-pop shops, all closed due to the late hour. Two televisions in the T.V. repair shop window are on. One is playing the nightly news, the news crawl reading **"How Many are Missing?"**

<hr>

Mike keeps walking until eventually he's in a seedy area where men, women, and those who identify as both work the corners. Reaching into his pocket, Mike approaches a trio of prostitutes. They look at him strangely and back up little, not sure what he is about to pull out of his pocket.

"Is this a stick-up?" a woman asks, hiding her unease behind a chuckle. Mike laughs out loud at her question, pulling out a handful of change.

"Only if you're a cigarette, doll," Mike says, offering her the coins. "Can I buy a smoke?"

The woman reaches into her purse, pulling out a pack of cigarettes. She taps one out, handing it to Mike. "Why you all wet, darling?"

"I went swimming." Mike replies. It takes a few flicks for his lighter to catch fire, but he eventually lights the tip. He inhales.

"You always go swimming in your clothes?" she asks.

"Every day," Mike says.

"Honey, you got concrete on your pants," a male escort says.

"Perks of the business," Mike quips. "Thanks for the smoke, ma'am." He heads down the sidewalk. After walking only a few feet, he pauses, spinning on his heel. "Hey, you guys ever see a wacky German around the neighborhood?"

One of the male prostitutes huffs, crossing his arms over his chest. "You mean that old bastard in the delivery truck?"

Mike shrugs his shoulders. "Maybe?"

CHAPTER 9

"This old German guy picked me for an overnight," he explains. "Took me back to some seedy abandoned factory on the west side of the wharf—some creepy shit in there, I'll tell ya. Anyway, I should have known it was a gag. I get ready in this foyer. He made me put on this white robe and wants to tie me up. I mean hey, if the money's right, let's do it, right?

"But here's the thing: I'm double-jointed in my wrists, so no restraints can hold me. He lays me on the ground and I'm like, 'Okay, this is new,' but hey, let's roll dice, right? Well, what a mistake! He pulls out this ax and I flip-flop my way off the floor like a fish, pull myself out of the restraints, and haul ass." He pauses to wiggle his fingers at the woman, grinning when she places a cigarette in his palm. "Thank you, gorgeous. Anyway, where was I?"

"I'm running around this huge ass factory in a white gown like some escaped mental patient, not that I can't relate to that. I'm screaming like a rat on fire, and I see these huge double doors. I crash through them and run off into the night. He was a killer, for sure. So much for the tie-up game." He shrugs as if to say *no skin off my nose*.

This guy can talk. Mike hands the man a ten-dollar bill. "Thanks. I think that's all I need to know." Mike offers them a little wave before continuing on his way.

"Hey, soggy shoes, at least let me earn my money. I can suck you and your clothes dry," the man calls

"I appreciate the offer, fella, but I'm on a case."

CHAPTER 10

The Dice Club is one of the coolest places in all of Valkyrie City. It's in a prime location, sitting just off the interstate, smack dab in the middle of downtown. The clientele spans from the super elite to the average Joe. Depending on the night, you can see live performances from world-famous crooners backed by brass bands to up-and-coming soloists.

The exterior of the club is sleek and modern, trimmed with miles of neon lighting. The front door is bright red and the spinning double dice on the top of the building can be seen from the interstate.

Johnny Martoni pulls up in his loud red Corvette, pulling his large ego behind him. "Not a scratch," Johnny warns the young valet, tossing him his keys.

Several onlookers—standing in the ever-expanding line that winds around the block— watch as Johnny straightens his expensive suit. A group of young men whisper animatedly to each other. It's not often that a bona fide gangster mingles with the locals.

"Yes, Mr. Martoni. Not a scratch," the young valet says.

Johnny walks toward the front door and a burly doorman opens it for him. As Johnny enters the establishment, he admires his home away from home. The Dice is set up like a theater, with a

CHAPTER 10

main stage big enough for a piano and singer. The walls are dark, with a wall-to-wall mirror at eye level. The bar is huge, spanning the entire back wall with several bartenders preparing drinks and making small talk with regulars.

The décor has an Old-World aesthetic. There are eccentric abstract paintings on the wall, separated by ornate sconces and other fixtures. There are ten statues on display throughout the club. They depict the Nine Muses and Osiris. There's Calliope, the muse of poetry; Clio, the muse of history; Euterpe, the muse of music; Urania, the muse of astronomy; Erato, the muse of literature; Polyhymnia, the muse of pantomime; Thalia, the muse of comedy; Melpomene, the muse of tragedy; Terpsichore, the muse of dance; and, of course, Osiris.

Johnny is greeted by a large man who barely fits in his suit, with a hat a little small for his head. This is Fat Eddie, one of Johnny's minions.

"Johnny, you're here. Wasn't sure you were coming," Fat Eddie says.

"Who're you, my mother?" Johnny smacks the man playfully on his cheek.

Johnny makes his way through the crowd, making sure that Wendy Washington sees him. It's important for Johnny to feel like a hot shot and big-timer in this club. After all, he is bucking for a cushy position within the criminal underworld. Wendy is onstage belting out a number; "It isn't fair for you to haunt me," she croons. It's a sultry tune with powerful notes. Johnny, as always, assumes she's singing the song just for him.

Fat Eddie escorts Johnny to a circular table close to the stage but set off in a dark corner. Reeko is waiting. He will gladly do the dirty work, whatever that entails. He doesn't bat an eye at murder, theft, racketeering, or kidnapping.

"Don't get up, Reeko," Johnny says sarcastically.

Reeko immediately realizes his mistake, jumping to his feet. He jostles the table in his haste. "Sorry, boss. I was just listening to Wendy."

"I get it. But next time, you fucking stand when I enter a building," Johnny snaps.

Reeko nods as he pulls out a chair for Johnny to sit. Johnny unbuttons his suit jacket, sitting down. As he does, Gina Reynolds walks over to him. She had her eye on him since the second he walked in.

"Hiya Johnny. You want an Old Fashioned?" the doe-eyed waitress asks.

Johnny grabs her around the waist, pulling her in close. "Hiya doll," Johnny purrs.

"Johnny, where have you been? I haven't heard from you in a week," she pouts.

"Working, baby. I'm a busy man," he says, slipping a ten spot into the pocket of her apron.

Gina nudges him playfully with her hip, giving him a wink. She walks across the busy club, passing several couples clearly having a romantic evening. Gina looks over at the in-house entertainment. Wendy Washington is waifish and dark-haired, one of the most beautiful singers in the entire city. She catches Gina's eye, giving her a wink.

The doorman returns with Leo and Jacky following him. He motions to the table near the stage and the men continue without him. Gina sighs. With all of Martoni's men here tonight, things might get a little unpredictable.

Johnny watches as Leo and Jacky approach. Johnny looks at his watch as if to say, "What took you so long?" Leo laughs a little, motioning to his dry suit. Johnny jabs his finger at the table. Leo and Jacky obediently sit. Smiling, Johnny looks at his table full of goons.

The songstress continues to belt out her tune as Johnny tries to suss out which one of his men is the Narc. *Each one might be the snitch. Jackey talks too much. Who's he talking to? Louie's a schlub, messy, maybe too messy. Has he been nabbed recently? I can't remember. Leo's a kiss up and his dame needs a new dress every day. Reeko likes jewelry, a lot. He's covered in gold—looks like a pawn shop. Zumba? Not a chance. Right? Geonetti is going to kill me tomorrow if I don't fucking kill one of these fucks tonight. I don't want to die like that. I'll murder all of them!* Johnny sips his drink. The men stare back at him, watching his eyes shift back and forth like a cat watching a mouse.

CHAPTER 10

Gina walks up with a tray of drinks, smiling. It doesn't quite reach her eyes. She seems just as worried as everyone else at the table.

"Here's your drinks, fellas. Please, no trouble tonight," She grins.

Johnny snatches his drink off the table, swallowing the entire thing in one gulp. He slams it back onto the table, sending ice everywhere. Leo looks around to make sure there aren't any city officials or politicians around.

Johnny isn't sure where to begin. He stares at the table, chewing on his cheek; he can still taste bourbon. He's sweating, his hair sticking to his forehead. He idly digs his thumb nail into the chipped shellac on the tabletop, peeling it up. His cigarette, forgotten, burns his fingers. Cursing, he jabs it into the ashtray.

Leo watches him spiral. *This is bad*, he thinks. He looks over the henchmen at the table, hoping one will twitch; it is imperative that they find the rat. Johnny wordlessly raises his eyebrows as if to say, *Any suspects?*

"Gentlemen, we have a rat," Johnny announces, steepling his fingers on the tabletop.

Louie does a spit take. The men look at each other.

"Ain't me, boss!" Reeko says.

Johnny shakes his head, swirling the ice around in his empty glass. Before he can speak, Gina walks over to the table again.

"Another round, fellas?" she asks. But then, she feels the tension; it makes the air feel thick like an impending storm. "I'll come back."

"Hold it, Gina." Johnny says. "Say, if you had to pick a snitch out of this group, who would you pick?"

"Oh, Mr. Martoni, I'm not good at judging people. I get judged all the time for being dumb. It doesn't make ya feel good." She starts to walk away but Johnny snags her by the arm.

"Which one? Just take a guess. No harm. I'm not going to shoot anyone in the club, doll," Johnny says, his fingers tightening despite his nonchalant tone.

"I already told you, Mr. Martoni, I don't like to judge anyone. My mother, God rest her soul, now, she was a good judge of character," Gina says.

"She was? How'd she judge your character then? The daughter who slings drink and ass for the right price? Shall we call her up and ask what she thinks of you?" Johnny asks.

Gina snaps her arm out of his hand with a grunt. "That's enough, Johnny," Gina says through gritted teeth, storming away.

Leo leans back in his chair, sipping his drink with one hand and putting his other on the snub nose .38 in his pocket. Johnny's glare is icy, and none of his henchmen dares to move. Except Leo, who is thoroughly enjoying his drink.

"I have been good to you boys. I've bought you houses, cars, dames! So many dames. Two or three at a time. I don't judge. I've put so much money in your pockets that your children's children won't have to work a day in their lives. And for what? So that one of you dumb rat bastards can bite the hand that feeds you? I've taken care of medical bills for your kids. This is the thanks I get. *This?!*" Johnny shouts the last word, slapping his palm on the tabletop. The rage makes him vibrate.

"Now, boss, let's just think for a moment—" Reeko starts.

"Think for a moment? All I've been doing is thinking since Geonetti put a little bird in my fucking ear. He said one of you fucks is running to the Ninety-Nine and blowing your gums out," Johnny interrupts.

"Well, at least Strong is in the drink, boss. That's one less worry," Jacky offers.

Johnny laughs. Reeko, Pete, and Louie look questioningly at Jacky, who grins like the cat who ate the canary.

"You guys got Mike Strong tonight?" Pete asks with a chuckle.

"Yeah." Leo says.

"Why aren't we celebrating?" Louie asks.

Johnny jumps up, grabs Louie by the hair, and slams his head down onto the table. All of the glasses rattle. Leo stands warily, looking for trouble in the crowd; violence tends to be infectious in places like this. Wendy Washington motions to her band to keep playing and she keeps singing. Thankfully, most of the patrons don't seem to notice the commotion.

"You dumb fuck!" Johnny hisses into Louie's ear.

CHAPTER 10

Johnny straightens up. His face is beat red, and sweat is pouring down his cheeks. His jaw is a right angle, rage making the vein in his temple jump beneath his skin.

"A rat!" Johnny screams as loud as he can.

Everyone in the club has no choice but to take notice now. The band stops playing, and Wendy stops singing. Gina, over at the bar, watches closely. The club manager, an older gentleman with years etched into his face, stares at Johnny. He holds his hand up. Johnny pulls himself together, his breathing slow. Leo's fingers curl around the grip of the snub nose, ready for anything. The club manager waves at Wendy to pick things back up again.

"Well, mister, that's a fine how do ya do," Wendy giggles into the microphone, making the crowd laugh. The joke backfires.

Johnny glares at the laughing crowd, sneering. "You laugh at me? I'm Johnny Martoni. I'm about to run this town," Johnny shouts.

"I have to ask, Mr. Martoni: you mind running it outside? We're trying to have a good time," Wendy says from the stage.

The crowd erupts again, and this sends Johnny over the edge. Johnny pulls out his pistol, waving it at everyone. Then he aims it at his own men. None of them dare move. They know the drill. This isn't the first time Johnny has swung his gun around like a lunatic.

"Perhaps we should go outside Johnny." Leo says.

Johnny presses the muzzle against Leo's forehead. Leo stares at him. He has known Johnny for twenty years. He knows Johnny wouldn't shoot him—especially inside The Dice. That would get him locked up for life. There are too many witnesses.

"Yeah, you're right, Leo. Let's all go outside."

Wendy motions to her band. They start right where they left off. Johnny and his men get up from the table and make their way across the dance floor toward the back exit. Johnny glares at Wendy, who is more clever and wittier than Johnny will ever be.

"Take a picture, kid, it'll last longer," she says.

The crowd laughs again. Johnny storms off to the exit like a defeated child.

"Let's get back to the show, folks. I thought the drama was up here," Wendy quips.

The back door to the club slams as Leo walks out, leading the other henchmen into the back alley. Leo is fuming. The rest of them

JOURNEY INTO HELL

are scared. Johnny pushes Reeko and Louie out of his way. Pete and Jacky keep their distance, trying not to get too close to him. Leo keeps his hand in his coat pocket, locked tightly around Becky's revolver.

Johnny walks around his men as they form a circle. He pushes Reeko again. Leo watches his leader descend into paranoia. Johnny snaps like a rubber band pulled too tight. He grabs Louie by his neck, slamming him against the brick of the building's exterior. Louie is shocked and fearful as Johnny chokes him with both hands. Just as Louie's body goes slack, Leo grabs Johnny by his shoulders, pulling him off the huge man. Johnny swings at Leo, but Leo expects it, stepping just outside the trajectory of his wild punch.

"You bastards," Johnny says.

"Get your shit together, Johnny," Leo says coolly. Johnny draws his weapon again, aiming it at Leo. Leo smiles at him. "I'm not the one," Leo says. "You know that."

Johnny turns his attention to Pete. "Is it you?" Johnny asks.

"It's not me, boss. I didn't do anything. I'm as loyal as Schwept's chewing gum," he insists.

Seemingly satisfied, Johnny places his gun against Reeko's temple. "Is it you, Reeko? You seem like the type to be a blabbermouth. You go off running to some friends at the precinct?"

"What? I'm no rat, Johnny," Reeko blubbers with his hands up.

Johnny turns around, eyeing Pete and Jacky who are huddled together as though there is strength in numbers He steps between them, his face inches from Pete's. "You, Pete? I've known you for a long time, so it'd be quite the trick you pulled."

Pete stares at Johnny. Then he does the unthinkable. "Fuck you, Johnny," he spits. "I'm done with this shit." He walks down the alley without so much as a second glance.

The gangsters watch in disbelief. Pete has the courage none of them have ever had. No one ever walks away from Johnny Martoni.

"Pete, you rat bastard. How could you?" Johnny yells.

Pete stops. "Johnny, I'm not your rat."

Johnny grins maniacally, aiming his pistol. His hand is steady. "Ya, I don't know that."

BAM!

CHAPTER 10

All of the men jump as if the bullet was intended for them. Pete's body falls to the cold ground. The gun barrel steams as the metal cools in the frosty air. Gina, standing in the doorway, screams, rushing back inside the club. Leo starts to go after her, but Johnny calls him off. "Forget her. We'll deal with her later. Right now, you sons of bitches are going to play a game."

"A game?" Reeko asks.

Louie, Reeko, and Jacky all step to one side of the alley standing next to each other. Jacky puts his hand in his coat, grabbing his gun but not daring to pull it out. Johnny puts his gun against Louie's forehead. Reeko and Jacky step away from him. Louie drops to his knees, pleading for his life. "Johnny! It's not me! It's not me!" Louie grabs the front of Johnny's coat.

"Get off of me, you sniveling pig." Johnny hits Louie in the forehead with the butt of his gun.

"Johnny, you gotta stop," Leo says, stepping up.

Reeko and Jacky both shuffle further away. Jacky pulls his gun. Reeko doesn't know what to think. He is starting to panic as everyone pulls out their weapons. Johnny aims his gun at Jacky and Jacky aims his gun at Johnny.

"You gonna shoot me Jacky-Boy?" Johnny asks.

"You're shooting everyone else," Jacky says, licking his chapped lips.

The two men stare at each other, breathing heavily. Louie clambers to his feet, watching in pure fear. The blow makes him unsteady on his feet, and he sways. Reeko looks at Louie with wide eyes. They are both just a dumbfounded. They should be spending their night drinking and dancing with women, not whimpering in a stinking alley like dogs.

"You've got to stop, Johnny. The cops are gonna show up real quick like. We gotta cut out," Leo urges.

Johnny looks back at Pete's dead body, blood pooling around his head. His face is distorted from the impact of the bullet, his eye socket mangled. Skull fragments and teeth litter the ground.

Johnny isn't quite finished. He keeps his gun trained on Jacky. With a sigh, Leo pulls out Becky's gun, aiming it at Jacky. Reeko and Louie both shake in their shoes not knowing what to do. Louie pulls his gun, so Reeko has no choice. He pulls his gun too.

"Jacky, I'm going to kill ya. I think you're the rat," Johnny says.

"Fellas, let's just all lower our guns. This is way out of hand and half the city's police force is probably on its way," Leo pleads.

Johnny's attention turns to Leo. Johnny steps up to him. Leo is far larger than Johnny and he's not afraid of him; he doesn't move. Johnny is too enraged to notice.

"You seem to know a lot about the coppers, fink," Johnny says. "Maybe you're the rat."

Leo laughs in Johnny's face. "*Me*? You're losing your goddamn mind, Johnny! Get it together before this night goes south for you."

Johnny is taken aback by Leo's words. "Are you threatening me?"

"Johnny, it's not a threat. It's an observation. Pete is dead, and Gina is no doubt calling the coppers. Get it together. We have to go. Not only do we have to cut out quick-like, but now we have to take Pete's body with us," Leo says.

Johnny stands there for a moment, contemplating. Then, he blows Jacky's brains out. The back of Jacky's skull splatters the brick wall behind him. His body slams back against the cold brick, sliding down the wall. Jacky's face is pulverized, and half his jaw is missing. The blood bubbles out of his remaining nostril. He gurgles. His body twitches and jerks for a moment as the steam escapes from the inside of his head.

No one moves. Louie vomits all over the ground in front of Reeko. Reeko doesn't even notice, his mouth agape. Louie falls to his hands and knees. "Oh Jesus!" he exclaims.

"Louie, take Pete's body and dump it. Reeko, take Jacky's body and dump it. Be sure to lay low tomorrow. Then we need to meet up. I gotta set up a meeting with Geonetti. I'm going to end this debate once and for all. Leo, where can we meet? Somewhere out of the way," Johnny says, all business now.

Leo stares at the man before him. *Johnny is a lunatic,* he thinks, *and so cold, too.* Louie and Reeko pick up the bodies, lugging them down the alleyway. The blood rushes in Leo's ears. *Wait, what is Johnny saying?*

"Leo, snap out of it," Johnny screams.

Leo shakes his head, and everything comes back into focus. His hearing returns and he breaths calmly. Looking at the man before him, he concludes his days are numbered as well.

CHAPTER 10

"Leo, a warehouse—you got one?" Johnny asks impatiently.

Leo thinks for a moment. "Yeah, there's that abandoned toy factory on 101st street," Leo says.

"Oh yeah, good place. Bring all the boys at nine p.m. It's time we cull the herd," Johnny says.

"You got it, boss," Leo replies.

Johnny takes off running down the alleyway, leaving Leo standing there. After making sure no one has come outside, Leo pulls up his collar and starts down the alley in the opposite direction. He can't believe what just happened. As he rounds the corner into the darkness, he fades into the shadows.

She's alone. Gina eases open the door, making her way out into the alley. She examines the pools of blood, the edges already freezing. Pulling her notepad and a pen from her apron, she jots something down. Then, she searches her pocket, pulling out a pack of cigarettes. She flips one out, popping it between her crimson lips. Lighting it, she pulls the smoke into her lungs.

The streetlight shines down on her. Her silhouette is as pretty as a photograph. Her black trench coat flaps in the breeze. She squats down, picking up the shells from Johnny's gun. Rising, she holds one up to the streetlight, turning it this way and that.

Her attention returns to the ground. Suddenly, a half-smoked cigarette floats to the asphalt in front of her. It bounces on the ground. She looks around to see if someone flipped it at her. There is no one there.

She looks up, tracing the fire escape to the roof. She catches the glimpse of someone's trench coat in the light. She smiles. The wailing of sirens pierces the air—the police are close. She flicks her cigarette into the pool of blood before going back inside The Dice.

CHAPTER 11

The cab pulls up outside of 1910 Mayfair Lane. It's a small little house on the corner of a quiet suburb just outside of Valkyrie City. The little house is made of brick and wood. The outside is a robin's egg blue with white trim. There's a beautiful porch swing, and a white picket fence. Becky steps out of the cab onto her lawn, shutting the cab door. Becky scans her street just to make sure she wasn't followed.

Looking at her watch, the time is 10:35 p.m. She walks up her driveway to the cute porch, climbing the wooden steps to her front door. As if waiting for her, Philip flips on the porch light and opens the door. "You're out late," he says. He was waiting. Becky nods, walking inside. "Working on this missing persons case," she says, putting her purse down on the kitchen table. "How was your day?" She shrugs off her trench coat.

"Fine." Philip says rather flippantly. His attitude says it all. He's upset with her. Becky understands his frustration. It is very late, and she hasn't talked to him since lunch.

"Modern communication, it's a drag." Becky chuckles, trying to lighten the mood. She starts to unbutton her blouse, giving him a smoldering smirk. But he's not having it.

CHAPTER 11

"I was worried sick, Becky! How could I not be? Knowing you hang around with that trashcan you call a hero all the time," Philip says, stomping into the living room.

Becky rolls her eyes, following him. "First of all, Strong is not a 'trashcan', as you put it. Second, he *is* a hero. You have no idea what he's done for this city."

"Oh yeah, you seem to love to get into trouble with him. The two of you are always off on your adventures," Philips grumbles. At the dry bar, he pours two glasses of bourbon, handing one to his fiancée. "He's gonna get you killed one day. Those people he investigates are horrible people, Becky." He takes a measured sip of his bourbon.

"Yeah, maybe, but he truly is a hero. You know who he's come up against. The filth of the city: mobsters, lowlifes, the dregs of society. I can't even count how many criminals and demons he's gotten out of the city. Or shot to death." Becky downs her glass of bourbon in one gulp.

"You say demons like he's actually fighting monsters. Get real, will ya! These mobsters will kill you just as quickly as they will him. And then what? You're dead. Where does that leave me?" Philip finishes his glass. "Do you have feelings for him?"

"Yeah, he's a friend. A colleague. An angel of sorts. Of course, I have feelings for him. You know how many times he's saved my life?" Becky takes her top off, tossing her bra on the back of a chair. Her figure is exquisite, with a thin waist, smooth creamy skin, and plump breasts. She is a looker, that's for sure. She walks over to Philip, draping her arms around his neck. His wool suit is coarse against her naked chest. "I may have feelings for him, but I love you. That means more than anything."

Philip shows little interest in her or her flirting. He nudges her away with a furrowed brow. "Are you two sleeping together?" he asks.

Becky laughs. "This again. I've told you like a million times. We are not sleeping together. We are nothing more than friends who get shot at together. Honey, please do not be jealous of Mike Strong."

"How can I not be? Look at him: smart, heroic, piercing eyes. He's a good-looking fellow. I can't help but wonder if there's more between you two," Philip says.

"I'm never going to cheat on you. What kind of dame do I look like?" she asks, her hands on her hips.

Philip walks through the house to the staircase. He takes off his Valentino leather wingtips, putting them neatly in a cubby in the hall. He takes off his silk tie, draping it on a rung on the hat rack next to a few others he'd discarded there. "I have to be in early tomorrow. I don't want to fight, but I can't help but feel jealous," he says, climbing the stairs.

Becky sighs, turning back to the dry bar to pour herself another drink. She kicks her shoes off, rubbing her foot with her free hand while using the other to balance. "These are some barking dogs," she sighs. Shuffling over to the television, she takes comfort in the thick carpet beneath her tired feet. She flips the television on, and a newscast slowly comes into focus. Becky takes a seat on the overstuffed couch with her drink in-hand, watching the anchorman talk about the city's high-end properties. She tries to focus on the program, but it is very difficult for her to do so. She dozes.

Her eyes open again as The Star-Spangled Banner plays loudly on the television. She blinks rapidly, trying to wake up. Her drink fell out of her hand during her nap, spilling over the couch cushion. "Damn it." Becky gets up to retrieve a washcloth from the kitchen.

Yawning widely, she scrubs the polyester. It's too late—the stain has set. She tosses the washcloth onto the dark oak coffee table. *I'll deal with it in the morning*, she thinks. Becky slowly makes her way up the long staircase to her bedroom. She craves the comfort of her bed—the luscious plump pillows and soft feather down comforter seem to be calling out like a siren on a rocky shore.

She falls face down onto the bed next to Phillip. He only grunts, rolling onto his side. Becky finds her pillow in the dark, bringing it to her face and snuggling into it. Her eyes close and, within seconds, she is out like a light.

The morning came quickly. Too quickly. The sun beats down on her face through the open curtains, warming her cheeks. The sudden heat penetrates her dreams, and, for a moment, she thinks she is on fire. She cracks her eyes open. The ray of light beaming through the glass window is a spotlight, emphasizing every speck of dust dancing in the air.

CHAPTER 11

The tranquil silence is broken by the sound of Phillip's exasperated voice. "You're going to be late for work," he says, looping his tie around his neck. "No shower today, love." He bends to kiss her forehead with his dry lips. "Better scoot if you're going to make it, baby."

Becky rolls onto her back, stretching out all her limbs. She suddenly thinks of Mike Strong and sits bolt upright. "Strong!" she gasps.

Phillip glares at her. "Is he always your first thought in the morning?"

Becky swings out of bed. "No! Phillip, he was taken by Johnny Martoni and his trio of goons last night." Becky rushes downstairs.

"What? Where? Did you see Martoni?" Phillip follows, seeming genuinely interested.

"Yes, and Leo Guzzo and Jacky Ribbasa. They tried to threaten me earlier in the day, too," Becky says. She rushes over to her shoes, slipping them on over the stockings she'd inadvertently slept in. Dialing Strong's number on the rotary phone, she finds herself murmuring, "Pick up, pick up, pick up." The phone simply rings. No one answers. "Shit."

"You saw Martoni?" Phillip asks again.

"Yes. Leo Guzzo had his hands on me."

Phillip stares at her. "I'll knock that fat gangster's block right off his shoulders," he says in all seriousness. "These dumb goombahs think they own the whole damn city!" Phillip's concern is drawn on his face, as plain as day. Becky notices. This is somewhat out of character for him. Phillip throws on his suit jacket as Becky finishes putting on yesterday's clothes and, together, they rush out the door.

"When is the last time you talked to Strong?" Phillip asks as they get into his blue Packard Caribbean Sedan.

"Yesterday, when Guzzo and Ribbasa took him from his office and kicked me to the curb." Becky says, lighting a cigarette. Phillip backs the car out of the driveway, nearly running over the neighbor's mailbox. Then he shoves the car into drive, stepping on the gas. Becky hands him the lit smoke and lights another one for herself.

"What's the plan?" Phillip asks.

"Well, I've got to know if he's alive or not. Though, he probably is. He is very resilient, especially when it comes to not dying," she says.

Phillip speeds down the narrow suburban street that stretches through their neighborhood. "What does that mean?" Phillip asks.

"I've got to get to his office," Becky murmurs, taking a huge pull off her cigarette. She pointedly ignores his question; *Phillip would never believe the stories if she told him. Who would?* She pretends to look in her purse.

"Where is your car?" Phillip asks.

"Still at *The Herald*. This all started with a lunch at Salvaggio's yesterday," she says.

"Salvaggio's? That's fancy," Phillip remarks, pulling onto the interstate.

Becky realizes he's going west instead of north. She smiles. "Not my idea, Ralph and the police chief were having a meeting there. Say, where are we headed?" She already knows the answer.

"Strong's place," Phillip says. "Listen, I know you too are like a dynamic duo and all, and there isn't much I can do about that. I know you love him. Not like a love affair but more like a brother, at least that's what I'm hoping," Phillip says.

"'Yes, my love. I love you. I love Mike in a 'I want to smash his head open with a flashlight' kind of way," she chuckles, making quotations with her fingers.

"I know, and that's why we have to make sure he's not dead. And, if he is, we have to stop Martoni and his gang of gorillas," Phillip says, resolute.

Becky looks at her fiancé as he drives. She is taken aback by his new vigor to help her and Mike. Phillip speeds, the pedal nearly touching the floor.

"How was Salvaggio's?" Phillip asks.

"I couldn't tell ya, I left before we ordered."

Phillip glances at her. "What? You left the most prestigious restaurant in the city without eating there?"

"Sorry, I wanted to track down Mike and see what all the hubbub was with Geonetti rushing out of there," Becky replies.

"Well, I hope it was worth it! Who knows when you're going to get the chance to eat there again. I'm going to say never. Like, I don't know, the half the city who can't get a reservation." Phillip is really disheartened about it.

CHAPTER 11

"Okay, I'm sure we can get in there. We are both lead reporters for *The Valkyrie Herald*, after all," Becky says, rolling her eyes.

The rising sun breaches the city's skyline. The orange sunburst encompasses the brick and steel buildings in a warm glow.

They pull off the interstate onto the ramp that leads into the industrial district toward Crown Center, where Mike's apartment is located on the fifth floor of an old building. The area looks similar to the wharf, minus the water—but keep the fish smell and dab of hot garbage. The buildings are just as old and mostly made of brick. Two large smokestacks rise out of the smog-like haze that most people equate to "A place that looks as bad as it tastes!" as Phillip says. The streets are lined with trucks being loaded with a surplus of fruits, veggies, and bread. The largest factory in the area, which was what really caused the smell, was a plastics plant. Sadly, the streets are caked with old dirt and new trash.

Phillip pulls the car up to a high-rise tower, finding a parking spot close to the front doors. Becky hurriedly thrusts open the passenger side door; it protests with a loud squeak. Phillip also gets out, putting on some nice designer sunglasses. Becky also dons sunglasses, black with a cat's eye lens.

The door to Mike apartment on the fifth floor opens with ease, as he rarely locks it. If it isn't stashed in his pocket or in a holster, he doesn't need it. The apartment is deserted. Becky and Phillip look around and everything seems to be in its place as far as they can tell. The apartment isn't pristine, but it isn't gross either. It's much better than the pigsty he calls his office.

Becky accepts the fact Mike hasn't been home. She walks over to the window, looking out at the busy city below. She turns her attention to the skyline. "Where are you, Strong?" Becky mutters under her breath.

Phillip walks into Strong's bedroom. He looks around but doesn't touch anything. He clearly hasn't been in his bed. It's right and tight, the bedsheets so tight that you could bounce a quarter off them.

Suddenly, Becky is startled by a beautiful female climbing down the fire escape, stopping on Mike's balcony. The metal clunks loudly beneath her feet. She is wearing a baby blue, Arctic fox fur-lined overcoat, with a matching woolen fascinator. She looks extraordinary. Becky has to take a step back just to admire her. Her silhouette, with the rising sun behind her, makes her look like a Christmas elf. Natasha curtsies to Becky from behind the snow-frosted glass

    Natasha slides open Mike's window, making her way inside. She trips a little as she crosses the threshold. The two women study each other. Phillip walks out of the bedroom, surprised to find Becky speaking to a rather beautiful woman with a Russian accent.

"You must be Natasha," Becky says.

"Ah, yes, and you must be the girl on the other end of the line," Natasha purrs.

"What?" Becky asks.

"The woman on the phone. You must be Becky," Natasha clarifies.

Becky chuckles. "Oh, yes. That's me."

Natasha makes her way further into Mike's apartment. She nods to Phillip, who leans against the door frame to Mike's bedroom.

"You are prettier than he says," Natasha says to Becky, flashing her a bright smile.

"Does he talk about my fiancée often?" Phillip asks.

Natasha unabashedly looks Phillip up and down. His suit is tight-fitting, straight out of a fashion magazine. His two-tone wingtips match the color of his gray suit. She feels something is off about him, but she can't quite put her finger on it. "No, we're busy fucking," she says.

Phillip chortles. Becky plays it cool, picking at an imaginary fleck of dust on her coat sleeve. Natasha takes off her white gloves, securing them to her belt. Walking into the kitchen, she starts making a pot of coffee.

Natasha knows where everything is. She pulls the coffee and filters out of the cabinet, putting the pot under the running faucet. She is done in seconds. The coffee maker hums, the pleasant smell filling the small apartment. She opens the fridge, pulling out a tray of Danishes. They are days old, and stale, but the only thing edible in the apartment. Becky eyes the tray, knowing how much Mike loves raspberry Danishes.

CHAPTER 11

Stepping back into the living room, Natasha leans her shoulder against the wall. She pulls out a pack of Golova Byka cigarettes, an ox with huge, curved horns printed on the label.

"Coffee?" she asks.

"Sure, I'll have a cup!" Becky says, elated.

Phillip follows suit. "I'll take one too, I suppose, it seems like we're staying for a minute?" Becky doesn't seem to notice the question, nor his raised eyebrows.

"You seem to know your way around the place," Becky observes with a smirk.

"Yes. Why should I not? We are very intimate, Mike and I," Natasha says.

Becky is taken aback by Natasha's transparency; her eyes nearly bug out of their sockets, and her mouth hangs open. Becky tries, in vain, to rein in her expression; she is all too aware she looks tense and jealous. Phillip's face is twisted into an expression of acceptance and anguish. Becky suddenly realizes she's been silent for too long—that'll make her look even worse in Phillip's eyes. "I've heard all about it," she finally musters.

"Then you should know me very well then," Natasha says, puffing on her Golova Byka cigarette.

"Was Mike here last night? "Becky asks.

"I think so. No. I didn't hear him. But I got home late. Had some important business, as it were," she says.

"And what is it that you do?" Phillip asks. "Because your style leans toward modeling."

Natasha walks into the kitchen, pulling the coffee pot off the brewer. She laughs out loud. "You are too kind. No, unfortunately, I was with my sisters."

The coffee steams as it touches the inside of the cool coffee cup. Natasha hands the first cup to Becky. Phillip steps up, receiving his. He nods a thank you and takes a sip.

"I don't have sisters. That'd be nice, I think," Becky muses.

Natasha sips her coffee, looking over the rim at Becky. She gives a little smile and a wink. Putting the cup down, Natasha rubs her hands together, breathing deep. "We are all sisters, my love. You are more than welcome to become my sister whenever you want," Natasha says.

Becky smiles a little, acknowledging the sentiment. She instantly likes Natasha. Becky pulls out a small notepad and pencil, writing her phone number down. Not only is she happy to have met Natasha, now she can keep tabs on her. Becky hands Natasha the piece of paper.

"Here's my number. I'd love to have a sister," Becky said. "Also, what is your number?"

Natasha takes the piece of paper, looking at it with a small smile. "Thank you, darling. Give me." She reaches for Becky's notepad.

Natasha writes her information down inside. She hands it back to Becky. "Now we are sisters. Kind of. You'll have to meet us on a full moon and kill a goat but, hey, we are Russian. We kill lots of things," Natasha jokes.

"Nice. I may have been to a few of those parties in college," Becky laughs.

"Well, we should be going," Phillip says pointedly.

"If you see Strong, tell him to give me a call," Becky says as Phillip ushers her out of the apartment.

"Nice meeting you," Phillip calls over his shoulder. "We are way too late for work."

"Same. Tell him to call me," Natasha says as the door closes.

Becky and Phillip walk out of the apartment building into the parking lot. Becky scans the area, looking for any sign of trouble. All kinds of people—and things—want Mike's head on a silver platter. They could be lurking. But she doesn't see any sign of trouble. Phillip doesn't notice the subtleties in her movements—her side-long glances between cars and into alleyways, her ready to fight posture, the pauses she takes to surmise any situation.

The rush of noise is like a freight train. Becky and Phillip burst into The Herald an hour and half late for work. Both rush to their respective desks, but just as Becky sits down, a shadow eclipses her. She doesn't even have to look up to know who the shadow belongs to, though the overly exasperated cough helps give it away.

"Hey, boss." Becky says.

Ralph places several folders on her desk. "Six more cases," he announces, "Are you and Phillip fighting?"

CHAPTER 11

"No. Why?"

"You two were 90 minutes late," he says with a pointed glance at his wristwatch.

"Oh, no. We went to Strong's place. I'm worried about him. He was taken by Martoni's goons last night," she says.

"Johnny's men took Strong?"

"Yeah, Leo and Jacky. I mean, I'm sure he's fine but..." She trails off.

"I'll keep an ear out. In the meantime, can you please try and get to the bottom of these missing people?" he asks.

Becky nods glumly. Ralph draws a heart in the center of his chest before walking away. Becky picks up one of the folders, thumbing through it. She looks over the report: yet another young woman has disappeared. She was last seen just outside the wharf.

Becky's desk phone rings, and she puts the folder aside. "Strong?" Becky answers.

"It's Gina. Sorry to disappoint. We've got to meet up."

"See ya in forty minutes?" Becky asks.

"See ya then."

CHAPTER 12

The room is cramped and stagnant, its musty smell propagated by mold and old soil. Mike is up to his ankles in water as the room floods. He stares at his hands, both dirty and covered in dark blood. He's reasonably sure it's not his own. He breathes heavily as the water rises past his shins. He sloshes to the side of the concrete room, pounding on the wall, but it is of no use. There is no way he can punch through three-foot-thick concrete. His only hope is that the steel latch above his head will open. The other option is to crawl under the small opening that leads to the flooding hallway. *Guess, I could swim my way back,* Mike thinks. His inner monologue is always sarcastic.

Just then, a familiar voice shouts from above. "Strong!"

Mike looks up to see Major Leland Charland. "What are you doing up there?"

"What are *you* doing down *there*? How did you get in there?" Major Leland asks.

"I went left and got trapped in a dead end. Found a hole and crawled in," Mike says, keenly aware of the rising tide.

"Well, we've got to cut out, daddy-o! This whole place is gonna be flooded in ten minutes."

CHAPTER 12

Mike smiles wide, giving Major Charland a nonchalant shrug of his shoulders. "Yeah," Mike says. "I figured as much."

Major Charland yanks on the steel latch but it won't budge. Then he sees there are three hinges on the left-hand side. "Stand back!" Major Charland orders.

Mike looks around the cramped concrete room. There's nowhere to go. "Where?" Mike asks.

Major Leland fires, hitting the first hinge and knocking it loose. Then, he fires at the second one blowing it off the latch entirely. Mike ducks the best he can inside his quickly filling coffin, throwing his arms over his head. The ricochet sends bits of hot concrete and steel at him. Major Leland aims again, firing at the third hinge. It shatters. He bends down, pulling the latch with ease. He lays flat on his stomach, reaching as far as he can into the room.

Mike jumps up and the two men lock forearms. Pulling himself up, Mike grabs onto the edge of the structure. Leland rolls to his back, heaving with all his might. Mike can taste the dirt on the floor as he slides to safety. Leland stands up, pulling Mike to his feet. The two men watch as the room fills up. They men take off down the hallway, the sound of rushing water all around them.

Rounding a corner, Captain Maxwell staggers in front of them, covered in his own blood. Mike and Leland rush up to him. Suddenly, a strange, mutated soldier in a bloody, ripped SS uniform lunges from the shadows. Mike, Leland, and Maxwell stare at the monstrous thing as it snarls at them. The creature resembles a human, but its eyes are solid black, and from its cracked skin seeps a noxious green goo. Mike and Leland both pull their pistols, firing at the thing. It is seemingly unaffected, grabbing the wall and pulling itself up, defying gravity. Then it crawls up to the ceiling, its bones twisting and contorting under its skin.

Mike watches as the creature spider crawls toward them. All three men back up. The creature's void-like eyes focus on Mike. It leaps from the ceiling, knocking Mike to the ground. The pain ricochets up his spine as, together, they slide down the hallway. Mike moans. He rolls over on top of the grotesque thing, trying to get his hand around its throat. As he does, he puts his pistol against the monster's head, pulling the trigger.

JOURNEY INTO HELL

The creature's brains blast out the side of his skull, spraying Mike's face and the hall with dark blood. Mike stands quickly, firing twice into the creature's chest. Major Leland and Captain Maxwell run up with their guns drawn. Their weapons strafe up and down the hallway, expecting another attack.

"What the hell was that?" Captain Maxwell shouts.

"These fucking Nazis are messing with forces outside our dimension," Mike says.

"This is the most bizarre shit I've ever seen," Major Leland says. He can't believe his eyes or ears. The things they've seen since they've arrived in Romania are simply unimaginable. If they don't shut this bunker down, who knows what other evils will arise. "Let's keep going. We still have work to do."

The men start down the hallway again, reaching a large steel door with a locking, three spoke handle. Captain Maxwell slams some plastic explosives on the corners of the door. Then, he jabs a wire into the sticky material, connecting all four blocks of C-4. He unspools 30 feet of wire, ushering the men back down the hall for safety.

Captain Maxwell ties the wire to a small handheld detonator with a red handle. Once the wire is connected to the charge, he closes the contraption and pushes down the red T-shaped handle. The door explodes, throwing concrete and steel directly at the men. The dust kicks up, as thick as fog. The heavy door slams onto the concrete with a thunderous boom.

Mike snaps awake on the couch in his office. He is still in his clothes from the night before, though they are significantly drier. He rolls off his couch with a moan, stretching. His entire body hurts. Just walking seems to send jolts of electricity into his brain. He makes it to his desk, stripping his clothes off and dropping them where they lay. Naked, he walks over to his armoire, slinging the door open. He selects an undershirt, dress shirt, tie, and a pair of pants. Opening a drawer, he takes out some deodorant and aftershave, splashing it on his neck.

He is dressed in minutes and feels whole again. He looks into the mirror, nodding at his reflection. His reflection nods back. *Hey*

CHAPTER 12

stranger. He takes his shoulder holster off the back of his office chair, sliding it on. His boots are still wet. All he has is a pair of Chuck Taylor All-Stars sitting in the bottom of his armoire. He sighs but has no choice but to put them on. The black and white sneakers go with the outfit. Mike laughs a little, doing a few defensive moves, getting a feeling for the shoes. He smiles widely. *I like these.*

Mike picks up his phone receiver, cradling it between his ear and shoulder. Before he can dial, he discovers that there isn't a dial tone. Mike follows the cord to the wall, finding that it has been ripped out. *No doubt Major Dumb-Dumb and Captain Bozo ripped it out,* Mike thinks. *I can't wait to get those two in a boxcar one day and beat them to death. I'm going to knock out all of Leo's teeth.*

Mike scoops ice into his rocks glass; it tinkles loudly. The smell of the bourbon brings both happy and sad thoughts. The pungent aroma sizzles in his nostrils, but he clearly enjoys it. He pours the bourbon over the ice, sifting it around. He swallows it in one gulp. *Why sip it?*

Mike thinks about the missing person cases. *What is the connecting factor? Why are these seemingly random people disappearing? There has to be a connection. If the police chief has Becky working on it, that means none of his men have the time or none of his men want to do it. I wonder how far Becky has gotten on the case? Shit. Becky. I need to call her.*

Mike looks at his telephone, remembering it's been compromised. *Damn it.* Mike walks over to a large metal filing cabinet, opening the bottom drawer. He pulls out a large map of Valkyrie City, tacking it to the wall. He starts to mark areas on the map where he knows people had been reported missing. Mike admires his handiwork. *Becky would be proud of me.*

Unfortunately, Mike's map is lacking in data. *I don't have all the cases of missing people. Only the case file I'm working on. So pinpointing the exact spot will be difficult until I compare notes with Becky. For now though, I guess this will have to work.* Looking at the dots on his map, Mike tries to triangulate a rough center point. *Well, it has to be somewhere by the docks. All the cases I have are within a few miles of the wharf. There are plenty of empty warehouses there, so it wouldn't be hard to stash a few dead bodies.*

JOURNEY INTO HELL

The bell over Mike's door jingles. Mike looks up to see a couple in their mid-forties walk in. They look distressed and sad. Mike makes his way out to the front of his office.

"Hello. How can I help you?" Mike said.

"Hi. I'm Robert Hughes and this is my wife, Eleanor. We were told by a good friend that you might be able to help us," Mr. Hughes says.

"Recommendations are always nice. It means I've done something right," Mike jokes. "Please come in and have a seat."

The couple sit in front of Mike's desk. Mr. Hughes can't help but notice the crusty clothes piled on the floor. Mrs. Hughes stares at the strange artifacts on the walls. There is a weird dagger, a gnarled stick that looks like a wizard's wand, and a ceremonial headdress that resembles a gorilla. She also notices the map.

"What can I do for you two?" Mike asks.

"Well, our daughter, Elizabeth Hughes, hasn't been seen in three weeks. We went to the police, and the chief there said, 'Young girls get flights of fancy—she probably has a new boyfriend. Come back in a week.' We are at our wit's end. There's only so much we can do," Mr. Hughes says.

"I see," Mike says.

"What is this map for?" Mrs. Hughes asks.

"Oddly, exactly your problem. Those are other missing people cases I'm working on," Mike says.

"There's more than just our Elizabeth?"

"Unfortunately," Mike replies. "A lot more than the city can handle, that's for sure. It seems like more every day."

"Our Elizabeth came home from college for the holidays. We ran low on milk, and she wanted to walk to the store to get some for us," Mr. Hughes says.

"And we let her," Mrs. Hughes sobs.

"Now, now, sweetie, it's not our fault," Mr. Hughes says, draping an arm around her comfortingly.

"Where was she last seen?" Mike asks.

"At the corner market. Just down the street from where we live," Mrs. Hughes says.

"And where is that?" Mike asks.

CHAPTER 12

"GasPro, at the Hardy Avenue and Lewisville Street intersection," Mr. Hughes replies.

Mike stands, looking at his map. He follows Hardy Avenue with his finger until he reaches Lewisville Street. He stops in his tracks. The three cases he's working on are very close to this new case. In fact, he notices something very peculiar. There is a factory nearby called Bobby Boy's Toys. Mike gets a red pen off his desk and is able to make a circle around the location by tracing the missing people's last known whereabouts as waypoints. The toy factory is almost dead center.

What are the odds? Mike thinks. "I'll take your case."

Mr. and Mrs. Hughes hug each other, elated by the news, "Thank you so much," Mrs. Hughes says.

"Well, we need to know how much this is going to cost us, our funds are low. We don't have much. But what I don't have in funds I can trade in work. I'm very handy." Mr. Hughes says, looking around the office.

Mike stares at the map, his eyes boring into the tiny square representing the toy factory. Mike turns to look at the two parents. "Don't worry about it. You have enough on your minds. But if you fix that door. I wouldn't be mad at ya." Mike smiles.

Mr. and Mrs. Hughes cheer with excitement. They can barely contain themselves; hope is such a powerful drug. Mrs. Hughes' eyes start to tear up and she hugs Mr. Hughes again.

"I'm not sure what I'll find, if anything. But if I do, I will most certainly let you know as soon as I find out," Mike says.

Mike walks around his desk, ushering the Hughes's out of his office. They are all smiles and tears as Mike pushes them into the hallway. They turn around to say a final, breathless thank you, but he's already shut the door. His mind is on a mission now and he aims to find out if his instincts are right.

Walking back into his office, he makes a beeline for the map. He knows he's right. *I'd bet dollars to donuts that the toy factory has something to do with this. It's a stretch, but I think I know what might be going on. I have to get to The Herald, I need to see the archives.*

The elevator dings and the doors slide open, revealing the top level of the parking garage. Mike gets a huge whiff of old socks and urine, an aroma he is oddly used to. He makes his way over to his Plymouth Fury, getting in. The engine roars to life and he is off like a shot.

The double doors to The Herald open and Mike goes straight toward Becky's desk in the bullpen. She isn't there. No one in the bullpen asks who he is looking for. Not many of the reporters, salesmen, or editors give two shits about Mike. Most of them don't even know who he is and that's a good thing. Mike doesn't want a ton of people knowing who he really is—or what he really does—anyway. The sheer thought of one of these reporters catching wind that he sometimes puts down a demon (or worse, an angel) and they would lose their minds.

Mike hears a cough from behind him. Ralph waves him into his office. Mike snakes his way through the myriad of desks and fast-talking pencil pushers to Ralph's office. Mike gives a little knock on the threshold.

"Mike, what happened to you last night? Becky is worried sick!" Ralph asks.

"You know, some goons did some goonie shit and tried to drown me. But I kept telling them how much I love swimming. They didn't listen." Mike snickers at his own joke.

"Martoni's goons?" Ralph asks.

"Yeah, you know, Guzzo and Ribbasa. I got it handled," Mike shrugs.

"I don't doubt you do. I just want to make sure I keep Becky safe. Those nitwits will stop at nothing to act like big shots. They think they're fucking celebrities if they get in the paper from some big knock off," Ralph says.

"Speaking of Becky, where is she?" Mike asks.

"She's not at her desk?"

"Nope. I assumed she would be here at work," Mike says. "I know what a workaholic she is—especially if there's a juicy story on the hook."

"She went to your apartment to look for you this morning. Her and Phillip," Ralph says.

CHAPTER 12

"Ah, I slept at the office. When I say 'slept' I mean 'passed out, comatose.' Nothing gives you a good night's sleep quite like a brutal ass-beating and a near drowning. It just tuckers you right out."

"You should go see a doctor," Ralph says, his brow furrowing in concern.

"I'll be fine. I heal real quick-like. Any news on those missing people?" Mike asks.

"Not on my end. Becky has got a whole command center set up down the hall. Go have a look. Maybe you'll see something we don't."

"I think I may have something already. I'll go have a look," Mike says.

Mike leaves Ralph's office, going down the hallway. He passes a few rooms until he gets to the small closet where Becky has set up almost the exact same map and grid system he had. Only hers is much better. Mike stares at it for a moment, then traces down Lewisville Street again to GasPro station.

Her map has about three times as many missing people listed. Mike takes the red marker she has attached to the map with a piece of yarn and marks the toy factory. He can't shake the horrible feeling that the toy factory has something to do with the disappearances. Mike has a bad feeling that means that something ain't right and he's about to find out what.

Something out in the hall catches Mike's attention—a movement in the corner of his eye, a familiar voice. Mike looks out to see Phillip talking to a gentleman in the hallway. The two men seem to be standing a little too close. But that's just part of it. Mike watches as the other gentleman deliberately grazes Phillip's hand in a playful, flirtatious way. Mike simply observes this for a moment before ducking back into the closet. But the seed has been planted.

CHAPTER 13

The wheels of the car push the gravel into the earth. It makes an unpleasant grinding sound as Becky pulls up into a secluded spot just off an inlet near Valkyrie Bay. Becky navigates down a narrow stretch of hidden road past a beached sailboat that hasn't seen the water in several years. The faded blue gunwale blends into the white hull seamlessly. Old rope dangles, the cool gulf breeze making it clang against the aluminum mast.

The car comes to a stop behind some high sawgrass and a huge pile of discarded wooden posts. More than likely, they were going to be used for dock-making, but the time for that has long since passed. They are weathered and bug-eaten now. Gina is already standing on the concrete seawall, wearing a thick purple overcoat.

Getting out of her car, Becky fishes through her purse. She remembers that her pistol was taken by Leo Guzzo back in Strong's office. She does find the old breadstick, and, in a moment of weakness, considers eating it but she decides against it; it's stale and she'll probably chip a tooth. She walks the rocky path out to the seawall, stopping next to Gina who looks out toward the bay.

The view is impeccable here. The huge suspension bridge stands heroically before them. The city skyline is massive and rests between

CHAPTER 13

the clouds and the sea. The cool wind that blows off the water keeps the city at a cool seventy-five degrees most of the summer months.

Gina snaps open her lighter, holding it up to Becky's cigarette before she even has it out of the pack. Becky laughs, pulling in the flame to ignite her cigarette. A tugboat blasts its horn as it sputters along, pulling a larger schooner behind it. The seagulls caw overhead. Becky looks down to see a slab of concrete—once a slipway—that now has new residents in the way of big, fat, cuddly sea lions. They waste no time letting Becky know that they are there, barking animatedly.

"God, I love this spot," Becky says, blowing a plume of smoke.

"I love this city. Look at how majestic it is. Look at that bridge!" Gina says. "It's as pretty as a picture."

"How did you find this place again?"

"I dated a fisherman for a time. He would bring me out here and we would neck." Gina laughs.

"Sounds fishy to me."

The two girls laugh at her bad joke, but the mood goes right back to a more serious one. There's a reason why they are meeting so far outside the city limits.

"Johnny Martoni killed someone last night, possibly two people. Not sure who," Gina says without preamble.

"I'm sorry—*what*? He killed two people? Where? How do you know? Was one of them Mike Strong?" A flurry of questions spills out of Becky's mouth before she can stop them. It's certainly not becoming of a seasoned journalist.

"No. Not Mike. I'm pretty sure it was two of Johnny's goons. But there weren't any bodies once the boys in blue got there. But I saw it. Well, I saw him fire his gun and someone fall dead. I heard it. Best guess: Pete Zumba. But I had to run away because I yelped and knocked over a trash can like a rookie."

"Way to go, clumsy," Becky ribs. "Who was the second unfortunate idiot?"

"Not sure. I went inside. I didn't see who it was, but Leo Guzzo lost his mind and basically told Johnny to get his shit together," Gina says.

"This is insane. It's like the city has got funny juice in the water supply."

"Here's the thing. He thinks one of his boys is a snitch and working for us. He doesn't have a snitch in his gang. The police chief has one on his side, unfortunately. I know this because I report every day and they know stuff that only someone on the inside would know. I think Johnny is gonna try and take over. Maybe take out Geonetti." Smoke pours out of Gina's flared nostrils. "And then I'm gonna take 'em down."

Becky feels as though she's locked inside of her own mind. Mike floods her every thought. She stares out across the water, letting the cool air caress her face. She pulls herself together. "Wow. Johnny is certainly drinking the city water. You know when he's gonna make a move?"

"Tonight. At some abandoned toy factory. He set up a meeting with Geonetti," Gina says.

"Holy shit. If he kills Geonetti and takes over, that could start a huge turf war. We're not even talking about the Bloodhound Gang, the Takamota's, or the Russians. This will send shock waves through the city. This could be bad, Gina," Becky says.

"Okay. One, who are the Bloodhound Gang and two, who are the Takamota's?" Gina asks.

"Oh! I must have read about them in an old pulp novel. I can't get enough of *Murder in Racer Town* and *She's a Killer*." Becky plays it off as though she made it up. But what she was referring to are two of the most violent gangs in Mike's neck of the woods. The Bloodhound Gang is a pack of werewolves who spend their time drug-running, weapons dealing, and human trafficking. They are mean and take pride in the fact they eat humans as a sport. Then, there's the Takamota's, a Japanese gang that use supernatural rituals to summon ghosts, demons, dragons, and various otherworldly monsters to slowly take over the underworld of Valkyrie City. They are clever and take great pleasure in revenge.

"I definitely know the Russians! How do you know more about gangs than I do? I'm the undercover cop here," Gina says.

"I'm a lady on the street, see? I know people who know people," Becky says, doing a campy James Cagney voice. She looks at Gina. "You don't know *Kiss Tomorrow Goodbye*?" James Cagney. Barbara Payton."

CHAPTER 13

"You're a kooky kid, Detter. I gotta get back. I start my shift at 2 p.m. at The Dice."

"Be careful out there, Gina. This town is getting crazy," Becky squeezes her friend's hand.

"You and Strong stay out of trouble. You're gonna get yourselves killed one day., Gina warns before hopping off the sea wall and heading back the way they'd come.

The bullpen is hopping with activity. The reporters busily shuffle papers, talk loudly on the phone, and type on their typewriters. Becky loves the smell of the bullpen—the aroma of paper and ink mixed with old wood. It puts her at ease. She rather enjoyed being at her desk typing up some in-depth interview about a local politician. But her real passion was solving crimes with Strong and, later, reporting on them. The stories ranged from the latest goings-on of some mid-level gangster to a precious artifact being stolen from the museum.

For her, the front line was where it was at. It's a hotbed of activity where she has to keep her feet firmly planted to contend with her more respected male counterparts. She is tough in interviews and heaven forbid she digs up dirt on someone. She will doggedly chase a lead until the trail runs dry like a creek bed in the desert.

As she walks in, she is greeted by Ralph who is all smiles until it morphs into a frown. Becky doesn't find his giant frame remotely threatening, she sees him as cuddly. He was a hell of a replacement for her father who died when she was seven years old. How she longed for her father to see her today! A spunky firecracker, fighting monsters on the side, while exposing corrupt politicians and shady business owners.

"Hiya, Ralph!" She makes her way to her desk.

"Good news. Strong's alive. He was here looking for you. He looked like he took the business end of a snow shovel, but he was walking around like nothing happened," Ralph says.

Becky stops in her tracks, smiling wildly. "He is!" she exclaims.

"Try to hide your emotions, why don't you? Yeah, he was in your 'war Room', as I call it."

JOURNEY INTO HELL

Becky rushes off to her little closet. Upon entering, she notices he's been working on her board. He has tied the missing person reports to a centralized location: the toy factory. Becky shakes her head, flabbergasted. "Get out of town! There is no way that Martoni is meeting at the same place where missing people are being kept. What are the odds?"

Ralph leans into the doorway. He looks around at the organized chaos. He sees the map on the wall with the cluster of red dots circling the toy factory. The sheer number of missing persons hits him hard. "All those red dots are missing people?"

"Missing in the last year and half. Not all the missing persons in Valkyrie City. I almost want to go to the precinct and ask for all the missing persons files just to have a visual," Becky says.

"What's the toy factory have to do with anything?" Ralph asks.

"I'm not sure, but it looks like Strong thinks it's the center of the kidnappings. So maybe there's a gang held up in there doing some dubious deeds?" She hates to speculate, but it's all she can do until she speaks to Mike Strong.

"Are you going to check it out?" Ralph asks.

"Not unless I have to. Seems like I'd be going into the hornet's nest alone," Becky says.

"I don't want you anywhere near that place without a police escort."

"Oh, speaking of! I met with Gina. Martoni lost his mind last night at The Dice. She is pretty sure he killed two of his men. He thinks there's a rat in his gang."

"That's some serious news," Ralph says, folding his arms.

"But we can't run any of it. That would break my trust with Gina," Becky reminds him.

"Yeah, I get it. Okay, well get with Strong and find out what's at the toy factory so I can give the police chief a heads up." Ralph says.

"Yes, sir. Now all I have to do is find Strong. I haven't had any luck all day!"

Philip walks in. He taps his heels together like a soldier in uniform, then salutes with a smile. Becky salutes him back, tapping her heels together with a *click*. Ralph shakes his head, looking at them with raised eyebrows. "Permission to enter?" Phillip asks.

"Permission granted."

"What's the latest, doll?" Phillip asks, leaning in for a kiss.

CHAPTER 13

"Mike is alive!" Becky says as Phillip pecks her cheek.

"That's great news. Where was he?" Phillip asks.

"No idea." Becky looks questioningly at her uncle.

"He came in about an hour ago. He said he was looking for Becky, but he must have left without saying goodbye."

"I'm thankful he's alive. That guy is going to get himself killed one day," Phillip says.

"Or Becky," Ralph adds.

"That too," Phillip says.

"If you gentlemen will excuse me, I have work to do. Babe, do you want to get dinner tonight?" Becky asks.

"Yes, ma'am. I can make reservations at The Chateau. That prime rib is like putting heaven in your mouth," Phillip groans, patting his stomach.

"Is that the place with the tomato soup? That was the best tomato soup I've ever had," Ralph says.

"Yes," Becky chuckles, "The Chateau, please."

Phillip hurries to his desk, eager to make the reservation. Becky squeezes past Ralph's huge belly into the hallway. "Don't move or anything," she grumbles, annoyed.

At her desk, Becky picks up her phone and dials Strong's number. It just rings and rings. She dials his home number but there is no answer there either. Becky drops the phone in the cradle, heaving a sigh. Sitting down at her desk, she opens the folder resting atop the blotter. It's another missing person's report to add to the map.

CHAPTER 14

Leo Guzzo sits outside the dingy hovel known as Mugin's Motel, puffing on his cigarette. It is a small motel chain with locations up and down I-45. While not known for being clean, they are very well known if you want to find some company for the night or need a place to hide, no questions asked.

Mugin's is the kind of place that's been shot up once, twice, or three times. Leo is disgusted at all the trash on the ground: old cans crushed by a thousand cars, crumpled cigarette packs, rotting food, wet napkins, and ketchup spilling out of the trashcans. Or, at least, he hopes it's ketchup. One can't be too sure at a place like this.

Louie Venetti walks up to Leo's bench, holding two brown bags in his hands. He's breathless. His left pant leg is soaking wet, as are his jacket and shirt. Leo looks at him questioningly.

"I dropped my drink," Louie whines. "This has been a fucking endeavor, Leo."

Leo grabs his drink and brown bag before Louie can drop those too. "Turkey or Salami?" Leo asks.

"Salami and Turkey with horseradish," Louie replies, pawing through his own bag.

"Pickles?" Leo asks.

"Yeah, I got you pickles, for fuck's sake."

CHAPTER 14

"You know I hate turkey!" Leo complains.

"I told him 'not turkey, salami.' And he said 'turkey?' I said 'no, salami not turkey', so he says, 'turkey then?' 'No, you numbnuts,' I said, 'salami, not turkey.' Then he says 'salami, turkey, and horse-radish?' Then I says, 'are you bustin' my balls here, or what? Just make the fucking thing before I smash this place to bits.' Then he threw the sandwiches at me."

"I would've shot you," Leo snickers.

"Ah, fuck dat guy," Louie says.

The parchment paper is soaking wet. Leo unwraps his sandwich and digs in. He takes a huge bite. "Not bad," Leo concedes.

Louie squeezes onto the bench with Leo, forcing him to scoot down on the seat a little. Louie balances his bag on his lap. He pulls his sandwich out of the bag, hunching over it like a pig at a trough. Leo watches the idiot get comfortable; his own lunch forgotten.

"Why do you eat like that?" Leo asks.

"Like what? I'm fat. What d'ya want?" Louie shrugs.

"You're like a buffalo or something."

"And you're like an asshole. So what? Eat your fucking sandwich," Louie hunches even more.

Leo laughs. The men lapse into a companionable silence, enjoying their sandwiches. Occasionally, they have to cover their sandwiches as huge trucks blow by, kicking up clouds of dust and debris. Small rocks pelt them in the face.

Leo finishes his sandwich, crumbling up the paper and tossing on the ground. Louie isn't quite done yet. "For a fat ass you eat fucking slow," Leo says, getting to his feet.

"I'm enjoying my meal. Johnny might kill me today. Who the fuck knows?" Louie says.

Leo chuckles at the thought, but Louie's right. Johnny is going insane. Even he's not too sure what Johnny will do next. He just killed Jacky and Pete. Jacky was as loyal as they came. "You might be right" Leo says.

"I bet Geonetti put the fear of God into him and now he's taking it out on us. But I've got to tell you, Leo, that ain't no way to treat a fella. Pete was a good man. He never did wrong by Johnny or his father. And poor Jacky. He took a bullet for Johnny in '48, remember?"

"Well, just be ready for anything." Leo sighs.
"That's why I'm going to enjoy my lunch, probably my last."

The door to room 314 opens, a beam of light piercing the darkness surrounding Johnny's pounding head. Johnny rolls over, putting a pillow over his face. Leo quickly shuts the door, allowing the room to be dark once again. "What time is it?" Johnny groans from beneath the pillow.

"4:45," Leo says.

Johnny sits up in the near-dark room, throwing his legs over the edge of the bed. He fumbles for his pack of smokes on the nightstand. The flicker of the lighter brightens the room for a moment. The cigarette's burning cherry gives them enough light to faintly see one another.

"Anything in the papers?" Johnny asks.

"No," Leo sits in a chair at the small table.

"Not a word?" Johnny asks.

"Not a word, a peep, or even a jingle."

Johnny is slightly upset about this. He loves when he gets in the paper. In fact, he has all of his mentions framed on a wall inside his house. He even writes up his own articles for the paper which he sends along with a glossy headshot. *The Chicago Bugle* has run three of his stories "No problem. I'll write something up!" Johnny says.

Leo smiles widely at the thought. The unchecked ego on this guy! But he respects his initiative; he's certainly proactive when it comes to marketing. Leo takes a long sip of his drink from lunch. "I mean, if you're going to be the bad guy, be good at it."

Johnny laughs, pulling nicotine into his lungs. He stands, pulling his pants on before shuffling his way to the bathroom. He flips on the light but leaves the door open as he takes a piss. Leo chews on his straw. He's suddenly starting to have mixed feelings for Johnny. He is a loose cannon and has become increasingly unpredictable. *What if Johnny is going to kill us all? That's absurd, right?*

There is a three-tap knock at the door. Leo knows it is Louie. But Johnny shouts from the bathroom. "Who is it?"

"It's Louie," Leo says.

CHAPTER 14

Johnny walks out of the bathroom, finishing his cigarette. He tosses the filter in the ashtray. "What's that fatass want?"

"He probably wants to know the plan," Leo says.

"What plan?" Johnny cackles.

"It's open," Leo calls.

Louie walks in, pushing the door wide so that he can fit. Johnny puts both his hands up to block the low-lying sun from streaming in. He takes the blast of light as a personal affront. Louie quickly shuts the door. "Sorry, boss."

"Leo, did you talk to Geonetti?" Johnny asks.

"Yes, sir. He'll be there at nine sharp. Said he 'Can't wait.'"

"Good. I'm hungry. Where are we going for dinner?"Johnny asks.

"There's a great Italian place about fifteen minutes north of here," Louie suggests hopefully. While they just ate a late lunch, he's always game to eat again.

"What else?" Johnny asks.

"The motel lobby," Louie grumbles, no doubt thinking of the turkey snafu.

"Italian it is," Johnny says.

Louie brightens. "They've got a real good eggplant parmesan."

Shirtless, Johnny walks out into the parking lot. He strolls right up to his Corvette, opening the trunk. He pulls out a suit on a hanger in a plastic bag. He slings it over his shoulder, his cigarette dangling out of his mouth. His thin stature alludes to weakness, but what he lacks in muscle he makes up for in relentless brutality. Put a hammer in his hand and you don't stand a chance.

In the room, he changes quickly, eager to get on with it. Leo, Louie, and Reeko follow him to the parking lot. While his goons get into Louie's Packard Panther-Daytona, Johnny gets into his Corvette. He prefers to drive and always rides alone.

The sun drops behind the mountains. The sunset is beautiful with hues of purple, blue, green, and copper. Johnny drives with his top down, letting the cool air hit his head. He catches glimpses of the city with each passing valley. As the sky grows dark, Johnny finds himself mired in his own dark thoughts.

JOURNEY INTO HELL

Reaching over to his glove box, he pulls out a prescription drug bottle. He shakes it to see if there's anything in it. The pills rattle merrily. He opens the bottle, pouring the pills into his mouth. He chews, his face contorting as the chalky powder stings his tongue. He swallows the paste. He holds the bottle up, reading the label:

Chlorpromazine; NOT FOR SALE/EXPERIMENTAL/ANTIPSYCHOTIC

Johnny shrugs, tossing the bottle over his shoulder. He digs for some more in the glove compartment, but, alas, there is none. He slams the glove box closed. Turning his attention back to the road, he realizes he's lost Louie, whose car he was following. He looks in the rearview mirror to see the neon lights of the restaurant. He slams on his brakes and the sports car comes sliding to a stop. Johnny shifts, peeling out and doing a U-turn in the middle of the road.

The three men enter the Italian eatery with the swagger of cowboys sidling into a saloon The small family-owned business lacks the opulent décor that Johnny is used to. There were only five customers in the entire establishment, all sitting at one table.

Johnny leads his boys to the podium where a maître d' should have been but found only a stack of paper menus. A young twenty-something with her hair pulled back into a tight ponytail comes out of the back. Her shirt is covered in flour and there are red spots of dried marinera.

"Hi, welcome to Antonio's. How many tonight?"

"Three, please," Johnny says politely.

Without so much as a glance, she takes them to a table in the back of the restaurant. The corner booth is in a darkened area, and, thus, was perfect for Johnny.

"Here you go." she says.

"Perfect, just what I would have picked! How'd you know?" Johnny says.

She waits for them to sit. "Well, I figured Valkyrie City's most notorious gangster would want to sit in the back of the place." She smiles.

CHAPTER 14

This elates Johnny to no end. He laughs, grabbing the girl by her shoulders and giving her a kiss on each cheek. Then he ushers Leo, Louie, and Reeko to their feet to shake her hand and give her a hug. A man and a woman—presumably her parents or grandparents, judging by the silver in their hair—come out with a camera. The gangsters and the restaurant owners cluster together and take a few photos. Johnny is having a great time and forgets about the night before. Except, the Chlorpromazine is starting to take effect and he's feeling out of sorts.

"Okay. Okay. I've got to eat at some point, folks," Johnny says.

"You don't have to worry about anything, Mr. Martoni. It is on us tonight," the owner says with a final vigorous shake of his hand.

After about fifteen minutes, the owner and his wife walk out of the kitchen with some fresh bread sticks and a huge serving bowl of tossed salad. The girl carries two bottles of red wine. "I don't want you to worry about a thing, Mr. Martoni. You get what you want. This is our own house wine. We make it ourselves. It's a nice red," the owner says.

The owner hands the bottle of wine to Martoni, who checks the weight and feels the bottle over. The label reads *Vineyard di Antonio*. The owner spins a corkscrew around in his hand, being a little flashy. He takes the bottle back from Johnny, opening it with a flourish. He hands the cork to Johnny who gives it a good sniff. After Johnny nods his assent, the owner pours Johnny a sample in the wide wine glass. Johnny swirls the wine for a moment then downs the small portion.

"That's a good wine. Is that plum and walnut?" Johnny asks.

"Wow. Those are some good tastebuds," the owner exclaims.

Smiling, the owner pours the wine for the men. "Okay, I'll leave you to it. Your entrees will be out shortly, gentleman. If you need anything, I am Antonio. This is my wife, Angelica, and our granddaughter, Sophia."

Finally, Johnny and his men are alone at the secluded table. Johnny laughs while drinking his wine. When he looks over his men, something feels unsettlingly wrong. There is no Jacky or Pete. Johnny regrets acting so violently toward Jacky, in particular. But he is almost certain he was a cop. Wasn't he? Johnny looks at Louie and Leo. "He was a snitch." Johnny mumbles.

Leo and Louie stop smiling, sensing the change in the air. Neither man dares to say anything. They both avoid Johnny's eyes. Johnny just stares at his glass of wine. He gulps it then pours himself another drink, tossing that one back too. He is clearly troubled. Leo watches his every move out of the corner of his eye. Leo thought perhaps this was going to be the night.

He's going to lose his shit and spray the place down with bullets. That's the Martoni way. Leo checks his side holster for his gun, then his jacket pocket to assure himself that Becky's gun is still there. He feels a little safer. This new Johnny is different, erratic, unstable, and ready to snap at any moment.

"What's wrong?" Johnny asks Leo.

Leo realizes he's been silent for some time, staring at his wine glass. The liquid inside is the color of coagulated blood. He studies Johnny for a moment. "Nothing. The wine is strong, and I haven't had a drink in about two hours," Leo jokes.

Johnny and Louie laugh just as the owner walks up with a tray of different pastas and a variety of sauces for them to try. "I brought you guys a little of everything. Try it. There are meatballs, spicy sausage, German sausage, sliced prime rib, eggplant, and garlic bread. Eat up," the owner urges.

Johnny, Leo, and Louie dig in.

"Now this is what I'm talking about," Louie says around a mouthful of food.

The men eat themselves into a coma. Louie wears a bib around his neck fashioned out of a cloth napkin. It is covered in pasta sauce. He grips a piece of bread in one hand and a fork in the other as he chomps noisily on a meatball. Most of the food is gone and only remnants of the meatballs remain. There are breadcrumbs everywhere and four empty bottles of wine. They have thoroughly enjoyed themselves.

"Well, gentlemen, we must be off. We have an important meeting to attend," Johnny says.

"Oh, I reached out to Lucy. Twice. No answer," Leo says.

Johnny stares at him for a moment then looks away. He sinks into his seat and curls into himself, frowning.

"Go pick her up and bring her to the meeting," Johnny says quietly.

CHAPTER 14

The owner walks up with a huge smile. "I hope you enjoyed it." Johnny instantly changes and is all smiles, shaking the owner's hand with both of his. Johnny is clearly fighting with his emotions, and this scares Leo. "The best meal I've ever had. Who would have thought? I love this place—a family place. I'll be back this time next week so save this spot."

"Mr. Martoni, it would be our pleasure."

Johnny hands him a stack of crisp bills wrapped in a paper band.

"Mr. Martoni, I said it was on us," the owner objects.

"I know. Let's just say this is for the rest of the year," Johnny says.

The men leave as the owner stands with his wife and granddaughter. He reaches into his pocket, pulling out the stack of money. The band is labeled $5,000. They all hug. "What a night. We were blessed," the owner sniffs, happy tears trickling down his ruddy cheeks.

"Yeah, well be careful, grandfather. That's Johnny Martoni," Sophia says darkly, watching them pull away. "He's a dangerous man."

CHAPTER 15

The massive brick building is a void in the darkness, seemingly unaffected by the shimmering light of the city behind it. Its subtle features made it look more like an abandoned prison than anything else. The differentiating feature, however, is the giant sign that once read Bobby Boy's Toys in big red letters. The logo was a small child with a cartoonishly oversized head holding up a toy plane.

The entrance to the building once had a rotating rocket that spiraled around a futuristic space woman wearing a bubble helmet. Her once pristine white spacesuit is now old and dingy, with water stains and mold growing on it.

Most of the building hasn't seen any maintenance in about five years. After Gretchen and her son Robert Khan were killed in a horrible traffic accident, the owner, Lucas Khan, shut the facility down. He hasn't been seen since. The building is, for all intents and purposes, condemned.

Parked at the front of the building, Johnny smokes a cigarette. He looks up at the giant rocket ship he loved as a kid. He is planning something big tonight. *Things are changing tonight, I tell ya.*

Headlights bounce off the street as Louie pulls up in his yellow Packard Panther-Daytona. The gravel crunches beneath its tires

CHAPTER 15

as it stops next to Johnny's Corvette. Louie gets out of the driver's side, as Reeko gets out the passenger side. Leo gets out of the back, pulling Lucy St. George out by her arm.

Lucy is wearing a white coat dress with large black buttons that match the buckle at the waist. The collar and cuffs are fur-lined. Her makeup is striking, with red lipstick and a dark smokey eye. A fur-lined bucket hat completes the look. "Get your damn hands off me, you dumb goon!"

Leo gives her arm a violent yank, pushing her toward Johnny. Johnny looks at him in confusion. "I caught her heading to the train station," Leo elucidates.

"What do you mean? She was leaving? Where are you leaving to, doll?" Johnny asks.

Lucy jerks her arm out of Leo's grip. She adjusts her clothes and fixes her hat. Flashing Johnny a wide smile, she sashays over to him. "Johnny, I told you I was going to see my mother. Remember?"

"No, you didn't."

"Why, sure I did! I must have." Lucy presses her crimson lips together, her brow furrowing.

"Nah, listen up, darling." Johnny pulls her in real close. He squeezes her shoulders, staring into her face. She is tragically beautiful. as fragile as a child's porcelain doll. He truly loved her more than anything, but he doesn't trust anyone anymore. She will have to be sacrificed just like everyone else tonight. He plants a rough kiss on her lips, smearing her lipstick. Johnny kisses her more passionately than he's ever kissed her. Perhaps it's the only real emotion he's ever felt.

He takes it all in. Everything about her: the taste of her lips, the scent of her perfume, the way the back of her neck felt in his hand, the pressure of her breasts against his chest, and even the supple softness of her sleeve. He imagined what his life would have been like in another time. In another city.

Johnny grasps Lucy by her arm, leading her toward the factory. He kicks the front door open with a grunt. The glass inlaid in the door shatters, scattering all over the ground. Johnny pulls her through the threshold, basically dragging her down the hallway. It's pitch dark. Johnny pulls a flashlight out of his coat pocket, clicking it on.

Johnny looks for a spot to set up. He walks down a corridor with offices on each side. It is covered in years of dust and cobwebs. Johnny sees a door leading into a backroom.

The room has four concrete columns in the center. Old candles flank the concrete columns. Johnny rests the flashlight on one of the columns for a moment, the beam illuminating an electrical box.

He flips the breaker on. Several small bulbs click and flicker, lighting up a small area of the factory floor. The floor is covered in a thick layer of dust, but there's something beneath it. There's an engraving on the floor. Johnny walks to the center of the dimly lit area, placing Lucy on a specific spot that makes sense only to him.

"Stay put," Johnny orders.

"Johnny, what is wrong with you?" Lucy says. "Are you having a meltdown?"

"No, doll. I'm having an awakening. I'm finally starting to see everything how it should be. How it was meant to be," Johnny says serenely.

Louie and Reeko stand in the shadows, hoping to stay out of trouble. Leo walks up next to Johnny, examining the columns. Johnny shines the flashlight at his wristwatch.

"Okay, boys. Geonetti should be here in a moment. I can't wait to show you what I have in store," Johnny says, gleefully.

"Johnny, can I go now? I'd like to be at my mom's before midnight," Lucy says.

"What is wrong with you? You're part of my plan, babe!"

Lucy is frightened now. Leo keeps an eye on Louie and Reeko, making sure to angle his body toward the nearest exit for a quick getaway. He feels more and more uneasy as the seconds tick by. The two goons step a little further back out of the light, cowering…

Geonetti pushes through the front doors, almost knocking one completely off its hinges. He is followed by his crew: Vick, a rather skinny man with a suit that's a little too big; a barrel-chested fellow with a scar down his cheek who goes by Sisco: Bruno, who resembles a gorilla, muscles and all; and his driver, Salvador.

All the men are in nice clean suits and fedoras. Geonetti is wearing a fancy tan and black striped suit with matching wingtips.

CHAPTER 15

He walks with a black cane that has a polished onyx handle in the shape of a ram's skull. The eyes are inlaid with rubies. The tip of the cane is brushed steel and every time it hits the floor there is a distinct *ting* of metal.

"Martoni, where are you?" Bruno bellows.

"Straight down the hall," Johnny shouts.

Geonetti and his men walk through the dark factory to the sparsely lit room in the back. Geonetti instantly has a bed feeling. He looks over the room, noticing the columns and the strange excess of wax that has solidified over the concrete. There are strange symbols on each of the columns.

Shine your light on this," Geonetti says.

Johnny shines the light on the nearest column. Etched in it is an upside-down triangle with a line going through it.

"What the hell is this shit?" Geonetti asks.

"I don't know. Egyptian?" Johnny shrugs.

"Doesn't look Egyptian," Geonetti says.

"What do I know?" Johnny says.

"What's the point, Johnny? I'm playing your game. Why are we here?" Geonetti asks impatiently.

Johnny paces around the columns, looking them over. He's still not sure what they might be. Besides seemingly being dipped in wax, each column has a large metal ring that is bolted to it.

"Johnny, I want to leave now." Lucy says, wringing her hands.

"I'm sure you do, doll." Johnny says.

Johnny coolly pulls his pistol from its holster, aiming it at her. Lucy doesn't know what to do. She is in shock—everyone else is too. Leo puts his hand on Becky's pistol in his pocket. All of Geonetti's men pull out their pistols, not sure who to aim at. Geonetti only watches in amusement.

"I have a rat, doll. There's a little mouse in my crew, running their little mousey mouth to the coppers. A dirty, filthy rat. I realize that I may have been too hasty killing Pete Zumba and Jacky Ribbasa last night. God rest their souls," Johnny says.

"What are you saying, Johnny?" Lucy asks.

She starts backing up into the center point between the four columns. She holds her clutch tightly to her chest. Lucy looks around and knows that anything she says won't matter. She slides her hand into her clutch, pulling out a small snub nose .38 revolver. "Stand back, Johnny. I ain't no rat. I love you. We're getting married, right? I thought you loved me!"

Geonetti motions to his men to stand down. He wants to watch this scenario play out. He slowly steps around a column, and out of the line of sight of Johnny's gun. Johnny walks up to Lucy, his gun still trained on her chest.

"I thought, and I thought, and I thought. Who knows everything? Who is the one who knows me the best—who have I talked to the most, in the most candid sense? You love that pillow talk, baby," Johnny says. "I trusted you."

Lucy starts to shake. She loves Johnny with all her heart. "Johnny, I never ratted you out. Never. I am loyal through and through. You have to believe me, baby," Lucy says.

"Sorry, babe. I don't."

The pause is just long enough for Lucy to know that she dead. He's going to kill her. The sound of the metal hammer clicking back echoes throughout the room as if broadcast through a bullhorn. The noise is deafening. The flash of light erupts like someone took a photograph, blinding everyone for a moment.

Lucy's eyes widen as the bullet pierces her dress, ripping through her chest wall and out her back. She mouths the words "I love you" as she falls to the hard floor. Her beautiful smile is unaffected, though a trickle of blood leaks out of the corner of her parted lips. It is as red as her lipstick. Johnny stares at her for a moment. His focus is so trained on her that all the sound leaves the room. He finds beauty in her blood-splattered face. Blood pools around her.

"Johnny. Johnny!" Leo says.

Johnny can dimly hear Leo, but his mind is somewhere else. He is still looking at the love of his life. Her last breath leaves a trail of steam in the cold air. Johnny turns, looking through his tears at Leo. He blinks as if rousing himself from a dream, shaking his head. "Leo, hey buddy." Johnny says.

Geonetti is shocked that Johnny just killed his girl. *Maybe he does have what it takes to be a leader.* Suddenly, there's a metallic crash in the other room.

"Go check it out," Geonetti says, jabbing his finger at Sisco.

"You got it, boss," Sisco says. He walks off into the darkness.

CHAPTER 15

Geonetti looks back at Johnny, who looks completely changed. He is holding his gun up to Leo's face. Leo aims his own at Johnny's stomach.

"I think you need a break, buddy," Leo says softly.

"But then again, the rat could be you, Leo. You know everything I know. Sometimes I think that you are bucking for my position," Johnny says.

"Johnny—"

"Look what I found, boss," Sisco says.

The men turn around to see *The Valkyrie Herald's* very own fast-talking reporter, Becky Detter. Johnny recognizes her and smiles.

"You're a real looker, Detter. It's fortunate you are here. You can put this in the papers," Johnny says gleefully.

Becky is confused. She clearly didn't expect to find them here. "Hiya, fellas. Don't mind me. I'm just snooping for another case."

"Well, you're out of luck, darling. I kicked Strong off a dock last night. He won't be here to save you. Oh, and we dropped a car on him too. Leo's car to be exact," Johnny says.

Becky smiles, knowing that Mike is clearly alive. Whatever they tried to do to him didn't work. Becky then notices that Leo is holding her gun. "Hey, that's my gun. You've still got it. That's great, Leo. You're a real swell chap."

Johnny looks at her then at Leo, raising his gun again. "I knew it. I knew you was the rat."

Geonetti laughs. He didn't expect to see a show tonight. His men close in around him to protect him just in case Johnny starts firing his gun off. Johnny swings his pistol between Becky and Leo. Reeko and Louie haven't moved in fifteen minutes. They are just standing in the dark, watching. Louie starts to back away even more now. Reeko sees this and decides to do the same. They look at each other trying to communicate with just micro expressions, but it's useless. They're just rolling their eyes at each other.

Becky steps backward, tripping on Lucy St. George's body. She maintains her composure with her eyes wide. She looks back up at Johnny, who has his gun trained on Leo.

"So long, Leo," Johnny says.

"Johnny don't do—" Leo starts to say before the bullet mangles his lungs.

JOURNEY INTO HELL

Leo's back explodes at the bullet forcibly exits, sending a spray of blood all over Reeko and Louie. Leo falls to his knees, then heavily onto his stomach. Becky's gun falls out of his hand, sliding across the floor to Becky's feet. In an instant, she bends to pick it up, darting behind a column.

Johnny looks at Leo's dead body laying very near Lucy's dead body. He is immediately overwhelmed and starts to feel sick. He turns toward Reeko and Louie in the darkness. *Maybe, maybe Reeko is the rat! Or perhaps it's Louie, the prick!* He is about to raise his gun when there is another huge crash somewhere in the distance.

"Coppers are here, Johnny," Becky says from behind a column.

Becky keeps her guard up, looking for a viable escape route. Johnny's back is to her, his gun dangling at his hip. There are no doors or windows nearby. She looks warily at Lucy's body, realizing she's standing in some blood.

Moving her foot out of the way, she watches as the blood flows into the engraving on the floor. She follows the flow of blood as it starts to make a symbol on the floor. It is as big as the area between the columns.

As the blood follows the engraved path, it creates a circle on the floor. Then, it splits off into two hairpin angles toward the center of the circle. As it reaches the center, it separates again, stretching out in five different directions to form a star. She recognizes the symbol—it's a pentagram. Abruptly, all of the candles adorning the columns ignite at once. Candles along the back wall and on a nearby podium ignite too.

"Shit," Becky says.

Johnny panics. "Time to get out of dodge, gentlemen." He takes off into the darkness.

Geonetti looks back at the columns as the flames grow stronger. Lucy's body starts to move and contort. The corpse rises off the floor, floating in midair. The blood seems to flow back into her body and the ground starts to glow red, the concrete floor crumbling around the pentagram. Lucy's hair whips around but there is no wind. Her body turns upright as her toes trail on the floor. Her arms stretch out as though she is a crucifix. The blood from the floor snaps like a stringy tentacle, wrapping around Lucy's body. The blood crawls

CHAPTER 15

up her body until she is encased in a thick cocoon of gelatinous fluid. It dissipates as it is absorbed into her flesh.

Geonetti fires at Lucy's body, hitting it several times. Nothing happens. She continues to float as waves of light beaming out of the floor surround her lifeless body. Her skin starts to crack and break off. Her beautiful pale skin becomes almost translucent as her eyes turn completely black.

Becky wastes no time and takes off running right past Geonetti and his men. She darts out of the room and into the vast factory. Geonetti also runs, followed by his men. Lucy twists and turns, her bones cracking and snapping into place until she raises upright and drops to her feet in the middle of the pentagram. Flames burst from the pentagram, the light playing across Lucy's corrupted body.

Lucy looks around through her new eyes, finding Leo on the ground. She waves her hand over him, sending a red energy stream to awaken him. Leo's body starts to shake and flop on the floor as his skin thickens and his face expands. His jawline snaps and elongates as his mouth grows tusks and his nose becomes a snout. The hairs on his face, head, and back grow thick and dark. His ears become pointed with thick hairs adorning the edges. His muscular haunches rip through his pants. Leo stretches out his fingers as they grow huge dark nails, so sharp that they dig into the concrete. Leo gets on all fours. He is more warthog than human.

Lucy walks over to her new pet, giving it a gentle pat on the head. She looks down at her blood-covered hands and cracks her neck; the vertebrae pop, the sound as loud as a gunshot and its retort. "Let's go take care of business. We owe someone a visit," Lucy says.

CHAPTER 16

The door to the back storeroom slams closed behind Mike Strong. He stands in the darkness with a flashlight, examining the boxes and crates that litter the abandoned factory. Some of the crates have labels on them that read: *Tommy the Teddy Bear* in a font that makes him think of the circus. Mike looks inside one of the boxes, pulling out an oversized teddy bear. It's old and fragile. He tosses the bear back in the box.

A shot rings out, making Mike take cover behind a large pillar that stretches all the way to the ceiling. He clicks his flashlight off and listens. He can hear Johnny Martoni talking to someone, and other indistinct voices too. Mike sneaks his way through the mess of debris, but something catches his eye. He flicks his flashlight on, shining it on a symbol that has been painted on the wall. The symbol is an angled line with three more lines coming off it. Two are the same length and the third line is shorter. Beneath the line is a shape that resembles the omega symbol. Mike recognizes it as a protection sigil.

He looks for more, spotting another one on a different pillar. This symbol is slightly different, with a triangle traversed by two parallel lines. Mike walks over, touching it. Sweeping his flashlight around, another gunshot rings out. He ducks down and takes off

CHAPTER 16

toward the sound. Mike finds a spot to crouch, eavesdropping on the commotion. He clearly hears several voices, one of which is female. Then there is a huge gust of wind that draws past him as if something sucked the air out of the room.

Mike peeks over the crate to see Johnny running down the corridor. Geonetti and his goons come running out a moment later. Mike heads toward the direction Johnny went but stops in his tracks as a very unsettling feeling overwhelms him. He listens for a moment. It sounds as if there is liquid dripping down from the ceiling.

Mike shines his flashlight into an office where he sees a poster-sized advertisement for Robbie the Robot, made famous by its short-lived television show. The robot is complete with a huge glass bubble head, rubber arms, a laser for a right hand, and a spinning two-prong claw for its left. Mike smiles, thinking of how much he loves futuristic stuff.

He continues down the corridor, trying to catch up to Johnny, when a splat of goo hits his shoulder. When he touches it with his fingertips, he finds that the dark ooze is sticky. Mike shines the flashlight upward to find that the entire ceiling is wet with dripping goo.

Suddenly, there is a loud scream from another room. Mike pauses for a moment. He recognizes the voice: Becky.

Mike abandons his pursuit, making his way toward the scream. He listens carefully for any sign of Becky. He hears faint rustling inside a janitor's closet. Mike runs over to the closet, opening it up. Becky is stuck to the wall by the goo and it looks as though it's trying to consume her.

"Mike, am I happy to see you!" Becky says as the goo crawls up her neck.

"What are you doing in here?"

"You know, just hanging around," Becky quips.

Mike grabs her hand, pulling her out of the sticky goo and into his arms. She embraces him for a moment. When they try to pull apart, their clothes seem to be stuck together. They pull harder and finally rip apart.

"Mike, Johnny killed Lucy St. George," Becky says.

"He did what?"

"But that's not the kicker. She came back to life on some sort of ritualistic alter. It looks like a possession of some kind," Becky says, picking bits of goo off her pink dress.

Somewhere nearby, gunshots ring out. Mike gestures for Becky to lead the way and they exit the janitor's closet. They jog down a long corridor that leads to the front of the building when they see Sisco running toward them. His big frame looks funny running at full speed.

"Monster!" Sisco screams.

Mike holds up his arms, getting the terrified man to slow down. Sisco runs right up to them, his flesh damp and pale. He gulps the air. "Monsters. There are horrible monsters in this place," he babbles.

"What are you talking about?"

"That way. A clown. There's a monster clown. It killed Gus," Sisco says, mopping his forehead.

"A clown? You mean Martoni?" Mike jokes, cracking himself up.

"No, a monster clown. It was like a toy or something. It came to life and jumped right on him."

"Okay, let's check it out," Mike relents. He'll have to moonlight as a comedian some other time. This is a tough crowd.

"Hell no. *You* check it out. I'm checking out of here."

Sisco runs off into the bowels of the dark factory alone. Mike and Becky watch him for a moment then look back the way he came. Mike flicks his flashlight back on and they continue down the corridor, more cautious now. Becky aims her pistol down the hallway. Mike unholsters his own pistol. "Good idea. I see you got your pistol back."

Becky stops in her tracks. "Oh, yeah. From Leo. Johnny shot him, by the way. Shot him right in the chest. Did you know he killed two of his boys last night too?"

"He did? Who?"

"Judging by who wasn't in the room. I'd say Pete Zumba and Jacky Ribbasa."

They reach the end of the corridor, stopping at a blue door. Mike opens the door, leaning in with his flashlight in one hand and his pistol in the other. The air is damp and smells a bit like sulfur. He can almost taste it on his tongue, musty with a bit of a tang.

CHAPTER 16

He enters and sees a series of doors that lead into separate offices. There are three doors on each side of the hallway. The carpet beneath his feet is old and dusty, not unlike the cabinets that line the hallway. Two of the office doors are open, one on the left and the other on the right. Mike gestures for Becky to follow him and, together, they creep down the hallway.

"You think Martoni's got a demon attached to him?" Becky whispers.

"Nah, sometimes people are evil because they're born that way. They don't need any extra help from outside sources. Just evil through to the bone. Those are the truly dangerous ones."

"Where the hell have you been, Strong?" Becky asks, brushing aside a cobweb.

"I went to the office and passed out. I went to *The Herald* in the afternoon. You weren't there so I came here early and fell asleep in my car for like three hours. My body hurts."

Mike places the flashlight under his chin, showing her the bruising, swollen jaw, and black eye. His face looks like someone beat him with a bat, which isn't too far off from the truth. But, despite the beating, he still manages to have an award-winning smile and debonair charm.

"You've looked worse," Becky says. "Did they try to drown you? Johnny was bragging about it, his chest puffed up like a proud rooster."

"Yeah, they threw a car on top of me," Mike says.

"Sorry, that was me. I was trying to cause a distraction," Becky admits.

"Well, it worked, I suppose." Mike chuckles.

As they creep down the hallway, Bruno crashes through one of the walls. His face is contorted and his eyes bulge from their sockets, blood and bile dripping down his chin. He grabs Mike by his throat, picking him up and slamming him through the adjacent wall.

They crash into another office, stumbling over a large metal desk. Debris goes flying everywhere. Mike lands on his back with Bruno on top of him. The goon curls his fingers around Mike's throat, squeezing. Mike bashes Bruno's forearm with the butt of his pistol, trying to loosen his grip. It's not working. Mike brings his right leg up, wrapping it around Bruno's neck and prying him back. Bruno has no choice but to let go. Mike leaps to his feet then vaults over the metal desk, putting distance between himself and the now demonic Bruno.

Bruno grunts and snarls. Mike watches him warily. "You wanna talk about it?"

Bruno leaps over the desk like a kangaroo, landing in front of Mike. He's ready for him this time. Mike lands a solid right hook into Bruno's jaw, knocking him back over the metal desk. Mike finds his flashlight, the beam illuminating a dust bunny and the gossamer thread of a cobweb. He kicks it out of the room and right to Becky, who picks it up without missing a beat.

Bruno stands up again. Mike pushes the metal desk with all his might, pinning Bruno to the wall at his waist. Bruno is about to flip the desk over when Mike puts a bullet in his head. Blood and goo splatter the office wall. Most of what was inside of his skull is smeared on the cream-colored wall. The body falls limp on the desk.

"You alright?" Mike asks looking at Becky through the Mike-sized hole in the wall.

"Yeah. Are *you* okay?"

Mike nods, stepping out of the room. They compose themselves and start back down the hallway toward the lobby of the factory, where they assume everyone went. Upon reaching the lobby, Mike listens for a moment, trying to hear any commotion. The silence is eerie after all the gunshots.

One of the front doors is off the hinge and laying on the ground. But that doesn't matter, the black goo that was all over Becky is also all over the threshold, sealing them inside.

Mike takes the flashlight from Becky, shining it around the lobby. The goo seems to be seeping in through the walls. The main entrance had double doors, but Geonetti pulled one to the ground as though it was made of balsa wood and held in place by bits of Scotch tape. The front wall has two huge, framed advertisements of Daisy Doll, a cute blonde-haired doll famous for saying "mama" through a tinny voice recorder, and Baxter's Big Top, a circus playset that includes clowns, trapeze artists, a ringmaster, bearded lady, and Stanley the strongman. This advertisement was hand-painted on wood to look like an honest-to-goodness circus poster.

CHAPTER 16

The receptionist desk hasn't been used in some years, but still has a yellow desk fan and a matching rotary phone on top. The desk chair is also still there, stuffing bursting from the. cushion. Behind the desk is a door. To the left side of the desk is another door. There are dead plants in planters in the corner and stylish cloth chairs that are starting to deteriorate. Between the chairs is a wooden table that has a few dust-covered magazines laying on it.

Mike walks over to the door on the left, opening it slowly. It's another long, dark hallway. He shines the flashlight and finds it empty and quiet. Becky steps up behind him, trying to look in over his shoulder. Together they walk in.

"Can't get any worse," Becky says, her tone hopeful.

Mike looks over his shoulder at her with a raised eyebrow. They only get a few feet before the door behind them slams closed. Mike spins around, shining his flashlight at the door. When he turns back toward the hallway, his flashlight's beam illuminates a very evil-looking clown creature. Its plastic face is distorted with a giant jaw full of blood-covered, pointy teeth. It is wearing multi-colored clothing of red, blue, yellow, and green with a diamond pattern down both arms and legs. "Clowns!" Mike exclaims. "Of course, there's clowns."

Mike looks it dead in its unblinking eyes.

"Look," Becky breathes, pointing at the clown's chest. It has been impaled by Geonetti's cane. Mike watches as the clown monster growls. He puts his arm out to shield Becky from its gnashing teeth. The hallway is lit by a series of emergency lights that give off a dim yellow hue. They serve to illuminate the monster, but also deepen the shadows beneath his plastic cheekbones. But Mike's only thought was *how does this place still have power?*

Becky wastes no time and fires at the monster clown, hitting it in the chest three times. The creature stumbles back but doesn't go down. It snarls loudly, opening its huge mouth wide. Mike fires, hitting it in the chest as well. The creature leaps, grabbing onto the ceiling with its claws before twisting its legs up. Suspended upside down, it crawls toward them. Mike and Becky both fire up at it, but Becky's gun clicks empty. As the creature crawls over their heads, it swings to the far wall then leaps toward Mike.

Mike takes the hit, landing on his back. He loses his grip on his gun. The monster's claws dig into his rib cage. With a roll, Mike flips the creature off of him and down the hallway. Mike palms the monster's forehead with his right hand. As he pushes the creature back, its forehead starts to glow and smoke. The creature wails, the sound high-pitched.

The monster grabs Mike's wrist with both hands, trying to remove his grip. The monster is losing ground; Mike pushes it further down the hallway until it eventually succumbs to his power, its legs giving out. Suddenly, the clown explodes with white-hot energy, throwing Mike backward.Hitting the dirty concrete floor, Mike slides to a stop at Becky's feet. She looks down at him. "Going well?" she asks.

"Perfect," Mike says.

Becky aims the reloaded gun at the monster, hitting it several times. The creature eventually goes down. Mike stands up, walking over to the downed monster to make certain it's incapacitated. Becky hands Mike his gun back. Mike kneels, looking the creature over. "I've never seen inanimate possession before," Mike murmurs.

"Demons possessing dolls?"

"It's not unheard of. I just haven't had the privilege of seeing it yet," Mike says. The creature shudders, and Mike puts one last round in the clown's plastic forehead.

"I saw your board, by the way. Good stuff. I added to it," Mike remarks.

"I saw that. How did you figure this might be the place for the kidnappings?" Becky asks.

"I just had a hunch. I think there's a connection. I just can't put my finger on it. Why is someone kidnapping people and bringing them here? I have an idea, and with the monsters running around, I'm getting a clearer picture."

"Yeah, me too. I saw a pentagram on the floor surround by four pillars and a podium," Becky says.

"Take me to it," Mike urges.

"Uh, okay. It's uh... this way?" Becky's brow furrows as she tries to get her bearings. The toy factory is proving to be labyrinthine. Becky leads them down the hallway to another door. When they

CHAPTER 16

open it, they find a back stairwell that leads to the second floor. Mike and Becky look at each other. "Well, it's not this way." Becky says.

"Clearly." Mike says.

Mike and Becky turn to go back the way they came when a strange voice shouts, "Stop!" They turn back to the closing door just in time to see what looks like a ghost rushing down the stairs. The ghostly figure bursts through the door and Mike draws his gun. The ghost puts up his hands. "Don't shoot," he pleads.

The ghost isn't a ghost, but an elderly man. His hair is ragged and unkempt. His clothes look like he hasn't taken them off in months and they certainly haven't been washed. His pants are dirt-streaked with holes in the knees. His green sweater seems to be at least three sizes too big, the hem threadbare.

"Who are you?" Becky asks.

"I could have the pleasure of asking the same?" the man asks politely.

"Listen here now, there is some serious shit happening and you're not safe in here. Do you understand me? You need to stay put," Mike says.

"No! You don't understand. There are unimaginable elements at work here. Things you can't comprehend. You must follow me. I have a room of protection upstairs. Follow me. Now."

"Who the hell are you?" Mike asks.

"I'm Lucas Khan. I own this factory," Lucas says impatiently.

Becky recalls a story she wrote five years ago. The owner of this factory had disappeared and was presumed dead. She'd interviewed friends and neighbors who described him as troubled and grief-stricken. "You're still alive?"

"My dear child, if I could change it all I would," Lucas says.

"Change what?" Mike asks.

"Come with me, there is no time," Lucas urges, gesturing up the staircase.

"Alright. I'll go down the rabbit hole." Mike shrugs.

"I don't want to go down a rabbit hole. I hate holes. Though, I love rabbits, they're so fluffy and cute. Now I want a rabbit," Becky says.

"Is she always like this?" Lucas quirks an eyebrow.

Mike nods. The men start walking up the stairs as Becky loiters at the bottom of the staircase for a moment longer. She looks uneasily down the dark hallway, thinking about the clown monster they had left for dead.

"Okay, sheesh. Wait up," Becky squeaks.

CHAPTER 17

Martoni is in a panic. *There's no way out.* He found a back door, but it was covered in the now-familiar black goo. His nerves frazzled, he stops to light a cigarette, hoping the nicotine will calm him and help him organize his thoughts. Johnny notices Sisco off in the distance looking equally as frantic. Sisco, seeing the flame of Johnny's lighter, rushes over to him. Johnny puffs on his smoke. He feels calmer already. "This shit is crazy right?" Johnny says.

"Cut the shit, Martoni. What did you do?"

"Well, I'm cleaning house." Johnny shrugs.

"Looks like you're communing with the devil," Sisco says.

"Not me, pal." Johnny spits out a flake of loose tobacco.

Sisco punches Johnny right in his mouth. He follows that up with a left hook. Johnny stumbles backward but quickly regains his footing, hitting his attacker in the stomach. Sisco can take it; he is as immovable as a brick wall. Johnny hits him again, but it does little to hurt him. Sisco picks up Johnny like a ragdoll, tossing him several feet. Johnny slowly gets to his feet, panting. He dropped his cigarette, crushing it in the fall. Both men pull their guns. "Don't do it," Johnny warns.

"I should kill you where you stand, you lunatic," Sisco says, pulling back the hammer on his pistol.

"Where's Geonetti? Those things get him?" Johnny asks.

"Yeah, some fucking killer clown got 'em, I think. I ran. Why'd you do this?"

"What are you yappin' about? I didn't make those things. I don't know what's happening in this damn place," Johnny says thinking for a moment. "Geonetti's dead, eh? So now I'm the top dog! I'm in charge. Finally! I finally did it! Sisco, you work for me now, ya see?"

"Fuck you, Johnny. I don't work for no one. Geonetti's dead! I'm out."

"Where you going, Sisco? You're my guy now!" Johnny aims his gun at Sisco.

"Geonetti was right. You're a little whiny coward," Sisco says, turning back to Johnny, holding his gun in his coat pocket. Johnny shoots Sisco in the stomach. Sisco fires wildly but misses. Sisco rushes Johnny, grabbing his lapel and lifting him up high over his head. With a grunt, he slams Johnny onto the concrete floor. He's about to stomp on Johnny's face when Johnny shoots through his foot, blowing off some of his toes. Sisco falls to the floor but takes the opportunity to grab Johnny's head with both hands. He starts to squeeze. "I'm going to crush your skull, Johnny."

Johnny is a little worried because Sisco's squeezing is really starting to hurt. He imagines his eyeballs popping like grapes. Johnny puts his gun to Sisco's head. "Nothing personal," Johnny says, pulling the trigger.

Sisco's head explodes all over the floor. His body goes limp. Laying on the cool concrete, Johnny breathes deeply, glad that the pressure on his skull has subsided. Suddenly, he hears shuffling feet. Then he hears Geonetti's annoying voice. *Shit, he isn't dead after all.*

Johnny stands, taking cover behind a large pillar. Salvador and Geonetti run up to the exit, cursing when they find it covered in goo. Vick stumbles in behind them. Genoetti is covered in blood and is holding a large table leg in his right hand. The men mill around, tripping over each other in the dark. "What the shit is going on?" Geonetti pants.

There is a huge crash behind them. All three of them turn around but there's nothing to see. There is another loud bang; it sounds as if crates are being crushed by a gorilla in the next room.

CHAPTER 17

Geonetti shoves Vick toward the noise. "Go check it out," Geonetti orders. "And find my cane."

"I don't like this, Vick whimpers.

Cautiously, Vick peeks around a section of pallets stacked high with old crates stamped with the company's logo. Suddenly, something grabs his face. The entire fleshy part of his face slides to the floor. He falls onto his knees, screaming as blood pours down his neck.

Looking up, he sees a harlequin clown staring at him. Her face is painted half black and half white, a triangle over her left eye and teardrop underneath. Her right eye is adorned with the same designs, though the symbols are switched. The white part of her face looks like cracked porcelain with black cracks; the black half of her face has white cracks. She smiles widely, as if pleased by her handiwork. Without a word, she slams her fist into his chest, punching the fleshy muscle that was once his beating heart out through his back. Blood sprays the surrounding area.

Geonetti and Salvador scream and take off running again. Johnny, who is still watching in the wings, can't quite believe what he is seeing. He follows Geonetti and his lackey. The harlequin does a front cartwheel. Its long lanky limbs twist and turn like a contortionist's.

Geonetti trips over some debris on the floor, crashing headfirst into a large wooden crate. His face gets cut up badly. Salvador rushes to his side, trying to help him to his feet. Geonetti is a heavy man and getting him up proves to be exceptionally difficult. The harlequin closes the distance between them. Salvador drops Geonetti on his ass and fires at the approaching monster. The shots ring out, ricocheting.

Salvador pauses, breathing heavily. It's too dark to see, especially after the bright flashes emanating from his gun's muzzle. He reaches his free hand out to Geonetti, who grabs it. Just as he is about to pull him up, Geonetti falls back to the ground still holding Salvador's hand. But something's off, and it happens to be Salvador's arm. Geonetti screams, tossing Salvador's amputated arm away.

"Holy shit. Holy shit," Geonetti pants, skittering backward on the ground.

The creature snarls at Salvador who is staring at his shoulder where his arm used to be. Blood gushes out like a busted fire hydrant. The harlequin hisses. Salvador fires his gun until it's empty, never hitting the monster in front of him. She grabs his face with both hands and digs her razor-sharp claws into his ruined cheeks. With a yank, she rips his head from his shoulders.

Geonetti watches perhaps the most horrific thing he's ever seen. Salvador's vertebrae snap. The creature tosses Salvador's head at Geonetti, hitting him in the head. *Bonk!* Geonetti is dazed for a moment. When he regains his senses, he finds the harlequin squatting down before him. She's facing away from him, her teeth chattering; the sound makes his skin crawl. She extends one leg up over her shoulder, then rolls to face him.

Geonetti grabs for a plank of wood, shoving it right into her throat. He uses it as a crutch to regain his feet, then swings it like a baseball bat. Swinging for the fences, he hits the creature across the head, knocking it back into several wooden crates. "Go back to hell," Geonetti pants.

Geonetti relishes in his achievement for a moment, but it's short-lived. Johnny launches himself from the shadows, hitting Geonetti with everything he has. Geonetti's jaw cracks and he drops to a knee. Johnny knees Geonetti in the face, knocking him onto his back. Johnny stands over the dazed mob boss, rolling up his sleeves. "Geonetti, I'm going to beat you to death. And then I'm taking over the city. You wanted me to clean house. Guess what, asshole? I'm cleaning from top to bottom," Johnny crows.

Geonetti moans, slowly sitting up. He is in some serious pain. His face is swollen, his nose is broken, and he's bleeding profusely from his nostrils. He wipes his nose, looking at the blood smeared on his hand. The front of his suit is shredded.

"I took all of your shit for years," Johnny says. "You fat, dumb *fuck*."

Johnny aims a kick at him, but Geonetti catches his leg, flinging him to the ground and rolling on top of him. Geonetti squeezes Johnny's throat as hard as he can. Johnny puts his gun against Geonetti's temple, pressing it in hard, but Geonetti pushes his head back against the barrel of the gun. With his eyes bulging, his face red and covered in sweat, drool dripping out of his mouth, he growls in rage. "Do it, you prick!"

CHAPTER 17

Johnny pulls the trigger. The gun just clicks. Geonetti laughs, squeezing Johnny's neck more tightly. The cartilage crackles under his fingers.

Johnny's eyes go wide, though he's not looking at Geonetti. Geonetti watches Johnny's eyes dim as he slowly extinguishes the life from him, but there's an overwhelming presence behind him. Johnny watches as the harlequin monster hangs upside-down right above Geonetti's head, looking serenely at the two men. She reaches out with her impossibly long arms.

Geonetti looks up to find the monster dangling from the rafters. Letting go of Johnny, he falls on his back onto the factory floor. The monster untangles her legs from the rafters, flips in midair, and lands nimbly on her feet. Geonetti frantically crabwalks backwards. The monster's legs come up over her head as she rolls toward Geonetti. Her jerky, otherworldly contortions are horrifying, but Geonetti can't find his voice to scream.

Johnny lays on his side, alternating between coughing and inhaling huge gulps of air. The blood rushes back into his head, his flesh returning to a normal color. For the first time in his life, he felt weak. His life was almost over. He saw his father working hard on the assembly line for all those years, struggling to feed the family; his mother working endlessly to provide a home and clean clothes. He saw his own selfishness and how wrong that was.

Geonetti scoots backwards on his ass. The creature taps her long nails on the floor in a rhythmic pattern that sends chills to Geonetti's core. The monster crawls toward him, twisting and turning her body like a corkscrew, teeth chomping like a hungry machine. She rises, bobbing like a coiled slinky, raising her hand to deliver the killing blow.

The harlequin tumbles to the floor with Johnny astride her back. Johnny grabs the hideous thing by the back of her head, slamming it into the concrete floor over and over again. He screams with every consecutive slam. The creature twists her torso so that her legs are on backward. She stands up with Johnny still on her back. She contorts her arms, grabbing Johnny and tossing him. Geonetti watches as she straightens her limbs to their original positions. Geonetti punches her in the jaw with a fearsome right hook. Her thin frame rocks back and forth. *Boooiiii-nnnnnng!*

JOURNEY INTO HELL

On his knees, Johnny pulls a speed loader from his suit pocket and attaches it to his gun. The empty shells pinging off the floor is a familiar sound to Geonetti. He needs to buy Johnny some time to reload. Geonetti looks for any kind of weapon, spotting a fire extinguisher hanging on a wood pillar. Grabbing it, he pops the pin, releases the valve, and sprays foam at the monster. The cloud of dust from the potassium bicarbonate fills the air, making it hard for them to see.

When it sputters, empty, Geonetti bashes the monster in the head with the large metal canister. Now fully loaded again, Johnny fires. The creature retreats up into the rafters and out of sight. The two men stare at one another, breathing heavily. Johnny stands tall, holding his gun with a new air of confidence.

Neither man can decide if they should attack or hug it out. Either way, Johnny holds his gun tight, waiting for the creature to come back from the darkness. The silence is broken by what sounds like a brick wall exploding in the distance.

Then they hear what sounds like something heavy sliding across the floor. They look around but can't see anything. The noise is growing louder with every passing second. The slashing of crates and debris sliding across the floor has them looking in every direction. Abruptly, a large tentacle crashes through a pallet of crates right in front of them. It wraps around Geonetti's leg, pulling him into the darkness.

CHAPTER 18

The factory is bustling with workers alongside conveyor belts as the newest toys are manufactured. They flank the various stations painting, assembling, and packaging all kinds of toys. High above them, looking down from his office on the catwalk, is Lucas Khan, the owner of Bobby Boy's Toys. His office is large with a grand oak desk that has a brass goat head paperweight, a larger than usual Newton's Cradle, a leather notebook containing the scribbling of a mad man, and a high-backed leather chair.

Chalkboards line the walls, chalk drawings of schematics on every available space. In front of his desk are two oversized chairs. There is a large globe that doubles as a dry bar sitting against the massive multi-paned window that overlooks the front of the factory. Books stuff every available nook and cranny.

Lucas Khan isn't a very stout man; he's rather thin and distinguished, with a full head of hair and a thick mustache that curls up at the ends. His suit is perfectly tailored with a matching bow tie and a handkerchief in the breast pocket. His shoes are handmade from a local cobbler in Valkyrie City, as he tends to shop only at family-run businesses.

The door to his office opens as a very beautiful brunette in a black pinafore dress with a half coat and oversized hat walks in. A veil rests upon her high forehead. This is Trisha Khan, Lucas' wonderful wife. "Trisha, you look more radiant every day," Lucas says.

Trisha smiles brightly, her red lipstick making her teeth look dazzlingly white. A small boy runs in behind her, wearing a little blue suit with matching bow tie and handkerchief; his smile and laugh are contagious.

"Robbie, my son. Are you ready for your big day?" Lucas asks.

Robbie grabs a red rocket ship off his father's desk and starts to fly it around the room. He makes engine noises with his mouth. "Zoom, zoom!"

"Rockets will be the wave of the future. I just know it," Lucas says.

Trisha walks over to the dry bar, pouring herself a ginger ale. Then she pulls out a long pack of cigarettes from her clutch. She packs a cigarette then puts it between her painted lips. Lucas lights her smoke. Robbie continues to fly the toy rocket ship around the room. "Look how happy he is," Trisha says.

Lucas watches his son, sitting down in one of the highbacked chairs. He pulls Trisha onto his lap, kissing her. Her soft lips leave a faint red smear on his lips. He stares deep into her eyes. He is so in love with her. Her very presence makes him so happy.

"Okay, baby. We have to go. I've got to get Robbie to the doctor for his school checkup. I can't believe he's starting school in a week," Trisha says.

"Finally. Now we can have a few hours a day to ourselves," Lucas says with a coy smile.

"I can't wait. Maybe we'll finally get some sleep." Trisha laughs.

"If it's beauty sleep you think that you require, my love, you're quite mistaken. You are a princess among trolls," Lucas croons.

"Well, thank you, my love. But not enough sleep and this princess becomes a witch."

Lucas and Trisha laugh, untangling themselves from the chair. With a flourish, he spins her around the office then sets her down gently by the door, kissing her again.

"Okay, my love. If I must say goodbye, may it be for only an afternoon," Lucas says.

"Let's go, Mr. Khan," Trisha says, holding out her hand to the boy.

The small child runs up to his father and gives him a huge hug. Lucas kneels, looking into his son's twinkling eyes. "Go, my son. I'll

CHAPTER 18

see you for dinner. I'm working on something special for you. I can't wait to show you," Lucas says. "You're going to love it."

After his family leaves the office, Lucas walks over to the huge window looking out over the parking lot. He watches Trisha and Robbie get into her beautiful black Cadillac Eldorado. She straps Robbie in, then, as if sensing him there, looks up at Lucas in the window. They wave to each other. Lucas watches her get in and drive away

Lucas sits at his desk, scribbling on a piece of graph paper. The image is a robot prototype with mechanical arms, a swivel body, two rubberized legs, large red eyes, and a grill for a mouth. Next to the drawing he wrote "ROBBIE THE ROBOT" in his precise handwriting. Lucas traces the lines of the drawing again, going over every angle.

Later that day, he looks over a series of tin wind-up cars that he is producing. He holds one in his hand while looking it over. The design is simple enough and it winds up easily. He twists the key in the top of the car, letting it go on the production floor. It wizzes past a few of the factory workers, hitting an older employee's shoe. She picks it up, handing it back to him.

Lucas moves on to another area of the factory where the teddy bears are made. The latest line are larger models meant to be cuddled, standing at nearly four feet tall. A designer goes over different clothing options for the bears, including hats, bows, scarfs, neck ties, vests, and shoes. Tired, Lucas wipes his eyes, looking at his watch. It is getting very late—Trisha and Robbie should be back by now.

Later, Lucas waits at the window for his family, sipping a cup of coffee gone cold long ago. The sun is going down and his heart sinks. Three Valkyrie City patrol cars pull into his lot, followed by a black sedan. The cars come to a stop and two men in suits climb out, walking toward the building. Several uniformed officers follow.

Lucas stands frozen by the window. His secretary walks in with the officers, the expression on her face saying far more than words ever could. He knows what has happened. She runs up to him, grabbing his hand. The lead detective motions for him to sit down, which he declines with a sharp shake of his head. The detective explains to him that there had been a terrible accident—both his wife and son were killed in a head-on collision earlier in the afternoon.

The coffee cup shatters on the floor, but Lucas doesn't even hear it. His entire being is sucked inside out and everything goes dark. He stares at the men talking to him, but he only hears static. The officers would like for him to come downtown to formally identify the bodies as soon as possible. Lucas nods, grabbing his coat and following the men out of his office.

The morgue is cold and dark. The stainless-steel compartments line the wall from floor to ceiling. They remind him of the safety deposit boxes at the bank. The coroner introduces himself, but Lucas doesn't care to learn his name. The coroner opens a mid-level door, sliding the first gurney out. His wife is laying on it. Her face is largely untouched, but her legs are missing. His heart swells into his throat. "That's Trisha," he whispers, his tongue thick in his mouth. "My wife."

The coroner opens the second compartment, sliding out the gurney. The lump under the white sheet looks unfathomably small. It's so unfair. Why would a child be taken like this? Lucas grabs the corner's hand before he unveils his son's body. Lucas shakes his head, walking away. He can't bear the thought of seeing his son dead on a cold slab in a dark room.

Two weeks pass. Lucas sits at his desk in his office not moving, not eating, wishing he was dead. His life was over. Everything he worked for, everything he stood for, everything he loved was gone and there was no reason to continue marching on. He sinks into his chair, weeks of tears making his cheeks stiff. He can't bear to change or wash his clothes. He can still feel the ghost of his son's last hug on the fabric. He plays that afternoon over and over in his head. What if he had taken one second longer to muss Robbie's hair, or given his wife one last twirl?

He is ready to die. But what about his company? Bobby Boy's Toys is everything he's ever worked for. His life has no meaning now. He must correct this.

CHAPTER 18

Inevitably, the factory closed its doors, leaving 150 people out of work and looking for answers. Lucas became a hermit, living in the accounting office. Days turned into months, and months into years while Lucas sat in the dark, withering away. His genius mind turned inward, seeking refuge in knowledge.

Lucas found himself at the Valkyrie City Library looking for answers.

The library is immense, to say the least. Two large statues sit out front on the steps of the beautiful building. The first depicts Athena, the Greek goddess of wisdom and knowledge, poised in a fighting stance in golden armor. She wields both a shield, the icon of Gorgoneion in the center, and a long spear with a golden tip. An enormous barn owl with its wings spread flies in behind her. The statue on the other set of steps depicts Lü Dongbin, the Chinese scholar and poet who lived during the Tang Dynasty. He is depicted in ceremonial robes. With his left hand, he is protecting a beloved book of poems known as *Quan Tangshi*. In his other hand, he wields a sword to dispel evil spirits.

Both statues are glorious and massive. They are one of the largest icons in the city. The library is known for holding some of the oldest texts known to man, including a basement that contains books of the occult.

Lucas Khan found himself standing on the steps of the library. The rain pours down over his umbrella, but he can't get himself to move. He knew that if he takes the next step, he would stop at nothing to reach his goal. No matter what it would take.

Upon entering the massive building, he is taken aback. The lobby is three stories tall. The entire east wall is an inset bookshelf with thousands of old books. There are three balconies, each with a reading nook. There are at least a hundred people in the reading section alone.

The grand entrance is brightly lit. There is a long wooden receptionist desk that has a series of green desk lights. Ornate carvings decorate the desk's front and corners. The tile beneath his feet is a gold and black checkerboard pattern he suspects is hand-painted.

Lucas walks up to the receptionist, tucking his folded umbrella under his arm. He nods to the woman who returns a smile. "Where would one find information on witchcraft or the occult?" Lucas asks.

"Well, we have a religious section over by the bathrooms," she says.

Lucas makes his way over to the religion section. After perusing the area and examining some of the books, he realizes this is not the section he truly needs. These books are for hobbyists and lovers of long forgotten stories of folklore and magic. He wants real material. He needs real subject matter.

A young woman notices him looking over the books and makes note of his furrowed brow. "What is it that you're looking for?"

Lucas, now an introvert, moves away from her when she speaks. He glances at her all-black ensemble, complete with black nails and lipstick. She seems like she might be able to help. Lucas is hesitant at first, because he's not even sure what he is doing. He just wants the pain to go away. "I want to know more about witchcraft, I think," he murmurs.

The young lady smiles politely, motioning to the shelves in front of him. She reaches out, pulling a book off the shelf. "This might help. This is titled *Witchcraft and You: A Master Class in the Occult.*"

Lucas takes the book, looking it over. He opens it up, scanning the title page and thumbing through its contents. He reads for a moment, then hands the book back. "This isn't real, this was written in the last decade. I want something written in blood that contains facts, not hopeful wishes and nonsense love spells."

"What is it you're trying to do?"

"I don't know. Bury the pain. Bring back my life—my loved ones," Lucas says.

The young woman thinks for a moment, then smiles. She points to a sign that reads: BASEMENT—BY APPOINTMENT ONLY "You probably want what's in the basement. That's where they keep the good stuff." She grins.

Lucas nods politely, turning to walk away. He forgets to thank her or to say goodbye: social niceties aren't his forte anymore.

"You know, sometimes, the path we're on is difficult because we are much stronger than we perceive ourselves to be. I hope you find the answers you're looking for," she calls.

"I am too tired and lost to follow my path anymore," Lucas says.

"And yet, you're strong enough to stand with your convictions."

Lucas smiles at this thought. He pauses, turning to look at her again. "What was your name, dear?"

CHAPTER 18

"Trisha."

Lucas stares at her for a moment. He can't believe his ears. His eyes start to well up with tears. The room seems to spin out of focus for a moment as he tries to cobble his thoughts back together. He fears he is trapped in a delusion until his thoughts are broken by a voice.

"Sir, can I help you? You look lost."

Lucas snaps out of it. Trisha is gone. He swallows hard, coming back to reality little by little. Turning, he finds a librarian wearing a bright yellow swing skirt and pumps. She is only about twenty years old.

"Oh, I'm sorry. Where is the other woman who was helping me?" Lucas asks.

"I don't know. Did you get her name?"

"Trisha. The same name as my wife," Lucas says.

"I'm sorry sir, but we don't have a Trisha that works here. I'm Jessica. Jessica Baltimore. I'd be more than happy to help you," she says brightly.

The desk crashes to the floor as Lucas renovates his office. The wide bay door where Lucas used to stand and watch his team make fascinating new toys is now a de facto garbage chute. Lucas shoves another table out of the open window to the floor below where it smashes into pieces. The globe he once loved shatters into chunks as it bounces off the concrete. His old life is over, and his new life had a hold of him, pulling him into the darkness faster than a freight train. The evil hands of fate had him by the ankles. All of his humanity was sloughing away, leaving him wanting more than he had ever wanted in his entire life.

He hammers nails into the wall, securing dark curtains against the wide windows to block out the light. The stack of new books on his old desk replace schematics of forgotten toys. He writes new ones, with strange symbols. His studies now include the astrological, trans dimensional beings, and the art of dark magic. He is going to stop at nothing to bring them back, no matter what the cost.

The four pillars of concrete set within a few days. He handcrafts a wooden podium made from church pews he purchased from a local church. The crates stack up as his orders from various continents arrived. He pries the top off his newest arrival, digging through the straw packing to reveal his newest purchase: a ten-foot-tall crucifix made out of black onyx, shipped overseas from Africa. A tiger's skull is mounted on top, and symbols are etched into the dark stone.

Lucas slides the artifact into its place next to the three stone podiums. On the floor, he had painstakingly carved a pentagram with a chisel until his palms blistered, burst, and bled. The endless days and nights of back splitting work had paid off: he is close to completing his altar. Soon, he will try his hand at practicing magic.

His studies would be for naught without the proper ingredients. He needed real subjects. Chicken and goats were not going to be enough. He needed humans. The time came where Lucas stood before his company van, staring at it. He knew the path he was taking would lead him further down a dark road, but he didn't care. He wanted his suffering to end, and this was the only way. He is certain of it.

Lucas stood in his office, his thoughts clouded with anger, desire, and depression. He pours bourbon into the goat's skull that is now a chalice. He sips it, building courage for the night. He takes one last gulp, puts on his sweater, grabs the keys to the van, and locks his office behind him.

The garage door rolls up as he pulls on the chain. The van starts and he turns on the headlights, putting the van into gear. Staring out of the warehouse toward the harbor, Lucas allows himself to cry for a moment. He unfolds a well-worn picture from his pocket, looking at Trisha and Robbie's faces. He rubs his finger down Trisha's cheek, swallowing hard. Placing the picture on the dashboard in front of the speedometer, he steps on the gas. "I'm doing this for you," he says, through dry, cracked lips. "This is all for you."

CHAPTER 19

Mike understands exactly what Lucas has done. Becky sees the expression on Mike's face and knows she's seen this look before; things are about to get really bad. She leafs through some loose papers scattered on the old metal desk. Every page is covered in scribbles and diagrams, each subsequently darker than the last.

"So, let me see if I understand this. You lost your loved ones in a horrible accident. Instead of grieving and moving on with your life, like a normal person, you fell into the dark arts. In attempting to resurrect your loved ones, you unleashed some sort of demon," Mike says

"Yes. But you can do little about it. I can't stop her," Lucas says.

"Niefilium?" Mike asks.

"Yes. Her appetite is insatiable. She desires more and more souls," Lucas says.

Mike puts two and two together. "Which is why you started kidnapping prostitutes," Mike says.

Lucas is clearly ashamed. He avoids their eyes, hanging his head. Becky stares at Lucas for a long moment in disbelief. She writes some notes down in her pocket-sized notebook.

"What are you doing? Lucas says.

"Taking notes."

"What are you, some kind of writer?" Lucas says.

"No, I'm a journalist."

"Where is this demon?" Mike says.

"I managed to secure it inside of a holding sigil. But I can hear her every night. She calls for more and more blood—more and more souls. But she is locked away. She can't escape," Lucas insists.

"Well, I think she's out," Becky says.

"Impossible. I sealed her away. She can't be free. It would take a ritual to unlock the sigil. Not to mention human blood. Someone would have to sacrificed," Lucas says.

"Or killed," Becky says with an air of realization.

"Yes, or killed, I suppose…" Lucas trails off.

"I think she is free., Becky says.

"You saw her, Becky?" Mike asks.

"If by 'saw her' you mean I watched a dead Lucy St. George float into midair above a glowing red pentagram, then yes, I certainly 'saw her.'"

"You can't stop her. No one can," Lucas says.

Mike looks over the book a little more. It is bound in leather with symbols embossed into the front cover. The edges are rough. The spine is sewn together with thin leather cross stitching and it's apparent that Lucas made this book by hand. Mike puts the book in his trench coat pocket, turning to leave. He has work to do.

"Stay here," Mike tells Becky. "Keep this lunatic safe."

"There are things that reach farther than our own universe. You have no idea what is waiting out there. The worst thing imaginable. It will consume your very soul," Lucas warns.

Mike looks at Becky for a moment. Becky nods. Mike opens the door, slamming it shut behind him.

"Where is he going?" Lucas asks.

"To stop her."

"No one can stop her," Lucas says.

"You know the things that go bump in the night, the monsters, the really bad stuff? Things like that demon you let loose? Who do you think those things are afraid of? They're afraid of Mike Strong."

Lucas walks over to a large lever on one of the electrical panels, using both hands to push it upward. It snaps hard into place and all the power to the factory hums to life. Lights throughout the

CHAPTER 19

massive building start to flicker; several bulbs popping after years of disuse.

CHAPTER 20

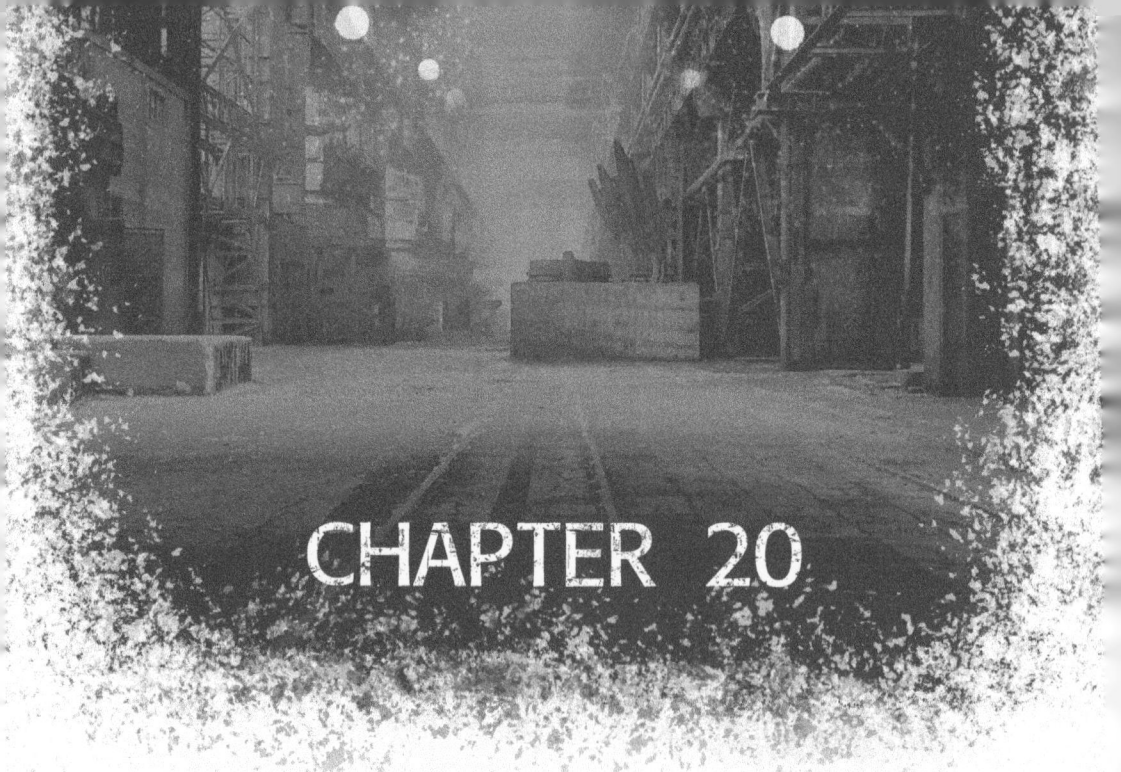

Mike walks down the old dingy hallway as the lights come to life. He makes his way to the cramped stairwell with the peeling walls, going back down to the first floor. Kicking the door open, he walks onto the main factory floor. He looks around, finding his immediate area empty, save for the stacks of crates and discarded packing materials. But, in the distance, he can hear what sounds like a slithering or dragging sound. He continues into the warehouse, itching for a fight.

The maze of crates and rows of forgotten machinery line the walls of the desolate factory. Mike can smell mold mixed with the old oil still saturating the gears that have long since stopped turning. The slithering sound continues all around him. Mike pauses to find its source. Just as he turns to go into an office suite, a large wooden crate crashes to the floor behind him. Something is trying to get his attention.

Looking over his shoulder, he sees the silhouette of something large behind him. Some- thing meant to be a sign of love and comfort. Shaking his head and taking a deep breath, Mike turns to see a large four foot tall teddy bear standing amidst the ruined bits of crate. The bear is ratty and matted, its mouth full of teeth. Tufts of stuffing stick out of its cute little ears. The snarling teddy

CHAPTER 20

bear stomps and staggers toward Mike. It starts to gain speed as it rushes at him, its oversized furry feet slamming against the concrete floor with a thunderous pounding.

The door splinters as he and the now demonic teddy bear crash through it into a room full of sewing machines. Mike's head cracks into a desk, and the heavy sewing machine falls onto his chest. He grabs the old Singer sewing machine, shoving it up into the teddy bear's chin. A bell rings out and several of the monster's teeth scatter across the floor. In a rage, the teddy bear stands to its full height, its eyes now glowing red. It roars, unsheathing its long claws with a whip of its wrists.

Mike's does a backward somersault, standing just in time to dodge the monster's swing. The claws catch the edge of his coat, leaving three tatters. Jogging backward, Mike manages to stay out of the demon's slashing range. Mike pulls his gun, firing into its chest, shoulder, and head. This slows the creature down but doesn't stop its onslaught. Mike would have to find another way to kill it. Bullets clearly won't do the trick.

Bolts of fabric line the back wall of the room. There are carts full of machine parts on either side of the room. The monster flings desks and sewing machines out of its way as though they are made of balsa wood, closing the distance between itself and Mike. It picks up a sewing machine, chucking it at Mike with a rageful snarl. Mike ducks out of the way as the old heavy machine slams into the dry wall. The stuck machine makes a mournful whirring sound as the bobbin becomes unspooled.

Mike slides across the room with a flourish, grabbing a long metal tube sitting by the bolts of cloth. He spins it around in his hands as the monstrous teddy bear lunges at him. Using the wall as a brace, Mike angles the pole like a lance, allowing the teddy bear to impale itself onto the pole. Despite the catastrophic wound, it keeps pushing toward him. Thick black blood and goopy stuffing pour out the back of the monster.

The teddy bear reaches Mike and, together, they crash through the wall back out into the warehouse. Mike's back and head slam into the concrete. The impact stuns him for a moment, but Mike uses the pole that was still in the creature's chest to throw it off him. Mike rolls on top of the monster's back, wraps his left arm around its neck, and pulls back as hard he can. The creature rises to its feet and blows through the warehouse at full speed, with Mike having no choice but to hang on. As they barrel through the warehouse, they crash into an open elevator. The cabin rocks back and forth and a ceiling tile crashes onto Mike's head.

Pulling the monster's head back, Mike is slammed into the back of the elevator. The monster flails wildly, slashing the control panel. The elevator dings cheerfully and starts to ascend. The creature slams its back—and, by extension, Mike—into the sides of the elevator. Finally, the elevator comes to a stop on the third floor and they both fall out into a room like nothing Mike has ever seen before. *Ding!*

The large room is stuffed full of an entirely new line of futuristic toys. There are toy rockets, spaceships, and weaponry. Mike slides across the floor and under a design table away from the terrible teddy bear. The creature flips a large table full of rocket parts, scattering them across the room. Behind Mike is a large panel window. The glass is stained from years of neglect. Outside, Mike can just make out the green glow of a streetlight.

Mike aims his gun again, squeezing the trigger three times in quick succession. He hits the monster in the head three times. The teddy bear finally falls to its knees and dies. Mike casually pops the clip out of his gun, reloading the gun with a fresh clip and cocking the slide back in. *Click!* "Okay, so bullets work. Just need a lot of them."

Mike walks over to the monster, giving it a closer look. Suddenly, he hears a clacking sound behind him. He turns to see a female figure standing in the doorway.

Mike smiles, but it quickly fades. He watches in horror as the svelte figure drops down, spider-crawling toward him. She leaps to the ceiling, crawling over him. With a sigh, Mike cracks his stiff neck. He isn't quite ready for another fight. The creature drops in front of Mike, hissing. In the green glow of the streetlight, he can get a good look at it. She's dressed like a harlequin clown, her limbs contorted.

The harlequin slashes at Mike's face, but Mike catches her wrist. Then, he punches her in the face, knocking her backward. The creature untangles her limbs, then bounds over to swipe at him a second

CHAPTER 20

time. Again, Mike catches her swing. Using Mike's chest as a springboard, the harlequin does a backflip, landing a few feet away.

Moving jerkily, the harlequin stands upright, cocking her head to look at her opponent. She leaps up into the air, lands on Mike's chest, and tries to slash at him. But Mike snares both of her wrists and, together, they pirouette around the room full of futuristic space toys. They crash into tall plastic rockets and a wall full of loose parts. The harlequin tries to stretch its legs all the way out, but Mike held her wrists tight. The two of them are locked in a tug-of-war, the harlequin acting as both his competitor and the rope. It was almost as if she was trying to shove her bare feet through his chest.

Mike backs into a long metal table and decides to use that to his advantage by giving in to the harlequin's strength. He would use her own power against her. He lay back on the tabletop, rolling off one side. The fall forces her to let go. The harlequin twists and turns, looking at Mike from under the table. Mike watches as her leg bends up and over her shoulder and her arm contorts to help her stand up. As they both rose to their feet, the harlequin looks into the barrel of Mike's gun.

Mike pulls the trigger, hitting her several times. Her porcelain shell cracks, pieces dropping to the floor. She falls to the ground lifeless, if only for a moment. Mike walks around the table to get a better view of the now fragile creature. His eyes widen. The harlequin twists and turns, separating into two creatures. The process only takes a few seconds as one pulls itself free from the other. The creatures are exact mirror opposites of one another: one with black face paint and the other with white.

With synchronous movements, they attack furiously. slashing at Mike. He blocks every attempt they throw at him. His trench coat takes the brunt of their attacks, becoming shredded. Mike dodges to the left and right by ducking around their wild swings. They attack haphazardly and with blinding rage. Mike is skilled in fighting and as long he can keep pace, he can stay out of harm's way.

However, the relentless attack from two enemies is a little more than he can bear. As soon as he would dodge one hit, the other harlequin would continue the assault. He was breathless, his own counterattacks becoming sloppy. His forearms and neck are stiff, crisscrossed with deep scratches. He couldn't take another second of the berserker barrage.

He pushes a table between them, trying to get enough space to stand his ground. He falls down onto one knee.

One of the harlequins jumps up and over him, putting him smack dab between the two. It certainly wasn't where he wanted to be. Mike picked up a wooden chair, throwing it at the creature. It smashes into its chest, knocking it into a rocket ship. The toy, and the monster, fall into a heap.

The other harlequin grabs Mike by the sides of the head, digging her claws into his scalp. Mike slams his back into her, pushing her into a large wooden pillar. She nimbly twists her body up and over him, still holding onto his head. Mike headbutts her in the face. Then, he pummels her with a series of left and right hooks until his knuckles crack and bleed.

He moves fast, breathing out with each punch. His hands are on fire, sweat and blood dripping down his face. The second creature twists to regain her footing. Mike picks up a wrench from one of workstations, beating each of the creatures in quick succession. He bats them back to the other side of the room.

One of the harlequins drops to the floor, sliding toward Mike. She wraps her legs around his knees, wrenching him to the floor. While knotted around him, she tries to claw at his face. Mike slams the wrench into her kneecap repeatedly. Suddenly, the other harlequin drops on top of him like a spider catching a fly, picking him up and tossing him across the room. He collides with a table, and it falls on top of him. Anger courses through him as he pushes it off.

Mike's right-hand glows. The double team was going to stop. It wasn't fair. With a yell, Mike rushes at both harlequins, tackling them to the ground. Rolling to his feet with the grace of a dancer, Mike holds out his hand. The streetlight is directly behind him now, casting his dark shadow over his enemies. As both creatures contorted their small, athletic frames into a standing position, the pentagram on his palm glowed red.

"Enough!" Mike shouts.

The blast lights up the room and the creatures fly backward. One hits a wooden structural pillar and the other slams into the elevator. Mike is blasted back through the window and out of the

CHAPTER 20

building. He falls three floors, landing on top of Salvador's sedan. The roof crumples beneath him, the glass blows out of the windows, and the trunk pops open. Steam rises from Mike's unconscious body, his right hand charred and smoldering.

CHAPTER 21

Disoriented, Geonetti jerks. He has a splitting headache. He tries to move, but he doesn't budge. His large body is cocooned in the smelly, oily goo. The more he struggles, the less he can move. Exhausted and red-faced, he lies still.

He watches as a very naked—albeit demonic—Lucy St. George walks up to him. She stares at his face, taking his chin in her hand. Her eyes glow as red as her hair and perfect lips. Behind her stands Leo, more animal than man. His drool drips from his gaping mouth, his snotty pig snout streaming.

"Where is he?" Lucy asks, looking into his eyes. Her voice is raspier now, hollow with a deep echo.

"What, who?"

"The one who concealed me in my tomb," Lucy murmurs.

"I don't know what you're talking about. Do you know who I am?"

Lucy smirks at Geonetti, running her long nails gently down his cheek. She sniffs him, taking in his scent. With a wave of her hand, the goo slides away, revealing his chest. For a moment, Geonetti remembers what it is like to take a deep breath. Lucy pushes her fingernails into his chest. Her fingers disappear into his flesh. Geonetti screams in pain as her nails scrape against his chest wall.

"Stop, stop," Geonetti wails.

CHAPTER 21

Lucy shoves her fingers deeper into his chest. The blood pours down her fingers, to her wrist, and drips upon the floor. Geonetti can't take the pain and is about to pass out when the door to the room bursts inward. Lucy, Leo, and Geonetti look over to find Johnny Martoni standing in the doorway, his gun drawn.

"Hi, doll. I think we've got some unfinished business," Johnny says.

Johnny opens fire, hitting Lucy in the shoulder. She leaps backward with a hiss. Waving her hand, a dark tentacle shoots out of the darkness, slamming into Johnny's chest. It knocks him back out of the room and into the warehouse. Johnny hits the ground hard, tumbling headfirst into a steel beam that supports the roof.

Dazed, Johnny tries to focus on the figure approaching him. When the fuzzy image solidifies, Johnny realizes it's Leo, more monstrous than before. Johnny scrambles to his feet and darts away from the pig man. He fires at Leo. Unaffected, the creature grunts, picking Johnny up by his coat and tossing him across the room. Johnny crashes through a refrigerator-sized crate, bouncing off the item inside. The wood shatters and scatters with Johnny as he slides across the floor.

Looking up, Johnny sees Leo charging him like a bull. Before he can move, Leo crashes into him again, shoving him into a metal shelving unit. Johnny and the items on the shelves come crashing down; the sound is cacophonous. Johnny is bleeding profusely from his forehead, but he is resolute. His gun never leaves his hand. Leo stomps over to Johnny, grabs him by his foot, and drags him out from beneath the debris.

Johnny's head pounds, blood pouring into his eyes. He can barely see or keep his eyes open, but that doesn't stop him. He puts the barrel of his gun directly against Leo's left hand, still holding his ankle. He fires and the blast rips Leo's hand apart. Leo rears back with a strangled roar. Johnny jumps to his feet as fast he can only to be tackled by Leo. The two fall to the floor, Leo pounding on Johnny's chest.

Lucy whistles, calling her pet off Johnny. On all fours, Leo bounds over to her. Lucy walks over to look down at the broken and bloody gangster. She places her bare foot on his throat, compressing his windpipe. "You sleep tight now," Lucy croons.

"I always thought you were stunning, babe," Johnny gasps.

Lucy stares at him then takes her foot off his neck. She squats down, putting her face directly over his. She licks his cheek, tasting his coppery blood. Johnny grabs the back of her head and kisses her aggressively. Lucy pulls back, looking into his eyes. The demon loses control for a moment as the real Lucy peers through. "Johnny?" Lucy's elegant voice cries.

Johnny stares at her beautiful eyes. "Hell was made for lovers like us." The cold steel of Johnny's gun presses against her temple. "Bye, doll."

Before Johnny can pull the trigger, Lucy grabs his wrist, twisting the gun out of his hand. She tosses it across the warehouse. Rising to her feet, she lifts Johnny off the ground with one hand. With her other hand, she squeezes his throat. Johnny kicks her in the stomach and chest, but it does little to deter her. He may as well be a mosquito. She throws him to Leo. "Keep this one. I've got plans for him," she orders, the raspiness returning to her voice.

Leo obediently follows Lucy, carrying Johnny under his arm. Johnny struggles to get out of Leo's grip, but he isn't strong enough; he's only wasting his energy. Leo stomps across the warehouse and back into the room where Geonetti is plastered to the wall. Leo holds Johnny up so that the gooey tendrils can grab him, adhering him to the wall beside Geonetti. Leo snorts at Johnny, something akin to a smirk contorting his mouth.

"Fuck you, Leo." Johnny spits.

Leo grunts, leaving the room. Johnny looks over at Geonetti, who looks dead. His body is gray, and he doesn't seem to be breathing.

"Gus?" Johnny calls hesitantly. Geonetti doesn't answer so Johnny calls to him again. "Gus!"

Johnny waits a moment and determines that Geonetti is, in fact, dead. Johnny struggles inside the goo, but he's not budging. The black slime seems to tighten every time he so much as wiggles. Johnny screams out—a man slipping into insanity.

CHAPTER 22

The large metal doors open to a vast, concrete room with twenty-foot ceilings. On the far end of the room is a huge Nazi flag, in the traditional red and black. In the center of the room, etched in the floor, is a massive Reichsadler with a swastika at its center. A concrete sarcophagus with restraints rests on top of the etching. Four-foot-tall pillars displaying strange artifacts flank the room, each standing ten feet apart from its brethren.

Major Charland, Captain Maxwell, and Strong cautiously enter the room, looking for more Nazi soldiers. It appears empty but the men don't buy it. They had already suffered great losses and couldn't take any more chances. The risk was too great. Wordlessly, the men fan out, leery for any sign of trouble.

Mike walks over to an artifact, studying it. By his estimation, it is an eighteenth-century heavy calvary sword, still stained with blood. The hilt is gold with purple rope weaving around the pommel. Mike looks over to see Archer, Baker and Campbell walk into the room as well. Mike smiles, reaching out to shake the men's hands. "I assumed you were dead" Mike says with a smile.

"The day is not over yet," Archer says through a puff of smoke. The men are ready for anything after weeks of fighting the Third Reich.

Suddenly, the ground vibrates beneath Mike's boots. The room cracks and the far wall explodes as if hit by mortar fire. A strange man in dark robes appears. Campbell opens fire immediately, but none of the bullets hit the man. It's as though there is some sort of energy field around him that deflects the bullets. Campbell is jettisoned into the air and floats toward the mysterious man. Campbell flails his arms as if trying to swim in the opposite direction, to no avail.

Major Charland fires his pistol at the man, but his bullets can't penetrate the force field either. Mike runs toward the man in an attempt to tackle him, but without so much as touching him, the man flings Mike across the room. Dangling in midair, Campbell's bones started to snap and break beneath his skin. He screams as his body is pulverized by an unseen force. His limp, motionless corpse drops to the floor with a thud.

Mike stares at Campbell's lifeless body, trying to understand what happened. He simply can't wrap his head around it. He looks over to Major Charland, who clearly isn't quite sure what to do either. Simon Archer, however, grabs an artifact sitting atop one of the pillars. It's a sixteenth century bronze crucifix, with curvy filigree and sharp points. Archer chucks it the man, hitting him in the shoulder.

The man grunts in pain, pulling the crucifix out of his flesh. He throws it back at Archer, who dodges the toss. The man waves his hands in a circular motion, chanting. A bright orange hue appears in the air. The electric hue seems to come to life and the man pushes the magic at Archer. It hits him with a crackling sound, slamming him against the wall.

The men watch in amazement. They aren't sure what is happening—this was far beyond their comprehension.

Eddie Baker barrels toward the man. Before the war, he was a heavyweight bare-knuckle boxer. If he got close, he knew he could beat the man to death. But his plan failed, and the man cast a red light that sent him flying across the room. He crashes into the far pillar holding the heavy calvary sword. It topples on top of him.

The man steps forward, chanting with his hands out in front of him. The floor beneath him glows and cracks. Flames push through the floor and his hand ignites into a ball of fire.

CHAPTER 22

"Ich werde de hölle auf Erden erwecken," the man spits.

"What did he say?" Maxwell shouts.

Archer slowly gets off the floor. "He said he 'will raise hell on Earth,'" Archer translates.

Mike watches the man wave his hand. Light appears in the middle of the room. Debris flies like shrapnel. The sand and small pieces of rubble pelt the men like hail. The structural integrity of the room is giving way.

Mike looks at Major Charland, who is on the other side of the room. They nod to each other and rush the man from either side, tackling him to the ground. They hit the floor hard, and Mike wraps the man in a bear hug. The man closes his eyes, whispering feverishly. A blast sends both Major Charland and Mike flying back. Mike slides into a pillar on his butt, rocking the pillar and knocking the artifact over. Mike deftly catches it. It's a Pugio dagger from Rome circa 50 B.C.. Mike fumbles with it, trying not to cut himself on the sharp blade. He stares at the amazing artifact with wide eyes.

Captain Maxwell runs, kicking the man in the face. His nose breaks, blood spraying all over the floor. The man whips his left hand, palm outward, and several pieces of concrete slam into Captain Maxwell, knocking him out.

"We have to stop this lunatic," Major Charland says, taking cover behind a large pillar.

Mike grips the dagger in his left hand, pulling out his pistol with his right. He sneaks toward the man. while Archer tosses a grenade into the corner of the room. The grenade rolls past the man's feet just as he notices Mike leaping toward him. Mike sinks the dagger into the man's chest just as the grenade explodes. In this same instant, the man whispers in Mike's ear and places his fingertips on Mike's forehead. The blast sends them both into the glowing sphere of light.

The entire room is engulfed in flames.

Mike and the man are suspended in midair. Mike's skin is on fire and his head feels as though it's being crushed by an unseen force. His eyes bleed and he watches, fascinated, as his skin cracks apart and light emanates from within. The man pulls the dagger out of his own chest, shoving it into Mike's.

Mike can barely move. He tries, in vain, to point the gun at the man's head. It is too heavy. Chanting, the man grabs Mike's hand holding the gun and it starts to burn. The metal of the gun turns bright red. The sensation is overwhelming and Mike howls in unholy pain. The man slumps against Mike, whispers one last phrase, and dies.

The man and the dagger evaporate into dust. The room is collapsing, but Mike can't move. He's hardly in the room now. Captain Charland, Archer, and Baker watch as the center of the room glows white and explodes. The blast is so bright that the men must cover their eyes.

Suspended in darkness, Mike floats, weightless. His body is flaking apart and disappearing. A giant hand reaches out from the shadows, grabbing Mike in its palm. A screaming face appears out of the darkness. The noise is deafening, shaking Mike to his core. His ears start to bleed, his bones hurt, and his body feels as though it's being crushed.

"What are you?" a voice asks.

Mike has no answer because he doesn't understand the question. The hand slams Mike to the ground so hard that his body leaves a small crater in the floor. The enormous fist pounds on him, but it can't seem to kill him. It only shoves him deeper into the crater as the ground gives way to Mike's weight. The pounding stops, Mike slowly rises to his knees. Mike drops his pistol, looking at his still-burning hand. There is a pentagram burnt into his palm. His gun suddenly flies up into his hand as though it's gained sentience. Mike looks at the gun—it too has a pentagram burnt into the handle.

A figure appears before him. It's tall, wearing a blood red cloak and hood. It floats down to the floor, landing one foot at a time. Mike stares at the figure as it walks up to him. It seems to vibrate in and out of focus, but Mike can feel its presence. Whatever it is, it is powerful. When it finally reaches Mike, the figure pulls its hood off, revealing a beautiful woman with black curly hair and bright green eyes. Her eyes glow amidst the darkness. She grabs his hand, turning it palm up. She smiles at him. "You are now cursed."

"What do you mean?" Mike asks.

"You interrupted the Necromancer's spell. Colonel Franz Fredric Geoffrey, a real piece of shit who dismembered children. He was

CHAPTER 22

trying to become immortal. Unfortunately for you, the dagger you used to stab his heart is the same one used to kill Julius Caesar and many kings before him. You should be dead. Yet here you are. This dimension is reserved for angels and demons. You are neither. You are something new. His spell somehow transferred to you, mid-casting," she explains.

She paces around him in a circle, looking him over. Each step leaves behind fiery footprints. Mike notices that, beneath her robe, feathers drag upon the floor. Mike eyes the sigil on the back of her cloak: three runes on top of each other The one on the top is a crescent moon meaning purity, spirituality, and psychic abilities. The second one is an arrow pointing straight up, which is Norse for warrior, sacrifice, and justice. The third symbol represents chaos, a series of arrows pointing in all directions, with a figure eight in the center meaning infinity.

She gently touches his face with her elegant fingers. She smells like lavender and jasmine. She leans in, kissing his cheek. "You are cursed to live forever, my son. Death can only take you by your own hand. Your weapon is bound to you forever, such as mine," she whispers into his ear. "Fight well, warrior, for I shall not see you again, I wager."

"Who are you?" Mike asks.

The words seem to echo throughout the void-like darkness. Mike's heart pounds loudly as he watches the ethereal being before him. She unclasps her robe and leaps backward, massive white wings lifting her up. They flap slowly and with great force. Then, light forms around her head and a golden helmet with wings solidifies, followed by golden armor encasing her body. In her right hand, a long, golden spear materializes. "It's time for you to go."

"Not yet." A wispy voice fills the room.

Mike looks over his shoulder to see a mist of pure blackness manifest out of nothing, swirling around until it forms a cloaked zombie-like entity. "He is breaking the rules," the creature says.

"Who are you?" Mike asks.

"I am the one who will never let you go. I am the traveler between worlds. I decide how, when, and where, you die."

"Hush your voice in my presence, vile insect! You feast on the suffering of those you needlessly kill," the Valkyrie says.

"He isn't going anywhere but with me. I'm taking his soul. He should be dead."

Mike glares at Death.

"If, not of Death, only you can choose your time."

Mike flips Death the middle finger. With that, the Valkyrie thrusts the spear into his heart. The light is so blinding that it burns Mike's eyes and skin. Mike screams as loud as he can as his body is ripped into a million pieces. He can't hear or see anything for what feels like an eternity.

CHAPTER 23

Becky paces the small room as she watches the madman flip through his spell book. He rocks back and forth, muttering under his breath. He looks like an insane person. "That's it. I can't take it anymore. It's been too long. Mike should have been back by now," Becky says, throwing up her hands in exasperation.

"He is dead. She kills everything," Lucas mutters.

Becky sits down in an old office chair, sighing loudly. "How long must I wait?" She can't relax. She springs up again, putting her hands on her hips and shaking her head.

"'Oh, just wait here,' he says. Until *when*, Mike? *For how long*? To hell with it. C'mon Mr. Khan, we're leaving."

"I mustn't," Lucas says.

"What was that? Get your ass up so we can get the hell out there. You started this and Mike is going to have to finish it. The least you can do is help," Becky snaps.

Lucas looks at his hands. How old they are now; cracked, weathered, his knuckles white from age. His heart and conscience are too heavy, adhering him to his seat. He pulls a picture off the wall, looking at his son and wife. His tears stream down his face. "I have been so foolish. Selfish."

Lucas stands, taking his trench coat off a coat rack in the corner and shrugging it on. He reaches under his cot, dragging out a large wooden box. Taking an old key from his pocket, he unlocks the old padlock. Becky tries peering over his shoulder to see what is inside, but before she can catch a glimpse of it, Lucas holds it high. It is an ornate dagger, the blade made of steel and the handle out of bone. Lucas rises to his feet. "We need this to kill her. We must thrust it into her spine, but I fear there will be unimaginable consequences."

"More than killing a hundred innocent people and summoning demons?" Becky says.

"Innocent? Those I killed were not innocent. They were whores, drug dealers, and thieves who sold their souls long before I met them."

"Exactly. You were sacrificing those with bartered souls. Those souls were no good, already spoken for by some two-bit demon or perhaps the Devil himself. No wonder your spell didn't work how you expected it to," Becky says.

"Perhaps. But now, it is time to end it."

"Good. Let's go." Becky swings open the door.

Lucas nods. Together, they walk down the long corridor to the stairwell. Becky pulls out her snub nose pistol, checking the chamber. Three bullets. She grimaces, hoping that'll be enough. But deep down, she knows she'll need more bullets.

On the main floor of the warehouse, Becky puts her hand out, stopping Lucas in his tracks. She closes her eyes, listening. She doesn't hear anything troublesome, so they continue onward. Becky and Lucas creep quietly through the destroyed warehouse. They jump when several crates topple over, crashing down onto the concrete floor. Leo's hulking figure appears from the darkness, snorting like a pig who's found truffles.

Becky shrieks, grabbing Lucas by his bony wrist. They run past machinery and tall steel pillars. Leo leaps over a conveyor belt with ease and lands directly in their path, cutting them off. Becky whips Lucas around and they scurry in the opposite direction. Leo gives chase, snarling and grunting.

As Becky runs, she notices a large tentacle sliding across the floor toward her. She pushes Lucas out of the way and jumps onto a pallet. She clambers up onto a stack of crates and leaps onto a

CHAPTER 23

high shelf. The tentacle smashes the crate she was just on, striking the shelf in the process. Becky holds on for dear life as the entire shelving unit falls forward, crashing into another shelving unit. Pieces of metal, cardboard, and wood tumble to the ground with Becky, who rolls with it before leaping to her feet again.

Lucas can't move fast enough. Another tentacle grabs him by his foot and drags him through the warehouse. Mid-slide, he manages to sit up and stab the tentacle with the knife. Abruptly, all of the tentacles retreat back into the darkness. Lucas and Becky dimly hear a roar off in the distance.

"Well, she didn't like that," Becky mutters.

Leo, however, is still a threat. He bounds over to Lucas who is still laying upon the floor, punching him in the face. Then he easily throws him over his shoulder.

"Hey, Leo. You're even uglier now. I didn't think that was possible," Becky shouts. Leo stops, turning to look at her. Becky raises her gun. "Put him down."

Leo grunts, walking away. Lucas dangles, his arms swinging; he's unconscious. Becky shakes her head in frustration, rushing after him. "Drop him," she says, stepping directly in his path.

Leo laughs, the sound akin to a guttural snort. "Okay." Leo tosses Lucas at Becky, knocking her down. She scrambles to her feet, rushing him. He palms her head in one hand like a basketball, pushing her away. Becky falls to the floor again, but that doesn't stop her. She rises to her feet, this time holding a large 2x4. She swings it, hitting Leo in the back as hard as she can. It does very little—he may as well have been hit by a feather.

"Mike, where are you?" Becky grumbles under her breath.

Becky swings again, the impact breaking the plank in two. She tosses what remains in her hands away, kicking Leo in the back of the leg. Leo backhands her, knocking her into the brick wall. Dazed and aching, she lays there for a moment, unable to do little more than watch as Leo picks Lucas up, carrying him away.

Lucas comes to, pulls the dagger out of his pocket, and stabs Leo in the shoulder. The wound smokes and Leo falls, dropping his prisoner. Lucas rolls under a table out of harm's way as Leo roars in pain.

Becky stands, only to be met by the two harlequins. They chatter their overly large teeth, clicking their nails against each other. Becky's face goes white. As if of one mind, the twins lunge, but Becky is quick. She picks up an empty pallet to use as a shield, blocking their onslaught. She is sandwiched between the brick wall and the pallet as the monsters slash and claw at her.

"Mike!" Becky screams.

Curled up beneath the table, Lucas holds the dagger tight, watching Leo's large legs approach. Leo flings the table away and sneers down at him, his glossy eyes tinted a sickly yellow. Lucas hears a familiar voice behind him.

"Finally," Lucy says with a grin, "I have you."

She kicks him and Lucas flies across the room, losing grip of the dagger. The weapon slides wildly toward Becky. It strikes the wall with a metallic *plink!* Becky glances toward the sound, but she has her hands full holding the twins off.

"I'm going to take great pleasure in eating your soul," Lucy says.

"I do not fear you, demon," Lucas says, clambering to his feet. He knows his mistakes and desire has cost a lot of lives, innocent or not. He turns to look at her. His eyes widen at her fiery hair and beautiful body.

"You don't have to. I'm going to eat you anyway." She laughs, her myriad teeth glinting.

Becky shoves the pallet at the twins, knocking them back a little. Their sharp claws cut several pieces off the wooden pallet. The integrity of the pallet is giving way and Becky's shield is about to be broken. "Strong! Get your ass in here!" Becky screams. "Mike Strong!"

CHAPTER 24

Mike snaps awake on the roof of Salvador's sedan. His body is in agony, but only for a moment—a perk of the curse. Mike feels his bones mending on the inside. The cartilage pops as his joints slide back into place. Mike rolls, dropping to the ground on the driver's side. He lands on his feet. He realizes then that he's outside. He looks up at the shattered window. He fell three stories. Cracking his neck, he peers in the trunk. "Thank you, Salvador," he murmurs, finding two Tommy guns tucked inside.

Mike grabs both of the Tommy guns, walking back up to the front of the toy factory. He idles in front of the double doors, adjusting his shoulders. With a grunt, he kicks the door so hard it flies off the hinges and falls into the warehouse. With a wide smile, Mike walks inside.

Suddenly, he hears Becky scream. Mike rounds the corner onto the factory floor to see Lucy, Lucas, the harlequin twins, Becky, and Leo fighting. Mike raises the guns up. "Hey, assholes!" The monsters stop, turning to look at Mike. "Did I miss the party?"

The twins stop attacking Becky, flipping toward him. Leo charges him as well. Mike opens fire on the twins. They scatter in different directions as Leo closes in on him. Mike turns his attention to Leo, firing one of the Tommy guns point blank into his muscular chest. The bullets rip through his body, decimating him. Leo drops to his knees and then falls onto his face at Mike's feet.

Mike puts the barrel of the Tommy gun against the back of Leo's head. He fires. Leo's skull shatters, spraying blood and chunks of brain everywhere. Mike spins, aiming the guns up to the ceiling knowing that's where the twins are waiting to pounce. The twins twist and spin across the ceiling, leaping from rafter to rafter, trying to avoid being shot. It doesn't work.

One of the twins gets hit in the leg. The force of the bullet knocks her off her handhold to the ground below. Mike aims both guns at her. The barrage of bullets pushes the creature across the floor, pieces of its body chipping off. Then an arm. Then one of her legs. Finally, Mike blows her head apart. The other twin drops onto Mike, but he slams the guns into the creature's head before she can dig her claws into his scalp.

Becky darts over to the dagger, scooping it up. She turns to see Mike fall to his knees. She jumps onto the harlequin's back, wrapping her free arm around her neck to wrench her off of Mike's shoulders. She spins the creature around, stabbing her in the chest with the dagger. The harlequin screams and turns to dust before their eyes.

"Took you long enough," Becky says, raising her eyebrows at Mike.

"I went to get a coffee," Mike deadpans.

Mike looks at the two Tommy guns in his hands and gives the triggers a squeeze. Both guns click, the chambers empty. Mike tosses the guns onto the floor. Mike looks for Lucy, but she is gone. Lucas lays face down on the floor but something's off. Mike kneels, gently rolling Lucas over to find that his heart has been ripped out of his chest.

"His grief led him to do stupid things," Becky says, her voice wobbling.

"A man knows no bounds when it comes to love. He loved them so much he did anything to see them again," Mike says, closing the dead man's eyes.

"Well, he's with them now."

"No. Unfortunately, he'll live the rest of eternity in a horrible place, full of darkness with unimaginable monsters torturing him," Mike says.

CHAPTER 24

"Is there no redemption for a man who has lost everything?" Becky asks.

"His redemption could have been the success of his company—making a million other children laugh and smile by making toys. He was selfish and lonely. Mistakes humans make."

"Too bad the powers that be won't see through his sorrow," Becky says, wiping her eyes. She is heartbroken for Lucas. He did so much just to be with his loved ones again and it was all for naught.

"We need to find that demon," Mike says, leading the way.

A familiar voice calls out. He follows the voice into the back room where Johnny and Geonetti are trapped in their slimy, black cocoons. "Looks like you found your place in life, Martoni," Mike chuckles.

"You're alive? I thought I killed you!" Johnny says.

"I get that a lot."

"Get me out of here, ya gotta!" Johnny chatters.

Mike walks closer to examine the goo, then looks him in the eye. "I couldn't even if I wanted to. I don't know what this goop is. Some sort of corporeal slime? Ectoplasm, maybe? Dimensional amniotic fluid, perhaps?"

"Are you a spaz or something?" Johnny sneers.

"Says the man stuck to the wall like fly paper."

Becky takes out the dagger, tentatively slicing at the slime. As soon as the blade hits the goo, it retreats into the wall, freeing Johnny who falls on his face. Mike simply steps back, laughing. Johnny pops up, brushing off his suit. He shouldn't bother—it's covered in dirt, blood, and remnants of goo. Johnny adjusts himself as if to show he's still somewhat in control of the situation.

"You're lucky—" Johnny starts, but Mike punches him in the face.

"Keep your yapper shut," Mike warns.

"Do you know—" Johnny manages, but Mike hits him in the face again. Johnny staggers back, blood pouring out of his nose and mouth.

Johnny puts up both his hands like he wants to fight, but Mike decks him in the face again. Johnny staggers back, trying to regain his balance but falls to the floor in a heap. Becky looks down at the gangster.

Johnny moans, giving up. He's had enough of all of it. He raises himself onto his elbows, looking at Mike. He reaches out his hand for help up. Mike grabs his hand, pulling him to his feet. Johnny grunts.

"Should we cut Geonetti down?" Becky asks.

"No. Fuck 'em," Johnny says.

Mike nods to Becky who cuts the goo. The goo retreats again and Geonetti's dead body falls hard to the floor.

"Now I know why you laughed. That shit is funny," Johnny chortles.

"Now, let's find this bitch and end this," Mike says.

"What are you?" Johnny asks.

"Just a man with a curse."

Becky hands Mike the dagger and he looks it over. He puts it in his coat pocket for safekeeping and continues his search of the factory. Becky follows him, but Johnny lingers. Johnny looks down at Geonetti, giving him a solid kick to the ribs.

"I'm taking over, you fatass," Johnny says.

Mike storms through the warehouse, looking for Lucy. He has no choice but to kill the demon—Lucy's body is just a host now. Lucy's soul died when Johnny killed her. Mike has no issue killing the shell that once was Lucy St. George. Tiptoeing, Johnny rushes up behind Becky who is following behind Mike.

Startled, Becky jumps, almost punching Johnny in his face. Then she realizes it's just him and sighs in relief. "What's wrong with you, sneaking up on me like that?" Becky hisses.

"I ain't sneakin', doll. I just don't want to be left alone in here. This whole night has

been a little fucking whack-a-do, if ya know what I mean."

Becky stops in her tracks, shaking her head in disbelief. "What are you talking about? *You* started this whole thing. You killed Lucy St. George, you killed Leo Guzzo, and that's just what has happened *tonight*. Last night, you killed Jacky Ribbasa and Pete Zumba. Now there's demons running around trying to eat us."

"Okay, first, yes. I killed them. But that was *business*. I ain't the one who summoned demons, lady. That ain't on me."

Overhearing, Mike turns his attention to them. "No, you're not a devil worshipper, you're something else. You're real evil. You don't

CHAPTER 24

need to be possessed to be a monster—you just are." Mike jabs his finger at Johnny's chest.

The crates around them begin to vibrate. Suddenly, the crates slam against the wall with force, exploding into pieces. Bits of wood and nails fly like shrapnel. Lucy floats out of the shadows. *"I'm a monster and I'm going to kill you all,"* Lucy croons

Mike wastes no time, squaring up to face her head on. Johnny gets behind Becky, using her as a shield. "You're a real stand-up guy, Johnny." Becky rolls her eyes.

"Yeah, well, I plan on living through this," Johnny says.

"You're not going to," Lucy promises, her voice deepening.

Mike opens his coat with his left hand, sticking his right hand out in front of him. His gun flies out of its holster and into his hand.

Johnny seems unphased by this. "Well, that's a neat trick," he says.

Mike aims his gun at Lucy who continues to serenely float in the air with her hands out by her sides. "You'll need more than bullets to kill me," she says.

"Well, we'll start here," Mike says, squeezing the trigger. The firing pin snaps, striking the primer. Flame bursts from the muzzle, ejecting a bullet. Lucy simply waves her hand and the bullet slams into a wood pylon beside her. Mike fires again and again. She deflects the bullets with a casual flick of her wrist then grabs him by his throat. She lifts Mike up off the ground so that they are eye-to-eye.

Becky watches Lucy choke Mike until Johnny grabs the back of her coat, pulling her away. Becky wrenches her coat out of his hands, not wanting to leave Mike. She pulls her own gun out of her pocket and fires her remaining three shots at the floating woman. Lucy ignores it, as if she couldn't be bothered. The bullets bounce off, as inconsequential as mosquitos.

Lucy tosses Mike at Becky. Tangled together, they slam into a large machine behind her. Johnny is left alone on the factory floor, Lucy floating toward him. Fear is a thick lump in his throat.

Sprawled on the floor, Becky grabs Mike by his coat, whispering in his ear. "Use the dagger."

Mike stands, helping Becky to her feet. They both tumble again as Johnny is thrown at them like a bowling ball. Johnny's feet strike Becky in the chin. Frustrated, Becky pushes his feet away. Lucy floats down beside the breathless Johnny as Mike and Becky roll out of the way in opposite directions. Lucy kneels on Johnny's chest, but Johnny snares her wrists, pulling her in tight. He rolls on top of her, pinning her to the cool concrete.

Johnny punches her in the face repeatedly, his knuckles bleeding. On the last hit, Lucy's mouth elongates to twice its size, biting down on Johnny's hand. She gnaws on his hand like a dog chewing a bone. Johnny screams, trying to pull his hand out, but it is no use. With a loud crunch, she bites his entire hand off. Blood sprays out of the nub, speckling her cheeks. "My hand! You bit my hand off! You fucking bitch!" Johnny howls.

Lucy shoves Johnny off and stands, spitting his hand out. Mike spots a toolbox on a cart and picks it up, swinging it the demon. He hits her on top of the head, splitting her scalp. Blood pours down her face. Then, Mike swings the toolbox backwards, cracking her in the jaw. The force causes the toolbox lid to pop open. Tools scatter on the ground.

Lucy's cheek is split open, a flap of skin dangling. She tries to grab Mike by his throat again, but Mike blocks her attempt, knocking her hand away.

Becky rushes up to Johnny who is laying on the floor, holding his nub against his chest. Blood pours out, soaking him. Becky tries to help contain the blood flow, but only succeeds in being covered in his blood too.

"She bit my hand off. She bit my hand off. She took my hand," Johnny cries

"Okay buddy, calm down. You're gonna pass out," Becky says.

"Nah, fuck her," Johnny groans. He struggles to his feet, bolstered by his anger. He pulls his gun, firing at Lucy. He misses, grazing Mike's shoulder. Lucy drops Mike and turns her attention to Johnny, which gives Mike time to pull the ritual dagger out of his coat. He swings it down at her, he's slow now, bleeding form his shoulder. She catches his wrist, snapping the dagger out of his hand. She punches him in the face and Mike flies up, landing on his back.

The dagger skitters across the floor. Becky follows it with her eyes. As Lucy leaps on top of Johnny, Becky darts toward the dagger. Lucy and Johnny hit the ground hard, with Lucy's back resting upon his chest. It reminds him of how they used to lay on the couch

CHAPTER 24

while listening to the radio, his nose buried in her sweet-smelling hair. Lucy grabs his nub, pushing down on the open wound. Johnny screams, kneeing her in the butt in a feeble attempt to buck her off him. He wraps his arm around her neck, squeezing. She stands up with ease, carrying Johnny with her.

Becky tosses the dagger to Johnny. "Johnny, catch!"

Johnny catches it, stabbing Lucy in the chest from behind. Lucy freezes for a moment, and they tumble to floor. Johnny holds the knife in place and the ground starts to shake. Lucy's skin burns and starts to flake away. Johnny crawls on top of her, looking into her eyes. "I always loved you, Lucy. I've made some mistakes. But my love never faltered," he says.

The floor starts to crack as flames shoot up from the depths of hell. The whole building is shaking now. Johnny holds the knife between her ribs as Lucy screams. The sound is ear-shattering, beyond what human vocal cords are capable of.

For a moment, the demon looks up at Johnny with her eyes—Lucy's eyes. "We can be together forever, Johnny," Lucy says.

Suddenly, the concrete liquifies and, together, Johnny and Lucy melt into the ground with an explosion of light. Mike and Becky cover their eyes to protect them from the blast. The imploding hole in the middle of the floor begins to suck debris toward it. Mike manages to grab a steel beam sticking out of the floor. Becky slides into a brick pillar. The hole explodes, a massive energy blast shoving both Mike and Becky into the wall just as the roof starts to collapse. Mike is hit with a shelf, and Becky rolls under a table just before a piece of heavy steel nearly crushes her. The table takes the brunt of the weight, but the legs collapse, trapping her. Mike and Becky are both knocked unconscious.

CHAPTER 25

The sun comes up just as the dust settles. Nearly half of the roof had fallen on top of Mike and Becky. In the light of day, the monsters are gone; all that is left is heartbreak and rubble. The once proud building dedicated to making children smile is now empty. Empty of its laughter. Empty of its horror. Empty of everything it was once or could have been.

Mike slowly opens his eyes, pushes the debris off him, and staggers to his feet. He looks around at the destruction. He first thought is of Becky. He climbs over the large chunks of concrete that stick up from the ground, ringing the circle of burnt steel, wood, and concrete where Lucy and Johnny were sucked into hell.

Mike pushes some rebar out of his way, making a stack of bricks fall. Mike could see the bay through the gaping hole that was once the factory's back wall. From where he stood, it was apparent the factory was damaged beyond repair.

Then he heard the faint call of Becky's voice. Mike rushes over to a section of the warehouse with a large pile of collapsed brick and steel. He pushes aside a big piece of rebar, exposing a small hole. Becky is barely able to stick her hand out, her fingers shaking. "Help!"

Mike grabs a large slab of concrete, moving it with ease. He painstakingly moves piece after piece, digging to reach her. Finally,

CHAPTER 25

he can grab her, pulling her to freedom. She falls on top of him and they lay amidst the debris field for a moment, holding each other.

Both Becky and Mike are crusty with dried blood, mud, and goo. Becky rests her head on his chest and breathes a sigh of relief. She is safe. Once again, she had witnessed an amazing event brought on by misdeeds, demons, and magic. She grips his trench coat tight, knowing that Mike is the only thing in the world standing between humanity and true evil. Regardless of what Mike thought of himself, she knew the city was safer with him in it.

Mike sighs, rubbing her back. There's only one thing in this world that kept him going and it was Becky Detter. Mike lays there with her for what seem like hours—there's nothing more that he wanted in life. But he knows the burden he carries. He knows that the things he wants most he can't have. But, for the moment, he is happy.

Mike pats her on the back, signaling that it is time to get up. They rise, taking one last look at the destruction. They don't look much better than the building. It looks like they died and came back from the grave.

"Shall we?" Becky asks.

"Let's," Mike says.

They stumble over fallen bricks and concrete. As they reach the front of the building, they find Johnny's Corvette, seemingly untouched. Mike and Becky exchange glances. Exhausted, Mike holds up the keys to the car. "He dropped these at some point. I thought why not."

"We can't take his car. That'd be unethical or something. Bad for sure. And I'm not wanting to add anything to my 'might make it hell ticket anytime soon."

Mike laughs. "You ain't going to hell, pencil pusher. I'll see to that."

Becky stares at Mike for a moment. Mike stares at her.

This is the part where the hero kisses the dame. I'd say damsel in distress, but she ain't no damsel and she ain't one to back down from fight. Her and I? I sure would like that to be the truth. But not in this lifetime. Or, from what I understand, the next few lifetimes. That's a train to another station I'm not riding. She's better off with me as a friend. I'm a terrible lover. Mike laughs out loud.

"What are you laughing at?" Becky pushes.

Mike shakes his head. "Just thinking, is all. Let's get out of the here." Mike holds her arm and escorts her to the road.

"Where's your car?" Mike asks.

"I took a taxi," Becky says.

"Here, let me give you a ride home."

They slowly—and sorely—walk to Mike's Plymouth Fury that is parked about a block away. The sidewalk seems impossibly long. Becky's feet hurt with every step. An elderly woman approaches them, walking her little poodle. She wrinkles her nose at them, assuming they are homeless. Mike nods at the old woman with a smile. As does Becky.

"Good morning," Becky says politely.

The woman hurriedly picks up her small dog and crosses the street. Mike and Becky laugh. Finding his car, Mike opens the passenger side door for Becky. Becky curtsies politely, getting in. Mike shuts her door and makes his way around to the driver's side. He climbs in, exhausted. His shoulders slump as though being dragged down by weights. Putting the key in the ignition, he turns to look at Becky. She's already asleep.

Mike watches the sun come up as he drives toward midtown, where Becky lives. He smiles and turns the radio on to hear one of his favorite songs—*Rag Mop* by the Ames Brothers—playing. He taps on the steering wheel in time to the music and sings along.

Pulling up in front of Becky's house, he taps her on the knee. She wakes with a start, looking at him. She smiles widely, leaning over and hugging him.

"Well, it was a night, Strong. See ya later, alligator." Becky opens the passenger side door, slowly climbing out. During the drive, her overworked muscles had stiffened.

"After a while, crocodile," Mike replies.

He watches to make sure Becky gets into the house safely then pulls away. He drives out of her neighborhood and back onto the interstate toward his apartment. The car races down the long stretch of road into the sun. Mike smiles, pulling a pair of black sunglasses out of the glove box and putting them on. He opens the center console on his seat, fishing out a pack of Ox Head cigarettes. He lights one, sucking in the smoke.

CHAPTER 25

"What a night," he says to himself.

He steps on the gas and the car accelerates with a roar. The exit is close, and Mike can't wait to take a shower. He'll be home soon enough. Then, a thought hits Mike like a ton of lead.

Why am I always in a warehouse getting my ass beat? He exhales a plume of smoke. *I need some sleep.*

Mike decides to keep driving to his office rather than going home. He could sleep there as well as shower. Something was calling him there and he often went with his gut.

The car races off the exit ramp and down the all too familiar street to his office. Mike always enjoyed driving his car. He thought about how much he was going to enjoy sleeping for the next two days even more. He pulls into his office building, putting his car in park.

Making his way to the lobby of his ratty complex, he is stopped by a woman in her forties. "You must be Mike Strong," she says.

Mike looks her over hesitantly. He smiles to look more presentable. Between the black eye, swollen knuckles, limp, and blood-stained clothes, he knew he was a shocking sight to behold. "How'd you know?".

"I just had a hunch," she chuckles.

"What can I do for you?" Mike asks.

"I need your help."

Mike gathers his thoughts, cracking his neck, the cartilage popping like gunfire. "Right this way." He ushers her into the elevator.

His job will never be over. He can never truly rest. He has a calling given to him long ago. It is his duty to keep his promise to his fellow soldiers. He would never let them down. No matter how tired, beaten, bruised, or bloody he was. He would fight until his dying breath to rid the world of evil. And that's exactly what he was going to do until the end of time.

THE END

BOOK CLUB QUESTIONS

1. How did you like the story overall?
2. Would you read a different Mike Strong title?
3. Should there be more or less Military sequences?
4. Is Becky portrayed as a strong or weak female?
5. Who is your favorite character?
6. Should there be more gore and blood?
7. Should there be more mystery and sleuthing?
8. What monster would you like to see Mike fight?
9. What part did you hate the most?
10. What was your favorite part?

AUTHOR BIO

Joe Davison's work spans twenty-five years of writing, directing, and acting. He can be seen in the Netflix smash-hit Stranger Things, where he stars as Nerdy Tech in Season 2. He has written over 38 screenplays and 7 novels: *Mike Strong; For Hire*, *Team Adventure Club: Cold Front*, *Zoey Saves Christmas*, *Infinite Chaos*, *Death's Campaign*, *Shindy Shine*, and *The Not So True Adventures of Sam and William*.

Joe Davison has also directed 6 feature films, including *Experiment 7*, *As Night Falls*, *Frost Bite*, *Mr. Engagement*, *Beauty is Skin Deep*, and *Sorority of the Damned*.

More Books from 4 Horsemen Publications

Crime, Detective, and Noir

A.K. Ramirez
Secrets & Photographs

Joe Davison
Journey to Hell

Mark Atley
Too Late to Say Goodbye
Trouble Weighs a Ton

Paranormal & Urban Fantasy

Amanda Fasciano
Waking Up Dead
Dead Vessel

Beau Lake
The Beast Beside Me
The Beast Within Me
Taming the Beast: Novella
The Beast After Me
Charming the Beast
The Beast Like Me
An Eye for Emeralds
Swimming in Sapphires
Pining for Pearls

Chelsea Burton Dunn
By Moonlight

J.M. Paquette
Call Me Forth
Invite Me In
Keep Me Close

Jessica Salina
Not My Time

Kait Disney-Leugers
Antique Magic

Lyra R. Saenz
Prelude
Falsetto in the Woods: Novella
Ragtime Swing
Sonata
Song of the Sea
The Devil's Trill
Bercuese
To Heal a Songbird
Ghost March
Nocturne

Megan Mackie
The Saint of Liars
The Devil's Day
The Finder of the Lucky Devil

Paige Lavoie
I'm in Love with Mothman

Robert J. Lewis
Shadow Guardian and the Three Bears

Valerie Willis
Cedric: The Demonic Knight
Romasanta: Father of Werewolves
The Oracle: Keeper of the Gaea's Gate
Artemis: Eye of Gaea
King Incubus: A New Reign

Discover more at
4HorsemenPublications.com

Milton Keynes UK
Ingram Content Group UK Ltd.
UKHW030412030224
437193UK00015B/279/J